Dedication

To my loves, always.

I0674337

The Rejected Princess

Katie Clark

The Rejected Princess

Contact Information: titleadmin@pelicanbookgroup.com

Cover Art by *Nicola Martinez*

Watershed Books, a division of Pelican Ventures, LLC
www.pelicanbookgroup.com PO Box 1738 *Aztec, NM * 87410

Watershed Books praise and splash logo is a trademark of Pelican Ventures, LLC

Publishing History
First Watershed Edition, 2018
Paperback Edition ISBN 978-1-5223-0020-5
Electronic Edition ISBN 978-1-5223-0018-2
Published in the United States of America

Also by Katie Clark

Enslaved Series

Vanquished
Redeemer
Deliverance

Beguiled Series

Shadowed Eden
Whispering Tower (coming)

1

Princess Roanna of Chester's Wake had only been to the dungeon once in her life, but that one trip had scared her enough that she never wanted to return. Now, ten years later, Roanna worked in the palace libraries side by side with Prince Benjamin of Lox, her lifelong friend and cohort in crime all those years ago, as they sorted socks, coats, and blankets to take to the Rejected in the orphanages.

"I just want to look around the dungeon for a little while." Ben's voice pulled her gaze toward him.

Roanna hated the dark and dank dungeon, which reeked of bodily fluids. The place gave her chills. Thunder boomed overhead, and Roanna gasped. Pressing her eyes closed, she took a deep breath to calm herself. Perhaps she was being silly.

Ben quirked an eyebrow at her and grinned. He leaned against the library wall and turned to the windows as rain dumped loads of water into the western gardens of her family's palace at Chester's Wake. Ben was taller than her, and his dusty-blond hair was parted messily to the right side. He was handsome, as so many hopeful girls had told him before. Not that he seemed to care about that.

Roanna finished tying a ribbon on the package she'd put together. She set it to the side and grabbed more supplies. Ben had been with her that fateful day in the dungeon ten years ago—the new cook's assistant had dragged them there after catching them stealing cookies from her platter. She'd said it was to teach them a lesson they'd not soon forget. The assistant was fired that very day, and Roanna swore off even the thought of a life of crime.

Now, the idea of returning to the scene of their punishment all those years ago did not appeal. Why would he want to explore the dungeons, anyway? Perhaps he was bored with sorting the donations. It could be why his mind drifted.

"I can hardly wait to see the reaction on the children's faces when they open their packages," she said instead. She arranged a few items on her lap. The gifts were for the children who'd been cast out for having been discovered to have anomalies. Sometimes they were simply considered unprofitable to society — but usually they were considered dangerous.

"We could play a game when we finish here," she went on. She finished her package and moved to the couch in the center, which was a strange spot to arrange the donations, but the perfect place for her to hide out. Roanna hated reading, which meant no one would look for her in the library. She needed refuge, as her parents wished for her to help entertain the Dawsonian ambassador and his entourage. She didn't want to spend time with the Fourth Prince of Dawson's Edge. Especially when he was twice her age and had proposed marriage three times this week.

In response to her suggestion about the game, Ben pushed away from the window's ledge. He took long strides across the room, knelt at her knees, and grabbed her hands.

Roanna watched in amusement, but his eyes held no mirth.

"Princess Roanna Hamilton, the thought of playing a game makes me want to leap from a twelve-story building," he said it in all seriousness, his brown eyes as deep as the muddy waters of the Edge River.

Yes, he was handsome.

Roanna burst into laughter to hide her emotions. She shoved him away as a grin broke across his face. "Have it your way." She walked toward the door to the library, attempting to be smooth. But inside, her stomach tightened. She didn't want to explore the dungeon, and she still didn't understand why it was so important to him. "Really, I don't know why I bother with you," she teased. "I could be spending time with the ambassador, you know. At least he has the good sense to propose marriage and his undying love."

She meant it teasingly, but Ben tensed. His jaw flexed, and her heart melted like a puddle of Cook's famous chocolate mousse. Why had she said that? Now things would feel strange between them. He would think she...expected something from him.

She swallowed her nerves as her hand slid from the doorknob, and she gripped her fingers together. "What, exactly, will we be looking for in the dungeon?"

Their eyes met. For a single moment she felt the familiar quickening in her heart. Ben and his family—the King and Queen of Lox—were visiting Chester's Wake to help negotiate a peace treaty between Roanna's kingdom and their mysterious and superstitious neighbors on the southern border, Dawson's Edge. The ambassador had arrived a week ago, and they had been haggling mercilessly over their negotiation points.

Ben was betrothed to the First Princess of

Dawson's Edge. The fact that Dawson's Edge had yet to produce a living princess did nothing to dissuade his parents' resolve to keep the peace between the kingdoms. They'd made a promise to link kingdoms, and they intended to keep that promise. The people of Lox were ever lovers of peace. Ben would marry into Dawson's Edge, and she would marry someone equally royal—it just wouldn't be him.

He gripped her pinky finger before she could reach the doorknob again. An ornery grin spread across his face. "Race you."

She jerked her hand away. "You have a match."

Without another word, she yanked open the door and bolted into the corridor. Her body collided with a solid, warm mass.

"Roanna Charlotte Jolene Hamilton!" Mother's voice wrapped around her like shackles. Father stood beside Mother, his face full of horror. That only left the Dawsonian ambassador...

Roanna looked up into his grinning, only slightly wrinkled face. He was nearly twice her age, but his olive-colored skin reminded her of her own. His dark hair glistened under the glowing hallway lights. His brown eyes sparkled and a smile danced on his lips.

So, he wasn't repulsed by a princess who barreled through the palace halls like a sportsman. Rats.

"My apologies," she muttered, backing away.

The ambassador took her hand and kissed it. "You are forgiven, Princess."

"We were looking for you," Mother said, saving Roanna from the embarrassing devotion emanating from the ambassador's eyes. "What were you doing in the library?"

Unfortunately, she asked at the exact moment Ben

stepped into the hall.

"We were preparing the monthly donations for the Rejected," Roanna explained.

"Ah, Prince of Lox," the ambassador said. "A pleasure to see you again." But his smile had dropped.

"The pleasure is mine alone." Ben bowed then turned to Mother and Father. "Your Highnesses," he said with another bow. "If you'll excuse me, I shall leave you to finish your walk."

Father nodded, and Ben strode away.

Roanna threw a glance at Father. His brow wrinkled as he watched Ben leave, but he held himself in check. He loved Ben, but he and Mother worried incessantly over the amount of time Ben and Roanna spent together. "Why spend time with a prince you cannot marry?" Or so Father said. He loved to remind her how the peace of many kingdoms rested on their shoulders. "It is never a flippant thing to consider war," he loved to say.

War. It was what might start between Chester's Wake and Dawson's Edge if this peace treaty didn't hold. With each passing year, Dawson's Edge encroached further on Chester's Wake's borders. The border villages were crying for relief.

And war would likely start between Dawson's Edge and Lox if Lox broke the marriage agreement they'd made eighteen years ago.

Awkwardness surrounded her in Ben's absence. Time for action.

Roanna took the ambassador's arm before he offered it, and he beamed. "Shall we walk?" she asked.

They headed in the opposite direction Ben had gone. Roanna sighed inwardly. It looked as though she had found the dungeon, after all.

2

The ambassador leaned closer to Roanna as they walked, speaking in her ear. "You must call me Roland."

A shiver broke out across her neck, but she held it at bay. She would examine the strange feeling later. She'd learned as a child that royals never showed their feelings unless it proved beneficial to do so. But what did the shiver mean? Surely she didn't enjoy the ambassador's attention. But she wasn't quite repulsed by him either.

"You will remember," Mother said, oblivious to Roland's flirting, "that the ambassador is King Dawson's brother."

King Bartholomew Dawson, descendant of the original Dawson who split from Chester's Wake.

"Of course I remember." Roanna smiled sweetly. "Shall I address you as Your Highness or Ambassador?"

Roland gave a mock bow. "Alas, you needn't worry over my title. I am but a fourth son. I serve my king proudly." His eyebrows raised then, and he spoke to her. "You say you were preparing donations for the Rejected? I'm quite intrigued by your interest in that area."

Roanna stared wide-eyed for a moment. So few showed any interest in the Rejected children. Of course, Dawson's Edge did not practice Termination—

the compassionate expiration of any fetus testing positive for strange anomalies. It made sense that Roland would admire her distaste for the entire process.

The Rejected were those who slipped through the cracks of the system—those who tested negative for powerful anomalies or physical defects in vitro, but then were born positive anyway. Roanna had first learned of the Rejected when she was thirteen. At that time Mother and Father had begun her training in being a Lady of the State. She had been drawn immediately to the children no one else wanted, though those with anomalies numbered less and less as they were bred out.

Ambassador Dawson's interest made sense. She nodded. "I want to show them that their lives matter in Chester's Wake. They may have been abandoned by their families, but they have not been forgotten by their rulers."

He lifted his eyebrows higher, and a slow and genuine smile spread across his face. "I couldn't agree more. As you know, we do not practice Termination in Dawson's Edge. Each life is valuable to us."

Father cleared his throat loudly—he didn't fully understand Roanna's compassion toward the Rejected—and started in on a different subject. Roland graciously joined him, and Roanna's mind was allowed to wander. Dawson's Edge refused to take part in Termination. Strange in itself, yes, but one of the main reasons they were considered backward and behind the times.

At least Ben, if he were to ever actually marry into the Dawsonian line, would continue to live in Lox as the future king. If she were to accept the ambassador's proposal, she'd be forced to move to his strange and dark kingdom.

Mother's reminder of Roland's heritage returned to mind. Roland was of royal blood, and he wanted to marry her.

A chill ran down her back, and this time she couldn't stop the shiver.

Roland paused mid-sentence and turned to her. "Are you cold, Princess?"

Roanna managed a smile and shook her head. "Don't worry for me. I'm perfectly fine."

He returned to his conversation, but Roanna's mind raced. She was the daughter of a king; she understood the way her world worked. Marrying for love was likely not in her future. Rather, marrying to keep the peace would be her fate. Keeping the peace was exactly what she feared in this moment. If Dawson's Edge desired peace and had sent the king's brother as ambassador, and the king's brother wished to marry her, would the marriage not produce the peace both kingdoms sought?

Father and Roland continued their conversation. Mother glided along at Father's arm, her smile firmly in place. They seemed content. Did they intend to marry her off?

Panic filled Roanna. As gently as she could, she slipped her hand from the crook of Roland's arm. "If you'll excuse me, I'm feeling a bit tired. I believe I'll rest in preparation for supper tonight."

Roland frowned, but he nodded. "Of course. I will look forward to seeing you again this evening."

Roanna smiled and hurried away without meeting Mother's curious gaze. How could she admit she didn't want to sacrifice her own future for the sake of the kingdom's? She knew without a doubt it would be selfish to follow through on her feelings. After all, she would be sending villagers to fight and die because she didn't want to marry a man twice her age. But it was a future she had yet to come to terms with.

"Where's the fire, sis?" Gregory's question stopped her.

She turned toward her brother. Of everyone in the palace, Gregory understood her most.

"I'm running from the Dawsonian ambassador."

"Does he still want to marry you?" Gregory's blue eyes danced with amusement.

Roanna rolled her own. "Unfortunately, yes."

"Would you like to hide in my room? I'll be out entertaining the ambassador's entourage." His voice held no enthusiasm.

Dear Gregory, always her hero. She should be out entertaining, instead of hiding away from the whole group. "No, thank you. I think I'll take a nap. I have a feeling I'll need to reserve my strength to get through supper tonight with my dowry intact."

Gregory chuckled. "Have it your way." She moved to pass him, and he teasingly tugged her hair pin loose. The pin slipped from its place, and dark curls spilled out.

Gregory's eyes widened. "You're growing out your hair?"

Roanna's cheeks burned, and she hastily shoved the curls back into place and secured them with the pin. She'd managed to keep the length hidden for months. "You must promise not to tell."

A slight frown pulled his lips down. "No, I would never tell. But..." He hesitated. Torn between being a gentleman and a brother? "But why are you hiding it?"

he finally asked.

The rule was a stupid one she'd endured since childhood. Mother insisted she keep her dark hair cropped short. Roanna had longed to grow it for years, and she had finally decided she had a right to do whatever she wanted with her own hair. It had taken a while to figure it out, but she'd learned to disguise it masterfully with hair decorations.

Roanna stepped closer to Gregory. She didn't need a servant overhearing and tattling to Mother. "Mother still insists I keep it short."

"I suppose I thought you'd outgrown that rule," Gregory admitted. "I thought you kept it short because you liked it."

Roanna studied his face, gauging his sincerity. "Mother still brings it up. I don't want her to know."

Now he smiled. "Your secret is safe with me."

Sweet relief.

"Thank you, Gregory."

"You're quite welcome. And while I'm keeping that secret, I will also keep to myself the proposal of the Dawsonian ambassador."

Roanna laughed. Mother and Father had to have heard about it, though she hadn't brought it up once, but she appreciated Gregory's effort. "Thank you."

Gregory was the perfect big brother, and someday he would make an excellent king. He didn't love the idea—he used to whine and carry on about abdicating the throne—but he'd purposed himself to do his best. Roanna wished him well. After all, at least one of them should be happy.

3

Maids buzzed around Roanna's room like bees in a hive. "This ribbon will work," one muttered.

"This bracelet."

"These shoes."

The chatter went on and on.

Roanna moved past her dressing area and into her main bedroom. The bed was simple but elegant. A white wood, polished to a sheen. White comforter, white walls. Pristine was how she liked it. Two small, electric lamps glowed from bedside tables, and other gas lamps were spread around the room.

Bette, her personal maid, popped into the bedroom. "You will adore your gown for tonight, Miss." She smiled.

Roanna nodded and returned the smile. She had resigned herself long ago to letting the maids dress her. Fashion wasn't one of her talents, as she would take comfort over style any day. Mother had decided the maids could be in charge when it came to Roanna's wardrobe.

The only part of her dressing she took care of was the styling of her hair. Occasionally, Bette helped, but she was sworn to secrecy regarding its length.

Roanna slipped out of her shoes and fell onto her bed. Her day dress spread around her in a wave of pale pink flowers. On a quiet day in the palace, she could usually get away with a more comfortable split skirt, but when they had visitors, the palace was anything but quiet. She rarely cared about the visitors, unless Ben was among them.

Ben.

She sighed. She ought to be focusing on Roland Dawson's proposal and what it could mean for her future. Or perhaps she should consider the strange sensation she'd felt when Roland whispered in her ear. Instead, all she could think about was the longing in her heart when she spent time with Ben. Did she imagine the same longing in his eyes?

They'd taken every chance to be together over the years, but things had never grown romantic. The distance between them was due to the "royals don't show their feelings" line of thought. She and Ben always knew there could be no romance between them. Neither had ever pushed the issue because, until now, there had been no threat. Dawson's Edge had no princess, and Ben was still free.

But what would happen if they never produced a princess? Would Ben be forced to marry into one of their noble families? Perhaps a part of the royals' extended family? It wouldn't be unheard of. After all, Mother had come from within the Loxian nobility when the royal family had no available princess. It was part of the reason Roanna and Ben had become so well acquainted over the years—she and Mother often travelled to Lox in her childhood in order to visit their family.

And as for Roanna? With tensions brewing between Chester's Wake and Dawson's Edge, the stakes were higher. Landowners along the border had been engaging in minor skirmishes for the last year, and the superstitious Dawsonian king believed every rumor of shadows trying to steal his kingdom.

With a marriage agreement between the countries, Roanna could put an end to the fighting. Roanna had thought the ambassador came only to negotiate a treaty, but was marriage the true reason he had visited? Mother and Father hadn't mentioned it, but they might have kept it from her intentionally.

What if she were to accept? She would have to move to Dawson's Edge and await Ben's own marriage into that royal family. What would Ben think? How would he feel?

Her stomach twisted in knots at the thought of letting anyone into her heart. The knots grew more painful with every passing moment.

"Miss?" Bette's voice interrupted her daydreaming.

Roanna focused. "What is it, Bette?"

"You must dress for supper, Miss." Bette plucked Roanna's day shoes from the foot of the bed, and Roanna looked to the window. Was it so late already?

Rain still pounded against the glass, but the clock on the bedside table read that two hours had passed. "I'll be a minute."

Bette nodded and hurried away, and Roanna reached toward her clock. A small note lay propped against it. She hadn't noticed it before, and she opened the envelope.

I hope I didn't get you into much trouble. And I apologize for not getting you into any mischief. I look forward to seeing you tonight.

He hadn't signed it, but she knew from whom it had come.

Benjamin of Lox.

Roanna's heart picked up speed. He had never sent her a note like this before. Why now? She reread the message and smiled, almost hearing the teasing in his tone. What mischief did he hope to find in the dungeon? Maybe he would fill her in tonight, though it was unlikely Mother would let her sit anywhere near him at supper.

Bette came into the bedroom carrying a black and gray gown with a silky, sleek black top and a billowing striped skirt. A ruffled swath of fabric accented the right hip. It looked heavy, but Roanna kept the thought to herself. Bette often reminded her there was a reason she wasn't in charge of her own fashion.

"Would you like to dress in here, Miss?" Bette asked.

Roanna studied Bette for a moment. Would she be sending Bette's family to their deaths by refusing to marry into Dawson's Edge? Could she live with herself for being so selfish?

"No. I'm coming." She slipped Ben's note under her clock and followed Bette out. Another maid stood in the dressing area, and she and Bette helped Roanna into the delicate gown.

"Time for your hair, Miss," Bette said with a curt nod of conspiracy.

Roanna turned to the other maid. "Thank you. You may go now."

The maid curtsied and left.

Roanna moved to her vanity seat. She pulled pins from her hair and let the dark locks fall. "Gregory discovered our secret today. He promised not to tell."

"Her Majesty will find out soon enough," Bette warned. She gently worked her fingers through Roanna's dark hair, which now fell to her shoulders. Mother preferred it no longer than chin length.

Roanna watched Bette in the mirror. "Maybe she

will," she said. "But maybe not." What if she did marry a Dawson? Mother would never need to know about Roanna's hair until it was no longer a parent's problem.

Bette worked through Roanna's hair with a wide-tooth comb then moved to the dresser. "I have the perfect clip for this gown."

Roanna turned her head to study her hair. It was growing nicely. Faster than she'd hoped. She ran a hand over the tresses, and a chilling shiver raced through her.

Roanna gasped softly. This was the same strange feeling she'd had when Roland whispered in her ear. What could it mean?

Bette returned and scooped Roanna's hair into its usual fashion, but Roanna couldn't forget the feeling.

"You don't like the clip?" Bette asked.

"What?"

"The clip," Bette repeated. "You don't like it? You're frowning."

Roanna checked her image in the mirror. The dainty clip was a brass turtle. Her dark hair was piled and pinned at the back of her scalp, with only a few short, loose ringlets around her face. The new hair clip glimmered all its own. Bette had positioned it prettily in the side of her hair. "I'm sorry, Bette. It's lovely."

With little of her own fashion sense, it always surprised Roanna when she saw her maid's work in the mirror. "You're an artist."

Bette beamed and curtsied. "Thank you, Miss." She had been Roanna's maid for six years now. Roanna needed her. Depended on her.

"Can I ask you a question?" Roanna asked. "What would you do if I were to marry?" She had never asked before, but it felt right for the moment.

Her maid shrugged. "If you would have me, I would be happy to follow you anywhere."

"Even at the expense of leaving your family behind?"

Bette smiled and took Roanna's hand. "I'm proud to serve my princess."

Roanna squeezed Bette's hand. "Thank you, Bette." She had a feeling she would need the support.

4

Once Roanna's makeup was finished, she made her way to the stairs at the top of the family wing. A small sitting area was situated in an alcove near the stairs, and Gregory sat in an armchair, dressed in evening wear, reading what looked like some type of report.

"Has Mother gone down?" She glanced around, hoping to score a few more moments before any type of marriage agreement was sprung upon her.

"She and Father went down earlier." Gregory stood. "I've been putting supper off as long as I could. Too many hopefuls."

"Ah, the girls from Dawson's Edge?" She offered a sympathetic smile. A year older than she, Gregory wasn't any more thrilled by the expectations of royal life than she was. Yet, he was gracious and courtly, gentle and kind, firm and authoritative. He would be a good king someday, even if it wasn't what he wanted out of life.

At least for now, she wouldn't have to face Mother and Father—and her fate. With her parents already mingling downstairs, she knew they wouldn't bring up Ambassador Dawson in front of others.

"Care for an escort?" Gregory held out his arm, and she smiled and took it.

"I thank you, Sir."

He patted her hand and started down the spiral stairs. Roanna gripped the wrought iron railing as they stepped in sync.

"We're a fine lot, the two of us," Gregory sighed.

No reason to ask what he meant. They both were barreling toward futures they didn't necessarily want. At least Roanna had Ben, for now. Their friendship ran deep, and the love she felt for him would never be swayed.

The thought filled her with angst. She had known her future since she was a child. Only now when faced with reality did she have reason to question it. Ben was her best friend. The first person she wished to speak to when something exciting—or sad or fantastic— happened. He was kind, and he smiled a lot. They had fun together, always. Was that love?

She and Gregory reached the bottom of the stairs and turned left toward the dining hall, situated at the eastern edge of the palace, facing the Edge River. One wall of the dining hall was made entirely of windows, allowing diners to view the workings of the city along the river.

Edge River ran through their capital then snaked southwest. Further down, it was the dividing line between Chester's Wake and Dawson's Edge, north and south. Lox was to the West, bordering both of their kingdoms.

Happy chatter rose as they approached the dining room. Gregory glanced at her. "Good luck, sis."

She smiled and they stepped into the lion's den. Chandeliers cast a warm glow over the guests who sat at a long mahogany table. The table could sit up to fifty guests, and tonight it was nearly full. The ambassador had brought along his entourage, including companions and their families. The Loxians, Ben, Queen Frieda, and King Neville, had a few others with them, as well.

As she'd feared, Ambassador Dawson sat to Father's right. The next seat over remained empty—saved for Roanna. Before she could be spotted, she glanced around for Ben. He sat beside Queen Frieda, and King Neville sat across from them. They were fair and kind leaders and had always shown great love for Roanna. Queen Frieda spotted her looking and smiled before returning to her conversation with her neighbor.

Roanna's gaze moved to Ben. He gave her a small smile and a wink.

He obviously knew they were being conspired against in their seating arrangements.

Roanna hid her smile and quickly turned away. No use provoking further ire should Mother or Father catch the exchange. She moved to Ambassador Dawson's side.

Roland jumped to his feet with a smile.

"Princess, how fine you look tonight." He bowed then pulled out her chair.

"Thank you, Ambassador." Why must he call her princess? Why not My Lady, or even Princess Roanna? He was goading her, trying to pull out an invitation to use her given name. Well, he would have to try harder than that.

A servant boy, only a few years younger than her, poured her drink. He stumbled but did not spill.

"Careful now." Roland smiled, but it didn't show in his eyes.

The boy's cheeks reddened. He finished pouring her drink then moved down the table to offer a refill.

"That gown is very becoming, Princess." Roland leaned closer, offering her a beguiling smile. He truly was handsome, but his proximity made her uncomfortable.

"Thank you, again," she said. Heat rose to her cheeks, and she took a sip of her cool drink. It wasn't that she'd never been complimented or pursued—she had. But it had always been harmless. Silly flirting that she knew would lead nowhere.

This was different. Ambassador Dawson had proposed marriage, and he was an acceptable match.

"Did you enjoy your tour of the palace?" she asked, eager to put those thoughts aside for now.

"Quite." He leaned closer still. "Though it was much more enjoyable when you walked with us."

A slight shiver hit her.

Roanna leaned away. "Flattery will get you nowhere, sir." She smiled to hide the sting in her words, but she hoped he would not notice her strange chills.

"What did you think of the observatory?" Time to steer the conversation away from herself.

"Quite modern," he admitted. "My brother, the king, will be interested to hear the advancements Chester's Wake has made."

"I particularly enjoy the telescope," she said. "It is the most powerful telescope available of our three neighboring kingdoms, though I believe it is old news across the ocean." She smiled again, proud of Father's interests in the sciences. After the gardens, the observatory was her favorite spot in the palace.

A shadow passed behind Roland's eyes. Did he not like his kingdom coming in second best?

"My nephew, Prince Stefan, married Isabella de Paul."

His switch in conversation confused Roanna. She blinked. "Yes, Mother and Father attended their wedding." Stefan was the crown prince of Dawson's Edge and had been married to a princess from across the ocean not a year before.

Roland's eyes narrowed slightly. "Isabella's father is privy to the most advanced of science technology."

Roanna's smile turned stale. "As I said, our telescope would be old news across the ocean."

Was he truly jealous? It had been a time since she'd had any significant interaction with a Dawsonian. How easily she had forgotten their suspicious and sensitive nature.

A crash drew her attention away. The servant boy from earlier had dropped a platter of vegetables behind Ben and his family.

"Boy!" King Neville chided as Queen Frieda brushed splatters from her clothes.

Ben had splatters on his white shirt, but instead of huffing, he flew to the mess the boy had made in the floor. He worked silently with the boy, scooping food back into the dish.

Roanna's heart swelled, as no one else around the table would have even thought of helping the boy.

Jacob, Father's head butler, rushed to Ben's side. "Prince Benjamin, you must forgive us. Please, return to your seat and allow us to clean this for you."

Ben ignored Jacob and helped until the mess was cleaned.

"Quite an incompetent little fellow, isn't he?" Roland drank from his glass as if the boy's embarrassment was of no consequence.

Roanna ignored the comment, her eyes glued to Ben as he smiled kindly at the boy and clapped him on the shoulder. He spoke something in the boy's ear. The boy looked up at Ben with relief written all over his face.

Jacob offered Ben a towel, and he accepted it. His gaze met Father's. "Your Highness, if you'll excuse me I will change into more acceptable attire."

Father bowed his head in acceptance, and Ben backed from the room. Chatter resumed within moments, but it was hard to focus on the ambassador's nonsense. She found it hard to focus on anything except Ben's return.

5

Supper continued uneventfully. Ben returned and ate his fill, laughing with the guests near him, including a few of the ambassador's companions. One had brought a daughter: Merry. Roanna had met her the day they arrived but spoke to her very little since. The girl had made a kind impression on her.

Might Merry end up the future queen of Lox? Ben smiled politely when Merry spoke, but he didn't fawn over her the way Roland was doing to Roanna.

Father tossed his napkin on the table, signaling the end of the meal. Roland jumped to his feet and magnanimously attempted to help her rise. She smiled. If she hurried, she might be able to catch Ben.

"Princess, might we speak alone?"

Roanna succeeded in holding in her groan. She pasted on her most sincere smile. "Of course, Ambassador." She led him to the sitting room where most of the other guests now mingled. The room was large and near the center of the palace. The walls were paneled in deep mahogany, and electric chandeliers cast a warm glow around the room. A piano sat in one corner, and groups of chairs and couches dotted the room.

She ought to lead him to a couch grouping, inviting others to join them. It would serve him right. But he had specified he wished to speak to her alone; and as she did have to marry someone at some point, she might as well get this discussion over with. She led him to a set of two chairs near the fireplace. No fire had been built as it was early summer, but the setting was private.

"Did you enjoy your meal, Ambassador?"

"It was a fine meal, but more than the food, I enjoyed the company."

She squirmed. The company—being herself—had been forced to stick to small talk because the one attempt she made at real conversation had produced tension.

"Princess, allow me to be frank." He leaned across the small space separating them. She could see the few graying hairs growing alongside his full head of black. "I did not come to Chester's Wake seeking marriage, but when I saw you, my mind changed. I felt an instant pull toward you, such as I have rarely experienced in the past."

Oh, merciful heavens.

"I have sent word to my brother, King Bartholomew Dawson of Dawson's Edge, asking permission to wed. It would bring peace to our kingdoms, ending this inevitable war on which we find ourselves at the brink."

The ambassador went on, but it all sounded like rushing water in Roanna's ears.

Where was Ben?

He stood near the windows, laughing with Merry, whose long blond hair reached nearly to her backside. Roanna was hit with the longing to let her hair grow even more.

"Princess?" Roland's voice held a desperate edge.

She'd missed half of his speech. "Forgive me, Roland."

He beamed at her use of his name.

"I'm so overwhelmed by your devotion. You will allow me time to consider your offer, I hope."

He nodded quickly, reminding Roanna of a lost puppy. "As long as you need, Princess. I have spoken to your parents, and they are most happy with the prospect."

So they did know.

"Now we must only await permission from my brother."

She smiled. "And my answer, of course."

"Of course."

Ben still stood near the window with Merry and her father. He caught her looking and smiled, but she turned away. What would Roland think of her making eyes at Ben only moments after he proposed marriage?

"I'm afraid I must ask your forgiveness yet again." She stood. "I have much for which to think and pray. I will see you tomorrow."

He stood. "I understand. Rest well, Princess."

She smiled one last time and hurried from the room. How quickly life changed! One week ago, she was as happy and carefree as ever. Then an entourage from Dawson's Edge arrived and her entire life's course was altered.

It wasn't that she didn't wish to marry—she did. In fact, she had always planned to marry. But maybe she'd held out hope for a romantic match. Being swept off her feet by a handsome prince from across the ocean. Someone who wouldn't make her long for her friendship with Ben.

The hallways were empty save a few servants scurrying about.

Roanna bypassed the staircase to her room and

made her way to the chapel instead. The family attended evening prayers together on any regular night. However, when company visited the palace, things were thrown into disarray. She had to pray alone as she found time.

Candles took the place of electric lighting in the chapel. Thick carpet quieted her footfall, and dark wood panels lined the walls. Pews covered in dark red velvet offered seating, and at the front was a prayer altar.

Roanna knelt at it, though she had no idea what to pray about. Marrying Roland? Peace for her kingdom? Love instead of repulsion when she looked at the ambassador? Bravery instead of fear when she considered moving to Dawson's Edge?

A hot tear slid down her cheek.

I want to marry Ben.

She sucked in a shuddering breath. She hadn't intended to pray that. Surely, such a request wasn't considered a legitimate prayer. It had probably bounced right off the ceiling and returned to haunt her forever.

She took a deep breath. She needed a real prayer this time.

I ask for wisdom to make good choices.

Yes, that was much better. A peace settled over her. Wisdom was good. One needed wisdom when choosing a marriage partner.

The door to the chapel creaked open, but Roanna didn't open her eyes. It could be another member of the family or any one of their guests. Even the servants were permitted to use the chapel, though they rarely came in when the royals were present.

Try as she might, no further prayers came. Roanna

stood and turned to go, but Ben knelt at the altar a few feet away. His head was bowed, his eyes closed. He had obviously seen her but had not interrupted. She would not interrupt him, either. But should she wait?

Before she could decide, he looked up. He smiled, stood, and then closed the distance between them. After his clothes had been soiled in the vegetable disaster at supper, he had changed into a fine, brown, linen suit with a white ruffled shirt underneath. The collar was unbuttoned, and now he shoved his hands in his pockets.

"You ran away." He left the statement open, waiting for her reply.

Roanna swallowed her nerves. Yes, she had run away. How much should she tell him? What was proper?

It only took a moment to decide. This was Ben, her very best friend.

"Ambassador Dawson has asked Father and Mother for permission to marry me. They have consented, and he has sent for permission from Dawson's Edge."

The words hung in the air between them.

His jaw flexed, and after a moment, he spoke. "So, it's not final yet?"

"No." It came out as a squeak. "It's not final."

He looked away a moment, and when he turned back to her his face had relaxed. The ornery smile was back. "Do you want to see the dungeon now?"

6

Roanna peeked from the chapel into the halls. "It's empty. The fastest way to get to the dungeon is through the servants' halls," she said.

Ben chuckled. "I remember."

They sneaked into the hall and hurried to the door to the servants' hallway underneath the stairwell. The dungeon was at the back of the palace, under the kitchens.

The door to the hallway was unlocked, and they slipped inside.

This part of the palace was different from the rest. Gone were the delicate paintings and fancy tapestries. In their places were beige walls, beige tiled floors, and beige lights that buzzed with cheap wiring.

In spite of the coloring, the halls were full of life. Farther down came the clatter of kitchen work and servants bustling about. A stairway to their left led into the depths of the earth.

Ben nodded toward it, and she followed him. The air turned cooler as they went the two levels below. Along with the cooler air was dimmer light. The fixtures were placed farther apart, and the air tasted stale. When had the electricity been added?

"What are we to do in the dungeon?" She shivered.

Ben slipped out of his suit coat and draped it over her arms.

"Thanks." She slid her arms inside the sleeves.

They swallowed her whole, but the silk inlay was still warm, and Ben's woodsy-scented cologne wrapped around her.

He studied her for a moment then gave a typical Benjamin grin. "I hope that old man at least told you how beautiful you look tonight before confessing his undying affection."

He'd used the same type of words a hundred times before, but tonight it felt different. Tonight, she'd been proposed to by a man she did not love but would probably accept. Tonight, her fate seemed sealed—they would never be together, and their friendship was almost at an end.

She ignored his question. "Again I ask, what are we doing in the dungeon?"

"I read something." He started down the dim hallway, leading her toward the dungeon.

"You read something?" She hurried to keep up, the hem of her gown dragging the floor and her feet aching. She should have changed shoes first. Blasted fashion.

"Yes. I read something. You are aware of reading instruments called books, are you not?" He winked.

She rolled her eyes. "Ha-ha. Yes, I am aware."

"Just checking." His teasing expression faded away, and he slowed his step. "I found an old book in Father's library at Lox. It was a handwritten history. Or rather, a first-person account."

Roanna frowned. "A handwritten account of something that happened here? In the dungeon of Chester's Wake?"

Mischief danced across his face. Or maybe it was the shadows. "According to the account, a doctor was kept prisoner here. A doctor from Dawson's Edge."

She didn't have to hide her sigh in front of Ben. "Call me dense, but so what?"

"When is your birthday?"

"December thirteenth, three hundred ninety-one post wars."

"That was the night the doctor was arrested."

Roanna stopped him with a hand on his arm. "What are you saying?" Confusion swirled inside her.

"I don't even know, except don't you think it's a strange coincidence?"

Strange, indeed. Almost impossibly so. "Why was a Dawsonian doctor present when I was born?"

"Exactly what I thought we could find out. They must keep records down here somewhere."

She nodded, and they resumed their walk. Ben's hand brushed against hers, and tingles raced up her arm. Should she pull it away?

But Ben made the decision for her. "There." He pointed, moving his hand. "It's just around the corner."

In spite of having only been there once, Roanna remembered the dungeon well. She stopped him again. "What if the guard won't let us pass?"

"He likely won't care as long as there are no prisoners. Are you keeping anyone right now?"

"How would I know?"

He quirked an eyebrow. "You are the princess. You ought to know what goes on in your own palace."

She smiled and rolled her eyes. "And I suppose you know every prisoner who comes in and out of Lox?"

The mischief faded from his eyes. Slowly, he nodded. "I am Prince Benjamin Bellevue, the future king of Lox. So, yes, I know every prisoner who comes in and out, because it is my duty to know."

First hurt and then shame and embarrassment spread through her. Was he chiding her? Making fun of her? "Well pardon me, Prince Benjamin Bellevue of Lox. It is unlikely I will ever be queen over anything. Unless, of course, King Dawson and his first two brothers happen to die all at once."

Tears burned her eyes for the second time that night. Why would he say such a thing?

He kept silent, so she chanced a look at him. His jaw muscles flexed once again. They were doing that a lot today. Had she angered him?

"This was a mistake." She turned back toward the stairwell. It had been foolish to sneak off with him. Irresponsible to spend so much time with him when she could never keep him. She was making issues out of nothing and causing tension for no reason.

"Roanna, don't go." He took her hand. "I didn't mean it to boast. Surely, you know me well enough to know that."

She did know him so well. But still she couldn't meet his eye. "Then why did you say it?"

He growled and let go of her hand. He ran his fingers through his dark blond hair. "I'm sorry. It was stupid."

"What was stupid?" She needed him to explain. What would make him give her a speech like that?

He shook his head, and two pink spots colored his cheeks. She had never seen him so flustered. Was Benjamin of Lox embarrassed?

"Ben, what is it?"

His gaze met hers at last, and she saw pain there. "I wanted you to remember who I am. I wanted you to…" He paused, studying her face then turning away.

"Never mind. Like I said, it was stupid."

Heat spread through her. What did he mean? They stood in awkward silence a moment more.

"If you want to go back, I'll take you." His voice was hoarse.

Was going back what she wanted? No. She wanted to spend as much time with Ben as she could before they were forced apart. She pointed ahead. "Let's see what's in the dungeon."

7

After the tension with Ben, Roanna composed herself. She had to be poised enough to pull off the act of authoritative royal in front of the jailor. The time to consider Ben's words would come later.

They turned the corner, and a guard met them at the entrance to the dungeon. He was tall—taller than Ben, even—with broad shoulders and an electricity stick strapped to his belt. He bowed slightly. "Your Highnesses. How can I assist you?"

"We came to see the dungeon." Roanna kept her shoulders straight, her chin high. If she acted as if she belonged, he might actually believe her.

"Of course, Princess Roanna." He unlocked the door and held it for them but frowned slightly. "The cells are on the left, and the offices are on the right. Knock three times when you're ready to exit."

Roanna could hardly believe it worked. They entered the dungeon, and the smell hit her immediately. It wasn't as strong as she remembered, but the scent of rotten fruit hung in the air. As Ben had predicted, the cells were empty. She nodded to the offices on the right. "Over there."

They walked to the offices, and Ben turned the knob.

"I haven't been here in ten years," she said, memories of those days swirling around her.

Ben smiled, probably remembering the same

scenes. "Come on. Let's find what we came to see."

They moved into the office. A desk sat in the center, and the walls were lined with filing cabinets. "How do you think they're filed?" she asked. "Alphabetically? Chronologically?"

He shrugged. "You start at that end, I'll start at this end."

It was as good a plan as any. She moved to the first cabinet and pulled out the top drawer. "So, what kind of account was this book you found?"

"It was a memoir." Ben slammed the first drawer and opened the next. "A Loxian, a friend of both our fathers. I think he was some sort of mentor of theirs. Anyway, he was visiting Chester's Wake on the night of your birth. He only made a small entry about the event with the doctor, but seeing your birthdate was enough to catch my attention."

Interesting. She opened her third drawer and kept scanning. "What made you read that book in the first place?"

His fingers paused their searching. He didn't look up. "Mother has me reading a lot these days. She calls it preparation."

Preparation to be king.

"Oh. Of course."

They resumed their search. Roanna gave up on the first cabinet and moved on to the next. She opened the drawer and gasped. "I found the right drawer! Year three hundred ninety-one P.W."

Ben moved to her side, and together they moved to the desk. She sat in the chair, and Ben sat on the desk. One by one they picked through the files dated for the year of her birth. "Did this memoir give a name for the doctor?"

"Unfortunately, no."

The files were listed by last and then first name, followed by the date of imprisonment and the length of sentence. It made for tedious searching. Roanna kept alert for her birthdate, but she passed file after file of dead ends.

"I wonder why these files aren't kept digitally," she mumbled. Most citizens across the kingdom had no access to higher technology, but at the palace Father usually afforded the best in technological advances. His interest ebbed and flowed, but he could usually be goaded into buying the latest inventions if for no other reason than to keep up with Lox.

Ben's kingdom never lagged. Their technology might even rival that of the scientists across the ocean. And then there was Dawson's Edge, the exception of their three neighboring kingdoms. They weren't nearly as interested in keeping up.

"You could discuss the filing system with Gregory," Ben suggested.

"Gregory?"

Ben looked down at her from his spot on the desk and shrugged. "He is the future king of Chester's Wake. I assume he is undergoing the same type of training as I am. That includes pet projects."

His words made sense, but she shook her head. "And what would I tell Gregory I was doing to learn the filing system of the dungeon?"

Ben's eyebrows shot up. Then he smiled. "Excellent point."

She returned to scanning the pages, and her breath caught. "Ben! Here's one." She moved to his side at the desk so they could look at the file together. Roanna's heart thundered. But what was she nervous about? So what if a Dawsonian doctor was present at her birth? What bearing did that have on anything?

"This man was imprisoned on the night of my birth."

"What was his charge?"

Using her finger, she scanned the page. "Upsetting the queen."

They read silently for a moment, looking for more information. The man's name was Dr. Richard Presnell of Dawson's Edge. He was later found to have attended the birth of Queen Katherine Dawson's stillborn daughter not two weeks prior to Roanna's birth. He was in his sixties and well respected before this point, as he often travelled between kingdoms.

Roanna didn't understand. "Why would he be imprisoned for upsetting the queen? Is it really so fair to jail him when Mother was in the throes of labor? It seems any woman would be easily upset."

Ben pointed to a line near the top. "He was held for nearly a month. It had to have been something significant." They flipped through the other pages, but most were various forms repeating the same information.

On the last page were a few handwritten notes. Ben scanned them quickly, then pointed. "There."

She read the words and chills broke out across her skin in spite of the warmth of Ben's coat.

"The prisoner was out of control, continuously shouting, 'You must cut her hair! Keep it short!'" She looked to Ben, seeking some type of reason in the madness.

His gaze moved to her hair, and he slowly touched a single curl near her temple. "The doctor upset her, but she listened to him." Ben knew of the rule about her hair—she had complained of it enough over the years. It was known widely that citizens of Dawson's Edge were superstitious and backward. Why had Mother trusted the doctor's warnings?

Roanna reached up and slowly unpinned her hair. It fell in awkward waves around her shoulders. Ben watched her, eyes widened. Finally, he said, "You're growing it out?"

"Mother doesn't know."

His eyes softened, and he gave her a small smile. "I like it."

They stared at each other for long moments, but the question remained. Why had Mother listened to the Dawsonian doctor?

8

Ben untucked his shirt and shoved the file behind his back. "Is it covered?" He turned his back to her.

"Yes, but why? What will you do with that?" Stealing from the dungeon seemed a strange thing to do.

"Don't you want to know more about this man? His words have dictated your life for the last eighteen years."

"Dictated is a strong word, don't you think? It's only hair." And hair went along with the world of fashion, in which she had little interest. But Ben was right. There was something strange about the entire thing.

He stepped closer to her. "Roanna, from the moment I read this account, I knew it meant something. Do you think I would drag you down to the dungeon otherwise? Now this Dawsonian peacock thinks he'll marry you." He ground his teeth and shook his head. "I'm not letting that happen without assuring myself you'll be well cared for."

Roanna held her breath. Did the prospect of her marriage upset him as it did her? Heat erupted inside her, and with it the fluttering of her heart. "What will you do?"

"I don't know, but don't make any decisions yet." He grasped her hands and pulled her all the closer. Her shoulders brushed his chest, and she became lightheaded from holding her breath. "Please don't make any decisions until you speak to me again."

She stared into his eyes, unable to look away yet unable to answer him.

The door to the dungeon squealed on its hinges. The guard was coming in.

Roanna stepped away as though she'd been caught stealing from the cookie platter again. Ben stepped in front of her and exited the office, ever confident. Roanna followed him, keeping her face averted lest even the guard witness her flaming cheeks.

"We're done now," Ben said. "Thank you."

But the guard didn't return the smile. "My lady. Your parents are looking for you." His frown deepened. "I hope my job will not be in jeopardy."

Mother and Father had noticed her missing? Had they noticed Ben missing as well?

But Ben shoved the guard against the wall. "You dare speak so to the Princess of Chester's Wake?"

The guard could crush Ben, but he had been trained well. "No, Your Highness. I only meant the king and queen have been searching for her."

Ben narrowed his eyes but released the guard. "You will speak of this to no one, and in return we will speak of it to no one."

The guard nodded.

Ben took Roanna's hand, pulled her along the corridor, and toward the staircase.

Roanna threw a look behind her.

The guard watched them go, shaking his head.

"Why did you do that?" she hissed. Again, she considered the Loxians' love for peace. Ben's actions were quite out of character.

"What do you think will happen if your parents find us here alone when you've just been proposed to by another man? You're practically engaged. Our time together is short."

"Why do you care?" It was an unfair question, and she shouldn't have asked it. Really, she was only begging for trouble.

He stopped short, his gaze spitting fire. "You really need to ask me that? Why I care if you marry another man?"

Her throat constricted, and she swallowed hard but said nothing.

He growled and restarted his fast footsteps. "You should go out the way we came in. I'll find another route."

"Ben, no. There is no reason to sneak. You're my closest friend."

"Don't you understand?" They were at the bottom of the stairwell now. His face was red and he gripped her hands. "They want to marry you off. Now. You and I cannot be together. We cannot be seen together like this anymore. Gone are our carefree days of childhood. Our friendship must end. Do you think Ambassador Dawson will react favorably to our close friendship now that he has gained your family's permission for marriage?"

Not favorably, no.

"I am betrothed to whoever they choose for me, and now you are practically betrothed to them as well." He let go of her hands, looked away, and shook his head. "Would you start a war just to remain friends with me?"

Friends? For some reason, in that moment, she had expected more.

She cleared her throat and in a tiny voice spoke. "No, I would not start a war."

He nodded once, seeming relieved that she was finally thinking. "Good. Then you will go out the way we came, and I will find a different way. I will find you when I know more. It may take a bit of time."

"What do we say when they ask us where we've been?"

"Say whatever you like. I have been nowhere but in the lower banks, sending my evening prayers."

She nodded. Time to leave him with this strange puzzle piece to her life tucked behind his back.

"Good-bye, Roanna." His voice broke, and tears sprung to his eyes. He turned back toward the dungeon without another word.

The tears slipped from her eyes, and she wiped at them furiously. Her hair hung around her shoulders, and she still wore Ben's coat. How could she face Mother and Father like this? She must find Bette.

She hurried up the two flights of stairs, but instead of exiting through the door they'd come in, she considered the layout of the house. There was a back staircase somewhere used by servants. She must take that up to her room. Turning right, she maneuvered through the empty beige halls until she stumbled upon the other stairs. Hopefully, these would take her to the right place. As she started up, a maid appeared at the top.

Bette!

"My lady!" Bette said breathlessly. She raced down to meet her. "What are you doing down here?"

"You must help me, Bette. Where are Mother and Father?"

Bette's worried eyes answered her question for her.

"Will you help me? I need to re-pin my hair before

41

I meet them in my room." She slipped out of the coat and laid it on the floor at her feet. "Can you also return this to Prince Benjamin? You cannot let anyone else see it. It must be you!"

Bette nodded and moved to fix Roanna's hair. Roanna wiped her cheeks again, and a moment later Bette retrieved Ben's coat.

"My lady, are you all right?" Bette bit her lip.

Again, confusion swirled through Roanna. "I'm fine, Bette. Thank you for helping me. You're always my friend. I'm so grateful."

Bette smiled, but the worry still shone through. "Come on, I'll make sure you get to your room without bother."

9

Roanna and Bette stood at the door to Roanna's room. Mother and Father would want to know where she had been. They had obviously checked around the palace already, if even the dungeon guard had been notified. She couldn't say she had gone out for air as Ben's story kept him outside.

She had decided on using bits of the truth—a story about praying in the chapel then visiting the kitchen for a headache remedy. She did have a headache...now. Bette had promised to fill in the kitchen maid. Roanna hated to lie at all, but she didn't see another way. Besides, Mother had been keeping something from her all her life.

"How do I look?"

"Disheveled, but that could be because of the headache."

Roanna bit her lip. Were things really as serious as Ben seemed to think? She hadn't given her answer to Ambassador Dawson, but with her parents' permission, there was really very little else to say.

She took a deep breath and strolled into her room as if it were nothing out of the ordinary for Mother and Father to be waiting.

"Roanna!" Mother hurried to her side. "Where have you been?"

"I'm sorry to have kept you." She kissed Mother's cheek. "Bette told me you've been waiting. Ambassador Dawson proposed, as he said you know."

She hit them with a pointed look. Why hadn't they told her? "I had much to think about, and I went to the chapel to pray. A headache developed, and I visited the kitchen to find medication."

"I found her on the way back from the kitchen," Bette chimed in.

Mother gave Bette a small smile and nod. "Thank you, Bette. You may go now. I can help Princess Roanna into her bed clothes."

Bette curtsied and backed from the room.

"Are you feeling better now?" Mother led Roanna to where Father sat near the windows. Two chairs and a lounge were situated in a semi-circle.

"I feel some better but admittedly not much."

Mother held tightly to Roanna's hand. "You do not wish to marry Ambassador Dawson." It was more a statement than a question.

Roanna's throat tightened. "No, I do not. But do I have any choice?"

Silence.

All hope for her future wilted. "That is what I thought and likely what gave me the headache."

Father stood and paced to the window. "Roanna, you have long known you must marry. This will secure peace between our kingdoms. Think of the lives saved."

"I have thought of it Father, which is why I see no reason to fight it. Do you think I want Bette's brother's blood on my hands?" It was true. She wanted to cost no one their lives. After all, she would continue to live in luxury, while the kingdom's inhabitants would struggle to make a living.

Father turned to her. He smiled sadly, but his eyes were clear. Relieved. While he didn't wish sadness upon her, he still wanted her to say yes.

"The ambassador said he must await the approval of King Bartholomew." Maybe the answer would be delayed.

Father nodded. "Yes. He sent word. We expect to conference him tomorrow."

"Conference him?"

"Digitally, in the observatory."

Ah. She had almost forgotten about Father's ability to speak to the neighboring king at the touch of a button. Which also meant the answer wouldn't be delayed.

"Why didn't you tell me?"

"We have been hoping you would come around to caring for Ambassador Dawson on your own," Mother said. "He expressed his interest the first day he arrived."

Roanna stayed silent. How could she come to care for him? He was a stranger to her. A generation ahead of her.

"We should never have permitted you to spend so much time with Benjamin." Mother shook her head and pulled her hand away. "At least not after you had come of age."

Dear heavens, hopefully Mother wouldn't start in on this subject. Ben's words from not an hour ago were too fresh in Roanna's mind. She didn't wish to cry again so soon, nor with an audience.

"The Loxians will be leaving for home by tomorrow afternoon," Father announced.

Roanna's heart clenched. Ben had the file from the dungeon, and he'd be exploring the subject even at home. Perhaps it wouldn't take him long to find answers, but he'd asked her not to give an answer to the proposal until she heard back from him. How could she keep that promise if King Bartholomew would be conferencing Father tomorrow?

"What happens next?" she asked.

"Assuming King Bartholomew gives his consent, we will prepare to travel to our border at Edge River, where we will sign the marriage agreement and the peace treaty with Dawson's Edge." Father clasped his hands. "We will have peace, at least."

She nodded slowly. "But I will have a say." She wanted to be sure she had time to prepare herself. To resign herself. "The marriage will happen in time."

Mother and Father shared a glance.

Roanna held her breath.

"Ambassador Dawson is well into adulthood. He wishes for an heir."

An heir? He was already planning a family with her?

Roanna stood and paced away. She might be sick. "I cannot stand the thought of marrying that man."

"Roanna," Mother warned. "He is a kind, decent, and handsome man."

Roanna spun on her. "Mother! He repulses me. He cannot stop complimenting me long enough to know whether I prefer roses or daisies, blue or green, chicken or pork."

"You think those things matter in a marriage?" Mother rolled her eyes. "They do not. And besides, he admires your heart and your brain. He was very interested in your compassion for the Rejected."

Mother's words were partly true, but Roanna still wasn't convinced.

"Roanna," Father sighed. "The marriage agreement is being pursued, and you will go along with it. Not because we are forcing it on you, but because such is the life we lead."

In spite of her best efforts, tears pooled in her eyes. She glanced between Mother and Father. She knew their story; they had not been allowed to choose each other. Still, they had found happiness. And hadn't she always known this was her fate? Her destiny was much harder to face than she had ever anticipated. Perhaps Mother was right. Perhaps it had been unwise to spend so much time with Benjamin over the years. Now every man she met would be compared to him. It would take many evening prayers to deal with seeing Ben and not being friends with him.

She swiped the tears from her cheeks and took a shuddering breath. "I do not pretend to like it, but I will do as you say."

10

Father left the room, and Mother helped Roanna out of her dress. The silence between them left Roanna feeling alone. How often would she get to see her family if she moved to Dawson's Edge? What would a life spent with Roland Dawson be like?

Mother folded Roanna's black, silky evening gown and laid it over the foot of the bed as Roanna slipped into her nightgown. "Sit down and I'll undo your hair."

"No, I'll do it. I'm going to stay up a bit more."

Mother's eyes narrowed a fraction, but she said nothing. If only she knew Roanna's behaviors had nothing to do with sneaking out and everything to do with hiding the length of her locks.

The short, handwritten note from the file in the dungeon haunted her. Should she ask Mother about the man who had warned her about Roanna's hair?

Maybe a different tactic. "Did you see that girl who came with the ambassador? Merry is her name."

"The Baron's daughter. I saw her, yes."

"Her hair is beautiful. Could we hold off on a wedding until my hair can grow long?"

Mother's eyes crinkled at the sides, and she tried to pull off a laugh. It didn't come through. "Growing your hair that long would take at least two years."

The longer the better.

"Besides, your hair looks lovely short. Even when

you pin it up you do it so well."

Roanna sighed. She didn't have the strength to pursue the issue tonight. "Very well."

A true smile spread across Mother's face, and she hugged Roanna. "It will be a lovely wedding."

"Have you been to Dawson's Edge recently?" Roanna never visited that she could remember.

A cloud passed behind Mother's eyes, and she shook her head. "Only once, for the crown prince's wedding."

"Ambassador Dawson became angry with me tonight. It was over the simplest thing." Roanna sat on the edge of her bed. "I can only imagine what a life with him will be like."

Worry showed in Mother's face, but she only said, "Tell me what it was about."

"He kept showering me with embarrassing compliments, so I attempted a real conversation by asking him what he thought of the advancements in our observatory. He grew agitated because he felt I was implying Chester's Wake was superior to Dawson's Edge. He brought up Prince Stefan and Isabella de Paul. The response was strange and uncomfortable."

Mother took her hand. "I'm sorry. Yes, they are strange people. But you will adjust. Perhaps you will even shed a little light into their world." Mother paused as if she wanted to say more. "Roanna, you must give up your friendship with Benjamin. It will no longer appear proper, no matter how innocent you keep it."

Give up her friendship? How did one give up a mutual and deep friendship?

But Ben had said the same thing, and they had

agreed. They would not start a war for each other. "Yes, Mother, I am aware."

"Good." Mother squeezed her hand and stood. "I will leave you to your rest. Should I send Bette back up to unpin your hair?"

"No, of course not. I'm perfectly capable of removing a few hairpins."

"Very well. Good night." Mother kissed the top of her head and left her sitting on the bed. When the door closed, Roanna moved to her vanity seat. Staring at her hair in the mirror, she removed the turtle hair clip and then the pins holding her hair in place. The tresses fell around her shoulders again.

Why should she keep it short? A warning so important that a man would shout it at a new mother and land in the dungeon over it. A warning that had so frightened Mother that she'd decreed Roanna must keep her hair short.

Truly, it was absurd. She grabbed the comb and ran it through her hair. Over and over and over. When Ambassador Dawson had whispered to her, a shiver had run through her. Then, when she'd messed with her hair before supper, the shiver had returned.

Now she felt nothing. Not even a tingle.

Roanna sighed and set the brush on the vanity. She had most likely caught a chill, and nothing more. The doctor from Dawson's Edge was an old superstitious fool, and he had succeeded in scaring Mother into following his advice. But Father must know about the whole ordeal, or else how would the man end up in the dungeon? It was unlike him to allow Mother to go along with such foolishness.

She climbed in bed and pulled her white blankets up to her chin. Tomorrow the course of her entire life could be changed. She could only hope for the best.

As she fell into a restful breathing pattern a deep shiver raced through her. Roanna sat up in bed with a gasp. Her hand moved to her hair and she felt the silky strands. The shivers continued for long moments, and Roanna endured them alone for as long as she could stand.

Finally, she climbed from her bed. In light of what they'd found in the dungeon, this was something Ben must see.

11

Roanna crept from her room. The hallways in the family wing were empty and the guest rooms only a few halls away. It was late, but any one of the other guests' doors might open, and she would be spotted. What would she say, standing there in her silky pajamas and dressing robe?

Down one hall, around a corner, past four doors, and around a second corner. The Loxians always stayed in the same suite of rooms. Roanna had never dared visit while they were occupied. Did she truly have the gumption to do it now? After all, appearances were everything. What if another guest saw her? Or a servant? They would get the wrong impression, and rumors would spread. Rumors were rarely able to be undone.

As she approached Ben's door, noise came from behind it. Voices. Roanna glanced around. She was alone.

Slowly, she placed her ear to the door. "Mother, nothing has happened between us nor will it ever!" Ben sounded irritated and defiant.

"The truth is not what matters when it comes to most peoples' perceptions. Rather, what appears to be true is what people will believe." Queen Frieda spoke in her usual calm manner.

The bite of her words burned. Hadn't Roanna just had the same thoughts about rumors and being caught?

"Why can we not wait until morning," Ben pleaded. "Why must we leave tonight?"

Leave? The Bellevues were leaving in the middle of the night because no one had been able to find her or Ben, and no one believed their story. Or rather, even if their families believed their stories, no one else would.

Her heart sank to the pit of her stomach.

"We will not hinder the peace between Chester's Wake and Dawson's Edge," Queen Frieda said. "The time has come to put away childish things. You are a man now, and you must take responsibility."

Something crashed inside the room, and Roanna jumped.

"Benjamin!" King Neville chimed in. "You will control your temper."

Ben had done that? Roanna took a deep breath and backed away from the Loxians' suite. First, he had threatened the dungeon guard, and now he was breaking things. This angry Ben didn't match up with the same loving and kind boy she'd always known. The boy who stooped in front of others to help a servant clean a mess. What had caused the change?

She knew without even forming the entire thought. He'd changed because of her. Because of their friendship—or rather, the end of their friendship.

She hurried back to her room. She would not see Ben again before he left. Tears clogged her throat, but she breathed deeply to keep them at bay. Once inside her suite, Roanna pressed her eyes closed and leaned against the door. Slowly, the urge to cry passed. Her shivers had left her.

Her hand went to her hair. Should she brush it again? Bring back the sensation? But to what end?

No. The shivers were useless unless she knew what they meant. Bypassing the vanity, she moved to her bed and resumed her curled up position under the covers. Try as she might, rest wouldn't come. Was Ben still here? Or had his family already left? The autos would take them directly to the small royal air station. They would fly out in an airship and be home by morning. Once Ben left, what recourse did she have other than to allow her fate to swallow her? Father didn't allow frivolous use of the technologies, and any mail between her and Ben would be screened at this point.

Gregory.

He had the same access to resources that Ben had in Lox. Could he pass messages through? Would he?

Gregory would help, she was sure of it. Peace found her at last. She was finally able to relax, and sleep overtook her.

In the morning, weak sunlight peeked through her windows. Someone bumped around from inside her dressing area. Roanna rubbed her gritty eyes, and she moaned because of a headache. She must have cried in her sleep.

"Bette, is that you?"

Bette breezed into the sleeping area. "Good morning, Miss. Did you sleep well?"

"Actually, I have quite the headache. Could you find me something for it?"

"Certainly, Miss." Bette turned to go.

"Wait."

Bette stopped and looked to her expectantly.

"Did you return the coat in time?"

Bette bit her lip, a nervous habit she usually hid well. "No, Miss. The Bellevues left early, and I did not have time to deliver it in private. I've hidden it in my room."

Bless Bette. "That's fine. I had figured as much." Roanna considered an idea. It was foolish and irresponsible, and she shouldn't voice it. "Can you bring it to me? Without it being seen? I should like to keep it."

Bette curtsied. "As you wish, Miss." She left, and Roanna rolled out of bed. A hot shower would help relax her muscles. She moved to the bathroom and turned on the faucet. Steamy water from thick copper pipes swirled around her, but the heat did little to make her feel better. Her head throbbed, but more than that her heart ached.

When she finished her shower, Bette had returned. She had laid out Roanna's brown, woolen day dress for breakfast. Roanna dressed but insisted on doing her own hair. It might be time to keep Bette away from it until Roanna could figure out what was going on.

How had a Dawsonian doctor known something would be wrong with Roanna's hair?

"Good luck with the ambassador today, Miss," Bette said.

Roanna smiled wearily. "Thank you, Bette."

They finished Roanna's wardrobe with a pair of shoes and she headed toward the stairs. She was anything but ready to put on a smiling face for her guests. As she descended the stairs, a manservant approached. Perhaps he was on his way to assist Gregory.

"Princess Roanna."

She stopped, surprised.

The servant held an envelope toward her. He stepped closer to keep it hidden. "This is for you."

Roanna looked down. It was a small, white envelope, and her name was written on it in Ben's handwriting.

12

"Thank you." She took the envelope.

He bowed slightly and stepped away. What was she to do with it? She had no pockets.

Two of Ambassador Dawson's companions were coming from the top of the staircase. She must hide the note.

Crushing it in her palm, she turned to them with a smile. "Good morning, gentlemen."

"Good morning, Princess," one answered. She recognized him as Merry's father, Baron Stern. "Can we escort you to breakfast?"

"Thank you, but I was just headed to the chapel for morning prayers."

"I see. We will meet you in the dining hall later then."

She smiled, and they parted ways.

Keeping a slow pace to the chapel was torture. The door squealed on its hinges as she pushed through, but the room was blessedly empty. She hurried to the front pew and tore open her note. The paper took a little smoothing out, but Ben's writing was clear. He gave no salutation.

By now you likely know I have gone home. I would have said good-bye, but I trust you will believe me when I say I had no choice. I will research the doctor from my end. He may still be alive. I do not know when I will see you again. Father will stay on top of the peace treaty progress, and I will glean what I can from him.

There is no time to write more. Father already calls my name, wondering what takes me so long. Please know I will keep you in my nightly prayers and also in my heart. You will remain there always no matter the path our friendship is forced to take.

He left it at that. Roanna's hands shook as she considered his final sentence. It felt so dramatic, this sudden end of their long friendship. Pressing her eyes closed against the tears, she considered her options. She could burn the note with one of the candles or hide it. Unable to bear the thought of destroying Ben's last words to her, she chose to hide it. A few small statues sat around the altar. They were fashioned into the likeness of scrolls, each with a different religious quote.

Pray without ceasing.

Love thy neighbor as thyself.

Thou shalt not covet.

Roanna lifted one statue and slid the note underneath. She would retrieve it later when the guests were gone.

She stood. Time to face Father, Ambassador Dawson, and the rest of the breakfast crowd. She hurried from the chapel, past the staircase, down the hall, and into the dining room. It wasn't nearly as full as it had been the night before. Many of the ladies chose to dine in their rooms. With the Loxian entourage gone, there was only Father and Mother, Ambassador Dawson and his two companions, along with Merry.

Roanna slid into the seat beside Merry, thankful the seats on each side of Ambassador Dawson were taken. "Good morning," she said with her best smile.

Merry returned her smile, and it put Roanna at

ease immediately. "Good morning, Princess Roanna. It's a much prettier day today, don't you think?"

Roanna looked to the huge windows facing the river and the cobbled streets of the city. The waters were calm, and the sky was blue. She hadn't even noticed the weather before now. "It certainly is."

A servant appeared with orange juice, and Roanna took a few slices of toast from a platter in the middle of the table.

"I wondered if we might visit the gardens today," Merry went on. "I haven't been able to see them yet."

A pang hit Roanna. She would have done better to have spent the last week with Merry rather than Ben. At least then he would still be in Chester's Wake.

"That would be lovely. Shall we go after breakfast?" The gardens were by far her favorite place in the palace. The flowers filled her with peace, and she'd had a knack for growing things since childhood.

Merry's smile brightened. "Yes, let's!"

Roanna returned the smile then bit into her toast. It would likely serve her well to make a friend who lived in Dawson's Edge. It would help keep her from loneliness once she was married to Roland.

"It's too bad King Neville had to leave so soon." Baron Stern's voice carried from across the table. He spoke to Father. "What the devil caused him to sneak away in the night?"

Roanna stilled, not looking toward the men but listening all the same.

"Urgent business in Lox," Father answered. "It's a pity."

Roanna took another bite of her toast. She took care to show no emotion over the simple statement.

They finished breakfast, and Roanna had just

stood when Ambassador Dawson approached. "Good morning, Princess. Did you sleep well?"

Not exactly. "Yes, thank you. How about you?"

"Quite well. I wondered if we might spend some time together this morning. Perhaps a stroll along the bay."

Thank heavens for Merry. "I apologize, Ambassador. I just promised to take Merry on a tour of the gardens. Would you like to come?"

He frowned slightly and glanced at Merry. "No, I wouldn't interrupt your time together. Perhaps this afternoon then, following our luncheon?"

There was no way around it. She smiled and nodded. "I look forward to it."

His smile returned. "I will wait for the hours to pass then." He moved away, and Roanna joined Merry.

"We have many beautiful flower species," Roanna said as they left the dining hall. "I'm sure you will enjoy it."

"I look forward to it. It's been quite dreary since we arrived." Her eyes widened. "Oh! It's not that we haven't enjoyed our stay. Your palace is beautiful. In Dawson's Edge the palace is so secluded. Here, the palace is right in the midst of the capital city. It's fascinating, in spite of the rain."

Roanna smiled to accept the compliment, but guilt hit her. She had left royal guests without a companion so she could spend time with Ben. What had Merry been doing while Roanna gallivanted about?

"I trust you've seen the observatory?"

"Yes, Prince Gregory has been a most gracious host."

Ah. Gregory. She had forgotten. She smiled again. "I'm so glad." She would have to thank him later.

They exited the palace on the western side, and Roanna led her guest into the large garden, bordered on two sides by a tall cobblestone wall. Another side bordered the palace, and one side was open to the river. They moved from bush to bush, smelling the roses, carnations, and morning glories that hadn't yet closed their blooms to the sun's heat.

"Do you have different flora in Dawson's Edge?" Roanna asked as they fingered the silky petals.

"Some different and some the same," Merry said. "But many flowers don't grow well in Dawson's Edge."

Roanna frowned. "Why so?"

"It's the heat." Merry sighed. "Only the rich are able to afford the upkeep of the blossoms that come naturally to our climate. We only have a small garden at the Stern Estate."

"How disappointing," Roanna said. "I love flowers." What sort of garden would Roland have?

"It's not as if we have no flowers, of course. The royals have more than others, but it is said that it is to aid their conjurers. The conjurers use the flowers' medicinal properties." The tone in Merry's voice piqued Roanna's interest.

Conjurers? It was rumored that the conjurers were the main reason the Dawsonians did not practice Termination, though Roanna had never heard any proof that the royal sorcerers existed. If it were true, Dawson's Edge wouldn't want to kill off those among them who held powerful anomalies.

"You do not agree with these beliefs?" Roanna asked.

Merry frowned slightly, but it didn't mar her beauty. "I don't, but what say do I have? Regardless, I will certainly enjoy the flowers you have here."

Uncertainty filled Roanna. Would Roland keep her from growing flowers in Dawson's Edge? She pointed to an area of shrubbery and led them to view it next. Like Merry, she would enjoy her palace home as long as she could. And once she was in Dawson's Edge she would hope for the best.

13

Ben

Ben paced his room, refusing to eat or sleep until he learned Roanna's fate. A few more minutes and his servant would be finished arranging his closet. Hansen would leave the room, and Ben would be free to find out what was going on with the peace treaty between their neighboring kingdoms. In one hour, Mother and Father would partake in the conference call between nations in order to serve as witnesses, and Ben intended to be present.

Roanna was to be married off to a man old enough to be her father. This might not be uncommon, but he couldn't stand the thought for Roanna. She was vibrant and young. She deserved better than to be whisked off to the obscurity of Dawson's Edge, never to be heard from again.

The conference call would begin soon, and he would have to be dead before he'd let them keep him away. He would know Roanna's fate.

"Will that be all?" Hansen asked. He had been attending Ben since Ben's childhood. He was tall and lanky, and he wore a tuxedo at all times even though Mother and Father insisted such formalities were long gone. He held that the royal family deserved his very best.

Ben owed him all the respect in the world. "Yes, Hansen. Thank you very much."

Hansen bowed deeply. "Welcome home, sir." He

left the room and closed the door quietly behind him.

Ben moved to his bed and pulled the file from Chester's Wake from under his pillow. He locked it in his desk then headed toward the state rooms. Mother and Father would be there, preparing to participate in the conference message. They wouldn't want him there—didn't want him to have anything to do with Roanna ever again. But they wouldn't keep him out, not if he insisted.

It had been reckless to drag Roanna to the dungeon after supper last night. Of course, people would be suspicious. Weren't they always? But he wouldn't have been able to get into the dungeon without her. Besides, he didn't regret it. For those few minutes—those few brief minutes—he'd seen the truth in her face. She didn't want their friendship to end. She didn't want to give him up, any more than he wanted to lose her.

For years, he had kept his feelings to himself. Never hinting that he wished their friendship could be more. Maybe he had been irresponsible last night, but why should he care? Hadn't he played by the rules all these years? What had it garnered him?

Regardless, what were her parents thinking to allow an engagement with Roland Dawson? Would they really subject their only daughter to live in such a dark and unharmonious country?

Ben hurried through the palace, making his way to the state rooms. The glass ceiling in the palace entryway let in rivers of light, and bright, open passageways gave way to various wings of the palace. Lilacs and greenery had been planted throughout the halls, and huge windows bathed the space with bright sunlight. At last, he reached the backside of the palace, where the state rooms were housed. He stomped across the marble floors. From these rooms his kingdom was ruled. One day, he would be the one doing the ruling.

"Your Highness." Father's secretary curtsied to him. "Queen Frieda cannot see you now."

He breezed past her. "I'm not here to see her. I'm here to join her."

"Prince Benjamin, wait!" She scurried out from behind her desk, her heels clicking against the marble. "The Queen said you are not to interrupt, no matter what."

Ben only paused long enough to answer her. "I will tell her I forced my way past you."

He pushed through the doors to the conference room. A large white screen hung against one wall, with a split down the middle. Two faces appeared on either side: King Bartholomew Dawson on one side, and King Hamilton of Chester's Wake on the other. Mother and Father sat at the long, cherry wood conference table. King Hamilton's real-time speech halted from the left of the screen as all eyes turned to Ben.

Even across the miles, the irritation in King Hamilton's face was evident. He didn't want to see Ben as part of the conference. Didn't want him upsetting the possible peace of his kingdom by insisting on staying in contact with his daughter.

Ben sat at the table as Mother and Father glared at him.

"I will speak to you when we finish." Mother's words were calm, but her eyes shot fire.

"I will hear the terms of the peace treaty myself. Won't I be king some day?"

"You are not king now," Father piped up. "Out."

Ben turned to King Dawson. "Your Highness, would you turn me away when I am to wed your own daughter some day?" It was a weak excuse, but he had no others. Father and Mother had lied to him, telling him the conference didn't start for another hour. They knew he would show up, and they hoped to be done with it by then. He should have known better.

To his surprise, Dawson laughed. "Stay if you like, Prince."

Father pierced him with a glare, but the conference resumed.

King Hamilton cleared his throat. "As I said earlier, the marriage between my daughter and your brother is agreeable to me," he spoke to King Dawson. "I would have only one other condition, and that would be for your border patrol to stand down. My landowners are frightened to be living under such scrutiny and fear."

King Dawson scoffed. "My patrol never interferes. If your landowners fear it is their own conscience."

"It is my condition." King Hamilton didn't flinch. "Roanna has agreed to the terms of the marriage, but she would also agree if I advised her against the agreement."

Roanna had agreed to the marriage? He'd told her to wait. King Hamilton must not have given her any choice at all.

On screen, King Dawson's nostrils flared at King Hamilton's threat. Off screen, Ben's stomach churned. How could King Hamilton give Roanna to this family?

"Think of the reign of peace," Mother said from the table. She spoke to the men on the screen. "Telling your guards to stand down by patrolling only a few miles further inland will not hurt anything, but it will help much. Let it be said of our generation that we are finally the monarchs to bring peace to our once broken nations."

Her softly spoken words seemed to resonate with King Dawson. "Our peace is not complete with only the marriage between Roland and your daughter, King Hamilton," Dawson said. "The peace of our three nations will not be complete until the marriage agreement has been fulfilled with Prince Benjamin of Lox as well, as he so eloquently reminded us a moment ago."

Ben didn't react. Unless King Dawson had a secret daughter he'd kept hidden away, he wasn't worried.

Father cleared his throat and spoke to the screen. "We have upheld our end of the bargain. Benjamin remains unmarried."

"I am losing hope of a female offspring," King Dawson said with a sigh. "I have been considering other options."

Father and Mother shared a look, but it told Ben nothing of what they were thinking. "Go on," Mother said.

"We have noble daughters in this country. Young women trained in the way of royalty and gentility, charity, and religion. Would one of them not suffice as the future Queen of Lox?"

"Our agreement was for a princess of Dawson's Edge, not a noble daughter." Mother straightened in her seat. Queenly.

Ben waited with his jaw tight. King Dawson meant to marry him off to someone other than his own bloodline?

"The marriage would achieve the same end," King Dawson said. "Peace. And do we not want to be the generation that can boast peace at last?" He waved his hand and a smile spoke more of his mockery than his words.

Anger spread through Ben, but Mother and Father remained calm.

"It is something we will need to consider," Mother said. "For today, we are here to witness the treaty between Dawson's Edge and Chester's Wake. That is all."

King Dawson smiled. "Very well. I will accept your terms, King George Hamilton. My border patrol will stand down, and you will send your daughter home with Roland."

King Hamilton's face turned red. "I will not send my daughter home with him. We will prepare the proper festivities for the engagement. We will meet at Edge River to sign the treaty. Then and only then will we move forward with the wedding."

King Dawson rolled his eyes. "So be it. We will set up a meeting for next week."

"That is acceptable to Chester's Wake," King Hamilton said.

Mother smiled. "Excellent. I will attend to witness the treaty."

Mother and Father would attend, but definitely not Ben.

He waited for the screens to go black before standing and storming from the room.

"Benjamin, wait!" Father's voice boomed.

Ben kept moving.

Father charged after him and grabbed his shoulder. "You will not storm away from me in this manner. Return to the conference room."

Ben ground his teeth, but he obeyed. Father led the

way, and once Ben was inside, Father shut the door and leaned close to Ben's face. "What did you hope to accomplish by barging in here like that?"

"I wanted to hear with my own ears the terms of the peace treaty."

"To what end?" Father spoke the words slowly.

Ben ground his teeth, his nostrils stretching. What could he say that wouldn't leave him looking like a weak fool?

He glanced at Mother. She stood erect, her shoulders straight. But her eyes were soft. Ben swallowed his pride. "I wanted to hear for myself that she was to be married." He looked away, his throat suddenly tight. "I needed to hear it for myself." Shame and embarrassment spread through him. He always knew it would end this way. As Father had asked, what did he expect to accomplish?

Father did not back down. "You will abide by the terms of this peace treaty. And if we choose a bride for you who is born of the Dawson's Edge nobility, you will abide by this as well."

Ben became stone. He nodded once, his features tight. "Yes, sir." He waited a moment. "May I be dismissed now?"

14

Father watched him as they faced off in the conference room. Studied him. Sized him up. Finally, he nodded.

Ben bolted from the room without another thought. He half-expected Mother to call after him, but she didn't. Ben strode from the palace, past the gardens, and toward the garage. It was huge, housing over one hundred automatic vehicles.

He shoved through the glass door, and Victor, the mechanic, stopped him. "Your Highness, what brings you to visit so soon? I thought you were in Chester's Wake."

Ben took a deep breath. He wouldn't do anyone any good by biting off Victor's head. "Father thought it was time to come home early. I would like to take out the Black Widow."

Victor's eyebrows rose. "Fast bike! Looking to blow off some steam?"

Ben stared at him.

Victor nodded. "You got it. Follow me."

Ben moved after the mechanic through the garage. Victor could fix any problem in any auto at any time. He had served Father well, and someday either he or his apprentice would serve Ben well.

With a Daswsonian woman at his side.

The reminder was like rotten meat in his gut. Why had it never repulsed him so much before? Maybe he had been living in a dream world. It hadn't felt real until this week. Until this day.

He had seen the way Roland Dawson looked at Roanna. From the moment Roland's entourage had arrived, he knew. He'd worked tirelessly to keep Roanna away from the man—sneaking her off to take walks around the palace in the warm summer rain, hiding with her in the library, debating bringing up the doctor in the dungeon. None of it had deterred the ambassador, and why should it? Roanna would improve his social standing—he was so far down the list of relatives to inherit the crown of Dawson's Edge that it was laughable. And besides, she was beautiful. Radiantly, blindingly, beautiful, inside and out.

"Prince?"

Ben focused on Victor, who stood two feet away holding out a set of keys. "Thank you, Victor." He took the keys and climbed onto the motorcycle.

"Enjoy the ride, Your Highness, and come back in one piece, or the queen will have my hide."

Ben gave him a tight smile and started the Black Widow with a roar. This bike was fast. So fast he might make it back to Chester's Wake in a few hours. Father would throttle him if he did. Mother would fume and fuss. King Hamilton would string him up, and war would likely start—at least, a war against him.

But Roanna would be happy to see him.

He positioned his goggles over his eyes, secured his helmet strap under his chin, gripped the handlebars, and pulled from the garage. The engine purred under his coaxing. He sailed through the palace gates and headed toward the flatlands at the western edge of their kingdom.

So, he wasn't going to Chester's Wake after all.

Ben pressed forward. He drove so fast his

shoulders ached with the force. He drove until the gas gauge inched toward empty. Well after dark he returned to the garage. Victor met him again. "I thought you'd driven off the edge of the world."

Ben shook his head. "No, only until I'd come back from it."

Victor gave him a quizzical look, but Ben didn't expound. His stomach growled, and he headed back for the palace. He was famished. He hadn't eaten since supper last night in Chester's Wake. He raided the kitchen and headed to his room. Hansen was there waiting, ever faithful.

"You can go on to bed, Hansen," Ben said. He slipped off his shoes and sank into a chair in his sitting room. "I'll dress myself for bed."

Hansen bowed. "Very well, sir. Your father has requested you join him at eight o'clock sharp in the morning. You are to work with him for the day."

"Thank you." Hansen left, and Ben bit into his sandwich. Work with Father. That could mean anything. More training? A diplomatic mission? A good will visit?

The slender brass messenger on his desk caught his eye. The bulbous light in the upper right hand corner blinked slowly.

Frowning, he moved to it and touched the light. The small screen glowed to life.

One message

The message loaded from Prince Gregory, and Ben's eyes widened in surprise, and not even bothering to sit in the chair, he read the missive.

We hope your flight home went well. Chester's Wake misses you already; however, we understand the importance of the issue calling you away. Rest assured that we look

forward to the next meeting of our peaceful kingdoms.
Sincerely
The Prince of Chester's Wake

Gregory had never contacted him like this before. They'd always gotten along, but had never been close friends. Roanna had been the one to capture his friendship as a child, her bright smile and contagious laugh, her adventurous spirit and fierce loyalty. She had found a way to send him a message, and he loved her all the more for it.

He considered whether to reply. After devouring his late supper, he stripped and tossed the dirty clothes into the basket, moved to the seat at his desk, and stared at the message.

"Type." The cursor blinked to life, and he spoke what should be transmitted.

"The flight was uneventful. I was happy to be allowed to sit in on the peace treaty between your country and our mutual neighbor, Dawson's Edge. I, too, look forward to the next visit between our countries. Until then, Prince Benjamin of Lox."

He couldn't hint at the marriage agreement. Couldn't cause a ripple. At least, not yet. Tomorrow he would work with Father. He would go along with this plan at marrying both himself and Roanna into the Dawsonian line.

But he would also work toward unravelling the mystery behind Dr. Presnell attending to Roanna's birth. The pieces did not fit smoothly together, and until he could put his curiosity to rest, he would not give up.

15

Father sat behind his desk, pen poised over paper. He looked up when Ben entered.

"Hansen said I was to meet you here."

Father resumed his writing, but a moment later, he put his pen away and stood. "You're going with me on a condolence mission today."

"A condolence mission? Who will we see?"

Father pressed a button, and a voice came through the intercom.

"The auto is waiting, Your Highness," the secretary announced.

Father nodded.

Ben led them from the office and onto the white marble floor of the bright, state room lobby. They walked silently to the exit, and a driver met them. Once they were seated and the auto in motion, Ben repeated his question. "Who died, Father?"

Father's eyes were sorrowful and understanding. "You need to see what war looks like, Benjamin. Your mother and I worry that you have been very sheltered from it. Even in Chester's Wake they live in relative peace, though it is worse along their borders. But wars and rumors of war hurt people. Not figments, but real people with real families."

Ben didn't understand what Father was getting at. He wasn't a boy anymore. Of course, war was real and it hurt real people. This wasn't a revelation to him.

They drove for two hours. Father spent most of the time with his head bent over a portable screen. A royal's job was never done. It was one of Mother's favorite quips.

Before long Ben would be working as diligently as Mother and Father. If he was to be married soon, he would be expected to pull his fair share. And let the work come. Ben loved Lox. He wanted to see her prosper. Wanted to help keep her peaceful. Peace was the Loxian way, as Mother always reminded him. He only wished Mother would consider that there might be better ways to do it—better ways than marrying one's children off to other kingdoms.

Roanna would say better ways than practicing Termination. Lox and Chester's Wake engaged in the practice for multiple reasons—it cut down on medical costs within the kingdom, it helped control population numbers, but most of all because it saved citizens from unnecessary pain and suffering. This was what they told the people. Roanna disagreed strongly, and while Ben hadn't settled his beliefs on the matter he was inclined to follow her thoughts on the subject. He'd seen the Rejected. They were worthwhile people, though it was true that some of their anomalies could be frightening.

His thoughts were interrupted as they they pulled up to a small border military base, only miles from Dawson's Edge.

The driver opened the door.

Father led them into the base.

A military general greeted them. He was dressed in a dark green uniform with brass buttons and golden lining. An eye—the Loxian symbol—was embroidered on the right shoulder.

"Right this way, Your Highness." The general led them through a string of dark hallways before finally pausing outside a white metal door marked *Morgue*. "It isn't pretty. I warn you."

Ben's gut clenched.

Father nodded. "We will see the soldiers."

Ben rolled his tense neck, not looking forward to checking over dead bodies.

Three black bags lay on three separate tables. The general unsnapped the first bag. The soldier was a man at least twice Ben's age. His hair was dark, almost black, but his skin was now a sickly blue color. Part of his face was missing, and the gaping wounds stared up at him.

"Tell us how it happened," Father demanded.

The general's chin lifted slightly. "They were ambushed, Your Grace. Dawsonian patrols mistook them for Chester's Wake soldiers. Attacked and killed. Once they got closer and saw their error, they ran."

"Why are they attacking Chester's Wake?" Ben asked. They had agreed to the peace treaty the morning before, and had been in the midst of negotiations during Roland's visit to Chester's Wake.

"Some would say Dawsonians do not trust King George Hamilton," the general said. "Personally, I believe King Dawson wants an empire."

"That will be enough," Father said. "Show us the others."

Ben didn't ask any more questions. Maybe they were much nearer to the brink of war than he had realized.

They left the morgue, and went to where tent housing had been set up for soldiers and their families. They would be visiting the soldiers' families. This would not be easy.

The green-clad military personnel bowed to them as they walked through the base.

Father nodded to each of them respectfully, and Ben followed his example.

The first tent they entered was a small but well organized home. A clothesline had been strung out front, and inside, a woman huddled on a pallet with a baby. Tears stained her face. Her eyes widened when she recognized Father. With the baby clutched to her chest, she moved to her knees.

"No, please," Father knelt in front of her. "I should show reverence to you." Tears pooled in his eyes as he took the woman's elbows in his hands. "I am truly sorry for your loss, but I respect your sacrifice more than you can ever know."

The woman hiccupped on a sob, but she managed a nod.

This was the father Ben knew. The fair man. The respectful and kind leader. It had been disrespectful for Ben to defy him.

The next two visits were no easier.

Ben spoke when the situation dictated, and he made sure to follow Father's example of comfort and respect for the widows and their families.

After three hours on base, they returned to the vehicle to ride back to the palace.

Father turned to him. His eyes were red rimmed from the honest tears he had wept. "Now do you see how necessary it is that we don't go to war?"

Ben's stomach knotted. "Yes, Father." Could he do that to his own subjects? Cause them harm and heartache because he wanted Roanna for himself?

No. This was the way of their world, and he

would accept and respect it. He swallowed down his words. "I understand, Father," he said more forcefully. "I intend to keep up my end of the agreement."

Father nodded slowly, his shoulders slumped. "I knew you would say that, once you had seen." He leaned his head back on the seat and closed his eyes. "You will make a fine king, and you will reign in peace."

16

Benjamin took supper in his room that night. The widows they'd met that day were alone now, struggling because of a conflict between neighboring countries. How would they buy food for their children? Where would they live when they left the military base?

He twirled his silver fork between his fingers, considering. Why was there so much animosity between Dawson's Edge and Chester's Wake? There had always been tension because of the split Dawson's Edge made from Chester's Wake, but that had been two hundred years ago. With the marriage agreement for Roanna and Roland Dawson going forward, he had believed there was little chance of war on the horizon. There should have been no attacks taking place.

Unless Dawson's Edge was planning a secret attack, he couldn't see a reason for the duplicity.

Ben pushed his plate aside and moved to his desk. He unlocked the door where he'd stored the file from the Chester's Wake's dungeon. He wanted to read it again with fresh eyes.

Dr. Presnell had been visiting Chester's Wake and was a guest in their home when Queen Hamilton went into labor. He'd helped attend the birth, told the queen she'd had a girl, and that the girl's hair must be cut short. Dr. Presnell repeated it several times, and the queen grew so agitated that Dr. Presnell was locked away for a month, an extreme punishment for what seemed to be innocuous advice.

Tucking the file behind his back, Ben left his room and headed to the library where he'd first read the account in the Loxian memoir. Maybe he'd missed something because he didn't fully understand the situation.

The library was on the first floor, just to the left of the palace's main entrance. Moonlight came in through the glass dome of the entryway, and it made the white marble glow.

The library was empty. Guests were absent because the Bellevues were supposed to be in Chester's Wake.

The main room was dim, lit only by an evening security light. Father and Mother prided themselves on the advanced knowledge available to the citizens of Lox compared to their neighboring countries. The Loxians had recovered and saved much of the art and educational tools lost from centuries ago. Mother said that was the reason the Loxians enjoyed more peace than the others.

Ben left the light off as he strode to the back room, to the place where he'd been studying history and political technique. Knowledge was power, Father always said. He pulled the small diary from the shelf where he'd left it and settled into his usual red armchair. "Lights."

The room was bathed in soft gaslight.

He pulled the file from behind his back, laid it out on the small table at his side, and then flipped through the diary until he came to the notes about the imprisoned doctor.

December 13, 391 P.W.

Whilst visiting our neighbors in Chester's Wake, Queen Hamilton went into birthing labor with her second child. It was early labor, as the queen was several weeks before her time. A doctor of Dawson's Edge happened to be visiting, to his great misfortune. He was able to attend the queen until her own doctor could arrive. However, the queen delivered long before a second doctor made his appearance. The doctor, superstitious Dawsonian that he was, caused such a fuss over the baby that he was thrown into the dungeon! It made for quite an entertaining evening.

The entry stopped there, and Ben grabbed the file he'd taken from the dungeon. The handwritten notes were brief and to the point.

The memoir stated again that Dr. Presnell was a superstitious Dawsonian. So what connection did a Chester's Wake baby have with a Dawsonian superstition? Dawsonian women didn't keep their hair cut short. Roland Dawson had quite a few ladies in his entourage, and they'd had long hair.

So, why would Queen Hamilton's child need short hair? A curse, perhaps? The Dawsonians employed conjurers. Maybe Dr. Presnell was one of them, despite being a respected physician who travelled between kingdoms. But why should Dr. Presnell care what happened to the Hamilton's baby?

He scanned the memoir, checking to see if the author had made any other references to the event. When he found none, he replaced the book before turning off the lights and returning to his room. He relocked his stolen file in his desk drawer and slammed the key onto the solid wood top. He knew nothing more now than when he'd started.

On his bedside table a square white note had been propped against his clock. In Hansen's fine handwriting it said;

Queen Frieda requests you meet her in her office first thing in the morning.

Another appointment. What tragedies did she and Father have to show Ben next? He didn't need more lessons on the importance of keeping the people safe. He understood, and he would not risk the lives of his people. Nor would Roanna wish him to. It was a pledge Mother and Father obviously did not trust.

17

Ben sat in the waiting area of the state rooms.

Mother's secretary had arrived a few minutes before, but Mother hadn't made it to her office yet.

"Can I get you anything, Your Highness?" the secretary asked.

He should ask for her name. After all, he'd likely be working in these offices very soon. The time for studying was almost at an end. Instead, he said, "No, thank you."

She smiled and went back to work, and he beat his pinkie finger on the smooth leather armrest. Where was Mother? She was rarely late, and especially not to a meeting she had called.

"Your Highness, the queen will see you now."

Finally. Ben bolted from his seat. "Mother," he said as he entered the office and closed the heavy wooden door. He sat across from her.

"Benjamin." Mother sat at her desk. She pushed a button on her Messenger screen and looked at Ben. "Hansen will begin packing your suitcases immediately. You will travel to Dawson's Edge for an upcoming ball."

Ben frowned. "Why?"

"King Dawson has determined the best way for you to meet a noble bride is by holding a ball where you can mingle with their people. See if anyone strikes your fancy."

Strikes his fancy? So, Father and Mother had decided to move forward with King Dawson's plan. Dread seeped through him, but the faces of the widows from yesterday passed through his memory. He would do his part in keeping peace between their kingdoms. He bowed slightly. "Very well, Mother."

Mother nodded, but her eyes showed her surprise at the easy response. "This will be a good thing. You'll see. I only warn you to take caution."

He leaned back in his chair, frowning. "Are you superstitious now, too, Mother?"

"No, just suspicious," she replied. "I do not always trust the Dawsonians. I warn you to take care, lest you be fooled."

He nodded. "Thank you for the reminder. I will keep diligent and hope to meet at least one woman worthy of Lox."

Mother smiled. "Of course you will. I am always proud of you."

He would need to see Father before he left. He was likely in his own office, which wasn't on the same floor. Father oversaw his own groups around the kingdom, mostly military matters. He preferred to work with his own staff and at his own pace.

Ben quickened his steps, though he wasn't sure why. He was in no hurry to be paraded in front of the women in Dawson's Edge.

Father met him on his way to his office. "Your mother has spoken to you, I take it. I will keep in touch with you. You leave tonight."

"I understand, Father," Ben said.

"Excellent." Father gave a curt nod.

The behavior was more tense than Ben usually witnessed from Father, but Ben didn't focus on it. He walked back to his room as his thoughts formed into ideas. If he was in Dawson's Edge, it could give him a chance to see if Dr. Presnell was alive. If he had been prestigious enough to travel between palaces in Dawson's Edge and Chester's Wake, surely, he would be remembered by a few people who could point Ben in the right direction.

Hansen was in the throes of packing Ben's suitcases when he returned. "Will I be travelling with you, Your Highness?" he asked.

Mother hadn't specified, but if Ben was to attend a ball he would appreciate Hansen's help. "Would you mind terribly?"

"No, Your Highness. I would be honored."

Ben smiled his thanks and then moved to his desk to figure out what documentation he might need. He eyed the Messenger, considering sending Gregory a note about the ball, but something kept him back. If he needed to let Roanna go, he should start now. A nagging voice told him he was fooling himself. He would never fully release her. But he could refrain from sending her notes and messages. It was important for him to be virtuous and upstanding, especially as the future king. He could not set a bad example.

Still, he slipped Dr. Presnell's file into his luggage.

Once he'd given Hansen all of his other paperwork, he left the room to seek out the chapel. He had much to think about.

18

Roanna

The flight to Edge River was uneventful. She, Father, and Mother had squished into a small airship because there were no air stations near the river territory, which meant they needed a vessel that could land easily on a grassy knoll.

Apparently, there was very little civilization in the region. Only the military base, which teamed with troops dressed in blue and silver: Chester's Wake soldiers and guards.

Across the expanse of the river was a different base, belonging to Dawson's Edge. Roland Dawson was likely there now, with King Bartholomew Dawson and perhaps Queen Katherine as well.

Roanna had never met them, had barely seen pictures of them when summit meetings were featured in news reports. Would she need to impress them somehow? Her stomach twisted, but she pushed past the discomfort.

Five days had passed since Ben was taken home; three days had passed since Roland Dawson returned to Dawson's Edge. Now, they were meeting at the river so Father and King Bartholomew—in the witness of King Neville and Queen Frieda, who smiled at her sympathetically—could sign their peace treaty as well as a marriage agreement.

Roanna gripped the sides of her ankle length,

cream-colored day dress. Bette had pushed her to dress up more, but with Roanna's insistence she had settled on something less formal. Now Roanna wiped her sweaty palms on the softly ruffled folds of material, wishing she were somewhere—anywhere—else.

Mother took her hand and offered a smile. "It will be fine, Roanna. Don't be afraid. All women have nerves when it comes time to marry; but we all make it through."

Roanna offered Mother a tight smile. Mother had gone through the same betrothal ritual. She came from within Lox. She had brought money with her, as her family had been one of Lox's wealthiest, though not royalty. She hadn't known Father, save a handful of prior meetings. But Father was kind, honest, and loving.

Ambassador Dawson had shown himself none of those things. He had also shown himself jealous and unsympathetic in the few days they'd spent together after their engagement. And her strange shivers had only increased since then.

Father stepped toward her. "It is time." He held his hand out to her, a large smile on his face. "Come."

She took his hand as she swallowed nerves. They were led by guards out the back of the base along the river bank toward a large pavilion, made of trellises but equipped with gentle fans to keep a cool breeze blowing. White roses had been brought in and wound through the trellises.

King and Queen Dawson approached as Roanna and her family entered the pavilion. Roland trailed behind them, a smile on his face. King Dawson was taller than she had imagined, and Queen Katherine was nearly as tall. They both carried themselves with surety. Queen Katherine's hair was a deep auburn, and her skin was pale. Roanna didn't know her origin.

The king, on the other hand, had tanned skin like his brother. His hair was dark and hung to his shoulders.

"King Bart," Father said, holding his arm out to the Dawsonian.

King Bartholomew gripped arms with Father and patted him on the back with his free hand. "It is good to see you, neighbor. It has been too long."

Mother and Queen Katherine hugged, always smiling.

Roanna hung back. Surely, she wouldn't be expected to approach Roland, but when a chance presented, she curtsied silently to the king and queen.

"So, this is the beauty Roland has told me about." King Dawson held out a hand to her.

Roanna stepped forward and curtsied again before taking his hand. "Your Highness."

"I am pleased to join our families in marriage at last." He gripped her hand and a warm sensation spread through her. She sensed no animosity from him, only open kindness, not a mere feeling, more like a definitive knowledge, something her senses told her to be true as surely as her ears told her of the rushing river water. A strange sensation.

King Dawson pulled her into a brief hug, and then she curtsied to and hugged Queen Katherine.

Roanna quickly moved behind Father and Mother so the small shivers that had started would draw no notice. She looked to her hands; they weren't shaking. Yet.

What could it mean? But more importantly, how could she hide it? They would think her odd.

Uncooperative and withdrawn.

Gripping her hands in her lap, she took a seat at the rear of the pavilion as Father and Mother sat with King and Queen Dawson, and Queen Frieda and King Neville. Roland met her eye, and she silently cursed herself for looking his way.

He smiled widely, his excitement obvious.

She indulged him with a small smile, but inside, she shook. She should have made a way to tell Ben about her hair. He needed to know that whatever the Dawsonian doctor had warned Mother about was coming true.

Pain throbbed behind her eyes, and she pressed them closed, taking deep breaths and willing the pain to pass. It did not pass, but grew worse, aching until she pushed the palms of her hands against her eyes to relieve the pressure.

"My lady, are you all right?" A guard beside her bent toward her.

"It will pass, thank you."

He backed away, but the pain persisted.

Peace at last. We will finally have the opportunity to expand our kingdom. Soon, we will have the resources to crush this cursed rebellion. King Dawson's voice resonated through the pain.

Roanna stilled. She glanced around, looking for anyone else's reactions to the words. But everyone went about their business as if the words had not been uttered. She hadn't exactly heard them, though they were in King Dawson's voice. But he could not have spoken them. Right this moment he spoke to Father, and Father would surely question talk of a rebellion.

Make sure to get the marriage agreement in writing, brother. She has a lover, and I don't wish to be jilted.

Roland's voice echoed when he hadn't moved his lips.

Roanna's breaths came in short bursts. Ambassador Roland had not spoken aloud. But then, how was she hearing them? Feeling them? Sensing them? Her shivering continued until she couldn't control it any more. She gripped her hands tighter.

A moment later the same guard reappeared with a small but stylish denim jacket. "You're cold, Princess," he said.

She smiled up at him gratefully.

Besides this strange phenomenon of her shivers, she had Roland Dawson's words to worry about. *She has a lover, and I don't wish to be jilted.*

A lover? Ben was not her lover. Still, the words had not been given kindly, but with a sound of warning. Perhaps she was being silly. Or going crazy. Or imagining things.

Torturous minutes passed as the kings and queens spoke and signed documents. Roanna could not get Roland's words out of her mind. Thoughts of Ben brought on a new pang, a new worry. Would Roland retaliate against Ben if he even suspected their friendship remained? The warning in the words she felt from him was clear.

The aching in her head relaxed little by little, replaced by the ache in her heart.

19

"We will hold a celebration!" King Dawson held a goblet in the air as if making a toast. The peace treaty had been signed, as had the marriage agreement. The Loxian Queen and King had departed, and now only the Hamiltons and Dawsons remained. A festive atmosphere permeated the pavilion.

"A party?" Queen Katherine suggested. She was beautiful, and like King Dawson, Roanna sensed nothing but kindness from her. "We could throw a ball!"

Roland sat on the edge of the table and smiled at her. "What about an engagement party?"

Roanna turned toward Mother and Father. Maybe they would refuse or postpone.

But Father smiled and nodded. "A fine idea. Where shall we have it?"

Queen Katherine beamed. "At our palace. I insist!"

"Yes," Mother said to Father. "Leave it to us. We will plan it all." She gripped Roanna's hand and gave her a big, excited smile.

Roanna forced herself to return it, but she doubted she pulled it off very well.

"Come along," Mother said. "Let's leave the men to speak, and we will make plans."

Roanna gladly left the company of Roland Dawson, who kept staring at her as if she should be happy. She pressed her eyes closed and took a deep breath. He did expect her to be happy, and rightfully so. He was going to marry her.

If she was to pull this off—protect her family, her kingdom, and Ben—she would have to do a better job at coming to terms with her life.

Mother and Queen Katherine led her to a small sitting area across the pavilion. Queen Katherine took her hand and gave her a smile. "I have always wanted a daughter, and while you will be my sister-in-law rather than my daughter-in-law, it is my hope that we can be great friends."

Again, warmth spread through Roanna. While she did not want Roland, she felt a kindred spirit in the queen. She squeezed Queen Katherine's hand. "Thank you, Your Highness. I hope so, too."

They talked about the engagement party they would throw. It would be held at the palace in Dawson's Edge, one week in the future. All the royalty and nobility around the continent would be invited. They would have elaborate foods, a live instrument band, and dancing.

The details overwhelmed her until the shivering started all over.

"Roanna, what's wrong?" Mother asked.

She forced another smile. "I'm not feeling well. This is a lot to take in."

Queen Katherine's eyes softened. "Oh, you poor dear. You must leave the rest to us."

Relief washed over Roanna. She sat back and tried to relax, but her mind would not rest. Chancing him spotting her, Roanna looked Roland's way. She couldn't forget how he had spoken to King Dawson, without ever opening his lips. Or had he simply been thinking it without King Dawson being able to hear?

And there was always another option, that he hadn't done any thinking at all. Roanna had imagined the whole thing.

Roland spoke jovially with Father and King Dawson. Someone said something amusing, and Roland threw back his head and laughed.

Roanna turned away before he could catch her looking, lest he think she held happy feelings toward him. Instead, she looked to King Dawson. If she truly had read his thoughts—or perhaps, sensed them—he was battling a rebellion. But where? In Dawson's Edge?

A thought came upon her, slowly at first but then all at once. Did royals have the genetic testing for the Termination process? What if she herself had an anomaly? How else would she explain the strange things happening to her?

The idea twisted her stomach with fear. If she had an anomaly, it would mean that she was one of the Rejected herself, a fetus who had a negative test result but then was born with defects anyway. Or maybe Mother had never had the tests at all.

She rubbed her forehead, the ache returning. How could she learn the truth? Dr. Richard Presnell of Dawson's Edge was the only person likely to have those answers now, but perhaps Roanna could learn more about whether Mother had had the genetic testing done. Then again, how could she ask Mother about it when she hadn't been able to bring herself to ask about Dr. Presnell?

At last, Father announced their meeting had come to an end.

Roanna hugged Queen Katherine and curtsied to King Dawson.

Roland stood to the king's right, and once King Dawson stepped away, Roland took his place.

"Good afternoon, Roanna." He spoke alone to her for the first time.

"Good afternoon, Roland."

He smiled and stepped closer, reaching for her hand. She tensed but allowed him to take it. What else could she do? He was to be her husband.

"Are you happy?" Clearly, he expected only one response.

"Yes, of course. King and Queen Dawson are lovely, and the engagement ball is sure to be fantastic." She couldn't bring herself to say *our* engagement ball.

He squeezed her hand and stepped closer. "I am glad you are happy. I fear I cannot wait long for a wedding."

Disgust washed over her, but she allowed him to continue holding her hand.

Silence spread around them. What did one say to a man she was engaged to marry but didn't like?

"Come, Roanna." Father's summons saved her.

She smiled at Roland. "I will see you soon."

He smiled. "Yes. Soon."

With relief, she pulled her hand from his and nearly ran to meet Father and Mother. They returned to their military base, and while Father spoke with two of the commanders, she and Mother climbed aboard their airship for the flight home.

"They weren't what I expected," Roanna said as she arranged herself in the seat.

"Quite kind, I agree." Mother leaned her head back and closed her eyes. "Are you looking forward to the party?"

"I suppose." She wouldn't lie to Mother.

Mother peeked at her through one eye. "You can be happy, Roanna. You are allowed. You must give yourself the freedom to live this life and not fret."

Roanna nodded, but she couldn't talk herself into smiling. At least her shivers had finally died down.

At last, Father climbed onto the airship, and the driver lifted off from the base. In a few days, they would travel to Dawson's Edge, and she would attend her own engagement ball. Tears pricked her eyes, but she refused to let herself break down. Soon they would be home, and Roanna could close herself inside her room to grieve alone.

20

The week at home passed quickly as Roanna and Mother made arrangements and preparations for the engagement ball. Soon, Roanna and her family flew from Chester's Wake to the air station in Dawson's Edge. From there, they drove an hour to the palace. The Dawsons provided a sleek, white auto that whisked them from the air station in full luxury and style.

The engagement party was in two days' time, and Roanna had a trunk full of gowns to choose from. Choosing what to wear to impress an entire kingdom was no easy task. Precisely why she had insisted Bette come along.

Roanna had spent the last week seeking information on whether royal mothers were subjected to Termination testing, but she'd found nothing definitive. She'd considered bringing up the subject to Mother, but like the mystery of her hair, Roanna never found the right time or the courage.

Now their auto neared a stone wall with a wrought-iron gate. Guards stood watch, large guns strapped to their sides. When the motorcade approached, the guards stepped forward and spoke to the driver. A moment later, the gates swung open, and the auto drove through.

Dawson's Edge was unlike anything Roanna had ever seen. The palace at Chester's Wake was positioned right at the edge of the capital city and up against the Edge River. The palace at Lox was situated at the base of a mountain, in a lush green valley surrounded by waterfalls and vegetation.

The palace at Dawson's Edge was a solitary, stone monstrosity with aging, gothic architecture and huge trees surrounding it. The trees weren't quite in full bloom. In fact, some of them were bare, giving the place the feeling of being partly alive, partly dead.

Rolling green hills sloped in the distance, but the green was different from the vibrant greens of Chester's Wake. These greens were dark and forbidding, more like the colors of winter, in spite of the heat.

Their auto was directed to the front of the palace where King Dawson, Queen Katherine, and Roland greeted them.

"Welcome to Dawson's Edge." Queen Katherine hugged Roanna tightly. "We are so pleased to have you."

Roanna smiled and thanked Katherine, drawn in by her warmth.

The inside of the palace matched the outside. Dark wood made up the main staircase, and dark green wallpaper lined most of the walls. Gaslights were spaced every few feet along the walls, giving a yellow glow to the entryway.

Once inside, King Dawson turned to her and bowed slightly. "We hope you enjoy your stay with us, and we welcome you to our family."

Roanna smiled at him, curtsying slightly. As she had searched for answers about her possible anomaly, she had taken time to consider what had happened at the Edge River. Her hair acted up when she brushed it vigorously, but especially when she was near Roland or King Dawson. Her strange shivers and long hair had to be linked to her new ability to sense thoughts and…intentions. What would happen if her anomaly was discovered?

No matter how she considered it, she had no answers.

Roland stepped close to her and took her elbow. The shiver was slight, like a small chill, but this time she expected it and was able to hide it well. Mother had warned her to not act coldly toward Roland, so she smiled kindly at him. "Good afternoon, Roland."

He took both of her hands and kissed them. "Good afternoon, Roanna."

She hid her repulsion at his lips touching her skin.

"I cannot explain my joy at seeing you here," he said.

"Thank you. I was wondering." She paused. She had practiced what she would say, determined to get to know him. To try. "I was wondering where your home is. I assume you do not live in the palace."

Roland released her hands and his smile grew. "You are correct. I have a modest palace to the east, along the coast, called Santa Rio. We can visit over the next few days if you would like."

"I would like it very much. Thank you." Her heart beat rapidly, but she took a relieved breath. She had done it. She had been kind to him, and things felt normal. Maybe her new life could work out after all. She could hide her anomaly, and pretend things were as they should be.

What is happening to me?

The sentiment had haunted her over the last week. She had sought divine guidance, but no revelation had revealed itself to her. She kept considering how she'd always been drawn to the Rejected—and now she understood why.

"We'll discuss business," King Dawson said, nodding toward Father and Gregory, who had come along to attend the engagement party.

Roland stepped to their side.

Queen Katherine smiled. "I will take the ladies to see their rooms." The women followed Katherine up the grand, winding staircase.

Servants buzzed around them, carrying rugs, flowers, dishes, and more.

"Is all of this for our benefit?" Mother asked.

"Not quite." Katherine smiled. "My husband has decided it is best to move forward with the marriage agreement with Lox as well. We will be hosting a second ball later this week for the prince to meet our noble women. Don't worry." They reached the top of the stairs, and she turned to them. "You all will not be expected to attend the ball. It will be for the prince, as well as the noble families with eligible daughters. As you will no doubt be exhausted from your own festivities, no one will think adversely if you do not wish to participate." Her eyes were kind and sincere, but Roanna longed to know more.

Ben was here? In Dawson's Edge? She hadn't heard that they were moving forward with his marriage agreement.

"There is to be a wedding, then?" Mother asked.

"Not yet, but hopefully soon."

Roanna glanced at Mother, but, of course, her face was a mask of serenity. Inside, she must be sighing in relief.

The thought pained Roanna.

Queen Katherine led them to their suite. "These are your rooms. Servants will be available should you need anything, and when you're rested, you can ask them to fetch me." She offered one last warm smile before retreating to the stairs.

The suite was masculine but stylish in dark browns and gold. A large sitting area was filled with three couches, and it separated three bedrooms. Each had a four-poster bed with full, golden bedding.

"It's beautiful here," Roanna said. "Different than I imagined, but beautiful."

Mother nodded as servants entered carrying their luggage.

Bette breezed in and Roanna pointed to the right. "I'll take that room, Bette." It was the smallest of the three, which suited her best.

Bette carried a bag into the room.

"I noticed you seemed quite at ease with the ambassador," Mother said.

"I practiced."

Mother sighed and took her hand with a squeeze. "I'm glad you're cooperating. I was quite surprised to hear of the other ball being held."

Roanna barely had time to process the second remark. The first one hurt too much. Why should Mother doubt her cooperation? She had never given her parents a moment's grief. Didn't she do everything they'd asked? She'd given up her freedom in order to prosper their kingdom, and she'd done it without complaining.

She hid the hurt, barely able to consider how they'd react if they learned she had an anomaly. Would they disown her, their own daughter? She had no choice but to marry Roland in such a circumstance.

"I'm going to rest for a while."

"Very well. I'll see you in a bit."

Roanna nodded and entered the bedroom where Bette already worked to put away their things. Roanna closed the door leading to the sitting room. A second door, leading into the hallways, stood open and other servants brought in the rest of Roanna's things.

"Any idea what I should wear for the party?" Roanna asked.

"I'll think on it," Bette promised.

The urge to get her dress right was strong. If Ben was to be there, Roanna needed to be as appropriate as possible. She could control her behavior, but she also needed to look the part of a devoted, engaged princess.

Roland's words—or thoughts, rather—from a few days ago rolled through her mind. *She has a lover, and I don't wish to be jilted.*

For Ben's safety, and the peace between their kingdoms, she must keep her distance. It would be best to be prepared.

"Bette?" Roanna moved to the hallway door and closed it softly. She glanced around to ensure they were alone. "Could you please find out who else is visiting Dawson's Edge this week?"

Bette smiled as she hung another dress in the closet. "I will do my best, Your Highness."

Roanna breathed out in relief. Bette wouldn't let her down, and then she would be prepared for whatever the Dawsons had to throw at her.

21

A few hours later, Roanna joined Mother and Queen Katherine in the library. It was a small space, but bright and tidy. Books lined the walls, and comfortable seating had been placed around the room.

"We have an entire section on gardening," Queen Katherine said as Roanna approached. "Your mother tells me you have a knack for growing things."

Roanna hid her surprise. After Merry Stern's strange words regarding gardening in Dawson's Edge, she hadn't expected to have access to her beloved flowers. "I do enjoy gardening. Thank you, Your Highness."

"Please, call me Katherine. You're to be my sister-in-law, after all."

Roanna smiled and nodded, but she doubted she would be able to bring herself to call the Queen of Dawson's Edge anything but Highness. She took a seat as Mother and Katherine resumed their conversation about the engagement party.

"We hope to announce the wedding date during the party," Katherine said. "Have you and Roland decided on a date?"

She and Roland? They had barely spoken, let alone determined when to have their ceremony. Of course, Roland had said enough to imply he did not wish to wait long. "We haven't set a date, but I imagine it will be soon. We can make a determination before the party." Dread seeped through every corner of her soul.

Time to change the subject. "May I see your gardens?"

Queen Katherine smiled. "I would love to show you. I don't have the special talent of gardening, but King Bartholomew is quite gifted with flowers. You will enjoy his work, I predict."

They stood and made their way to the center of the palace. The citadel was a circular structure, with a menagerie situated in the middle.

The air in Dawson's Edge was moist and hot, as Merry had described. Roanna didn't complain. It felt nice compared to the cooler air in Chester's Wake. The flowers seemed to thrive in the damp climate, and despite the bare trees she'd seen on arrival, the blooms in the garden were huge, some twelve inches in diameter. "It's beautiful!" she exclaimed.

Katherine smiled. "I agree."

They toured the gardens slowly, taking in different types of flowers in an array of colors. Had Merry seen this garden? She was so wistful back in Chester's Wake, as if she had never seen gardens like that before. Perhaps she could become better friends with Merry, and they could tour the gardens together.

As they walked, Roanna noticed garden ornaments among the flowers. There were statues of strange creatures, not like the religious quotes in the prayer chapel at home. A monster with two heads, a snakelike creature devouring a rodent, a flying varmint. Gods?

Unease crept into her belly. The royal Dawsonian garden was beautiful, but it was filled with their infamous superstition.

As they finished their walk, Roland came from the

palace. He smiled at her, his dark eyes gleaming in the sunlight. "Roanna, I'm glad to see you rested. Would you care to sit with me for a spell?"

She smiled as sweat pooled on her lower back. "I would love to. Might we go inside?"

His smile grew. "That was precisely what I had in mind." He offered his arm, and she took it. Mother nodded her approval, so Roanna followed him into the palace.

He led her to a small sitting area on the second floor. There were a pair of couches and a piano. She sat on a couch, but he moved to the piano bench. "What do you think of Dawson's Edge, Roanna?"

He began playing a light tune, and she stared in surprise. "You play the piano?"

"And the guitar as well as the trumpet. Does this please you?"

"I think it's lovely!" And she meant it. To think the man she would be marrying did have a few redeeming qualities.

"So," he reminded her of his earlier question. "What do you think of our kingdom?"

"It's beautiful here. I love the gardens."

"I don't have a garden at my palace, but I would be pleased for you to oversee one."

The consolation was a small one, and she expected it to bring a tinge of happiness, but she felt nothing. "I will look forward to it." She swallowed hard, knowing it would be best to press for a date as Queen Katherine wished. "Roland, the queen has asked we provide her with a wedding date to announce at the engagement party."

His playing stopped. He rose from the piano bench and took a seat beside her on the couch.

Her hands grew clammy, and she held them tightly to ward off the bad feelings.

"I do not wish to wait long, Roanna. I've told you this already. Soon is not nearly soon enough for me. So I will ask you, when would you like to be married?"

Why did he have to ask it that way?

She hesitated a moment too long. It opened the door for Roland to take her hands and draw closer to her. Repulsion swirled inside her, but worse, the shivers started at the base of her neck.

He leaned close to her. "Roanna, will you allow us to marry soon? Is a month acceptable to you?" Before she could answer, he leaned toward her as if he would kiss her.

Panic overtook her. She had never been kissed, not once. Her entire body shook, and just as his lips touched hers, she shoved him away. She stood from the couch and paced away.

Roland shot to his feet, his face red and his nostrils flaring.

This was not good.

Taking a deep breath, she ran her hands along the folds of her dress. "Forgive me, Roland. I'm quite unaccustomed to the ways of men and women." True, even if it was only an excuse. The memory of his lips on hers wouldn't be a pleasant one.

His shoulders relaxed, and he composed himself. "It's quite all right, my darling." He stepped closer to her, but this time he didn't reach for her. "Your confession brings me pleasure. What of the date? Is a month acceptable to you?"

She managed a smile as she nodded. "Thank you, Roland. Yes, a month is well."

This time he took her hands and pressed his lips

into her palms. "I will wait for it with every breath in me." He smiled and left the room as she stood shaking. This time, she wasn't sure if the cause was her hair or her fears.

22

The following day was a blur of preparation for the engagement party. Guests arrived throughout the day, and Roanna exhausted herself meeting each of them. She saw little of Father, King Dawson, or Roland, and she saw no one from Lox.

Roanna and Bette now stood in her bedroom. Bette was helping her into her navy party gown. Its full, lacy skirt ended just below her knees in the front and flowed to the floor in the back. Bette paired it with a thick black belt and black boots. Its scoop neck draped gently off her shoulders, and Bette had clasped a strand of pearls around her neck. She looked very grown up and very appropriate. "Did you ever learn who else the Dawsons are entertaining this week?"

"There are so many guests, Your Highness." Bette shook her head. "It's hard to make much sense of anything."

"But what about the guests who were already here?"

Bette bit her lip as Roanna turned to look her in the face. Bette was holding back.

Roanna's heart fluttered. He was here. "Bette? I promise not to get into any trouble, but I need to be prepared. I have to ready myself so I can steel my emotions." Admitting these things was safe. Bette knew Roanna inside and out, and Roanna could trust her.

Bette's eyes softened, and she nodded. "Prince Benjamin is here. I saw his servant, Hansen, in the kitchens. He's been out touring the kingdom with King Dawson's first brother, Prince Southerland."

The king's brother? Roanna hadn't even considered that she hadn't met the rest of Roland's family. She would likely meet them tonight.

"Will Ben be at the party?" If there was any mercy in the heavens, the answer would be no.

"I don't know, Miss. It wasn't appropriate for me to ask."

"Of course. Thank you, Bette. Did Mother tell you not to tell me?"

Bette went back to biting her lip, and Roanna chuckled. "It's fine. I won't mention it to her."

"How would you like your hair, Miss?" Bette moved to the small vanity, and Roanna turned toward the mirror. Her hair hung in limp waves around her shoulders. She had managed to stay away from Roland and King Dawson for the last day—or rather, they had stayed away from her. She hadn't felt a single shiver since Roland's unauthorized kiss.

"Mother would be unhappy to discover its length if we left it down, wouldn't she?"

"Yes, Miss. Besides, it would appear more appropriate if you put it up."

Ah, yes. She needed to look devoted and unavailable. "You're right. Let's put it up."

She sat, and Bette went to work. In little time, her strands were put into a nice twist, and Bette pulled out a small leather satchel. "What is that?"

Bette's eyes danced. "A gift from your mother for tonight. You may need to look unavailable, but there is no reason to look boring." She emptied the bag into her hand, and Roanna gasped.

"Are those diamonds?"

"Yes, my lady." Bette grinned. "Your mother had them specially made to clasp into your hair. Shall I show you?"

Roanna stared in wonder. "Yes, of course!"

Bette made fast work of placing the diamonds in Roanna's hair. One here, one there, until she truly looked like a princess. Next, Bette pulled out a small case. Roanna recognized this one immediately.

"My tiara."

"Yes, Miss. The one with the sapphires."

Bette placed it on Roanna's head, and Roanna moved to the full mirror. The tiara matched her navy dress beautifully. "Bette, you are fantastic."

Bette smiled. "Thank you, Miss."

Roanna hugged her maid—her friend—tightly. "I wish you could come to the party. I'm so nervous."

"You'll do well. These are your people, and they only expect you to behave the way you've always been trained. It will not be difficult in that respect. Just try to play your part."

Play her part. Like actors on the stage? She could try that. It might work.

"Thank you, Bette. I don't know what I'd do without you."

Bette smiled again then gently pushed Roanna toward the door. "You'd best go before Ambassador Dawson comes knocking on your bedroom door."

That took the excitement out of her mood. "You're right. We don't want him feeling comfortable enough to stop by."

Bette frowned slightly. "That wasn't quite what I meant, Miss."

"I know, I just—never mind. I'll head out."

Mother and Father were likely waiting for her in their shared sitting room, but Roanna wasn't ready to see them. She would explore for a moment to calm her nerves.

The hallway was empty as she exited her room. The guest wing was large, with bedroom after bedroom lining the hall. Hers was the second door to the right, with the door to her family's sitting room next, and Mother and Father's bedroom door following. Then, it was guest room after guest room for another dozen doors.

A door opened a few spaces down, and an older man and woman came out. They spotted her and moved quickly to greet her. Roanna had met them the day before—he was the duke of one of the southern provinces. The Maynes, if she remembered right.

"How lovely you look!" the duchess said. "Prince Roland is a lucky man!"

"Thank you." Roanna smiled. "You look quite beautiful yourself."

The woman beamed, and they moved on.

Roanna looked down the length of the hallway one last time before moving to the door to the sitting room. As expected, Mother and Father sat waiting. Gregory exited his bedroom at the back of the suite.

"Oh, Roanna!" Mother said as she came in. "The diamonds are exactly as lovely as I had hoped! You are breathtaking!"

Gregory moved in front of her and took her hand. "She's right, Roanna. You will be the belle of the ball."

She couldn't help but beam in their praise.

"Roland won't be able to take his eyes off you," Mother gushed.

Roanna's smile faltered. That was what she was afraid of.

23

Roland was waiting for them at the top of the stairs to the guest wing. His eyes widened slightly when he saw her, and he bowed. "Princess Roanna, you are stunning."

No matter how much she disliked him, his words rang with sincerity, and she blushed. "Thank you, Ambassador Dawson." She wasn't sure why the atmosphere felt so formal, but he obviously felt it, too.

He held out his arm, and she linked hers in his. They led the rest of her family down the staircase. Other guests joined them as they made their way to the ballroom. She smiled and greeted them as she was smiled at and greeted, but mostly she kept silent. All these people were here for her? No, not for her. For Roland Dawson, fourth son of the former King Dawson, and third brother to the present King Dawson.

They reached the ballroom door, and the noise coming from inside seemed to hush. King Dawson and Queen Katherine met them, and a trumpet sounded from inside the room.

"King Bartholomew Dawson and Queen Katherine Dawson!" someone announced.

The king and queen entered the ballroom, and the guests clapped. Father and Mother were announced, and then she and Roland. Gregory had slipped inside at some point without any fanfare.

When she and Roland stepped into the ballroom, the people clapped and cheered. Roland waved. His smile was large and genuine, and guilt hit her. She was being unfair toward him. He was truly excited, and she was truly not.

He leaned close to her ear. "Will you dance with me, Roanna?"

They would need to lead the first dance, but his breath on her ear started her chills once again. She pushed the strange feelings aside and gave him a tight smile. "I would be delighted."

He took her hand and the music resumed. They waltzed around the ballroom, and people clapped. After a few moments, others joined them on the dance floor. The atmosphere slowly changed from formality to excitement. The people were happy for Prince Roland, and they were happy for a peace treaty between their country and hers. Roanna found herself smiling and happy.

The dance ended, and Roland pulled her from the dance floor. "Would you like a drink?"

"That would be nice. Thank you." She wasn't thirsty, but she would humor him. Tonight, she would work on getting to know him. Giving him a chance. The people in their kingdoms deserved peace. Not only those in Chester's Wake—including Bette's brother—but the people in Dawson's Edge as well. They were brothers, sisters, fathers, and mothers. She owed it to them as her royal duty to help protect them.

Roland left her standing near a raised platform with fancy chairs—thrones—but he didn't insist she sit, thank goodness. She watched him for a moment, but the crowd swallowed him up. She scanned the ballroom, searching for Mother and Father or Gregory.

Gregory danced with Merry Stern, and Roanna smiled. She would have to speak with Merry if she got the chance. Father and Mother danced together in the crowd.

Roanna looked around for Roland, but she didn't spot him. Unease crept through her. She didn't know anyone else. These people were strangers to her, and she was alone. She glanced around for Roland again but still didn't see him.

Was Ben here? She hadn't allowed herself to look just yet, but now that she was alone she glanced around for him. She didn't find him.

So, Ben was in Dawson's Edge but not at her engagement party. That seemed wise.

"May I have this dance, Princess Roanna?" A man stood in front of her. His olive skin and dark but graying hair bore a striking resemblance to the other Dawson brothers.

"And you are?"

"Prince Southerland Dawson, Your Highness." He bent low.

She smiled at him and took his outstretched hand. "It is nice to meet you, Prince Southerland."

He returned the smile. "I feared my youngest brother would never find himself a wife. It appears he waited for the best."

Southerland swept her onto the dance floor, and she allowed herself to relax in his arms. He was older than Father, but not quite as old as King Dawson. He seemed kind, but something about him made her keep up her guard.

"Are you enjoying Dawson's Edge?"

"Yes, very much. Your family and your kingdom are lovely."

He smiled at her as he danced. "I'm glad to hear it."

They made small talk until the dance ended, and then he left her with Mother and Father at the edge of the dance floor. Again, Roanna looked for Roland but did not find him.

"He said he was getting us something to drink," Roanna said to Mother. "But I don't see him."

Mother smiled and patted her hand. "Don't worry about it, darling. Men get interrupted by other men and they lose track of how much time they spend talking."

Roanna had seen this happen to Father enough times that she knew it to be true. But this was their engagement party. Where had he gone?

She danced one more turn before she decided she would look around a bit. He couldn't be far if he had only been drawn into a conversation.

As she slipped from the ballroom, something in her stomach told her he wasn't simply having a conversation. Something was wrong. She could…sense…it.

A chill raced down her back, the same feeling she'd had at Edge River. An almost tangible aura. A sixth sense, and she knew how to find him.

Without another thought, she moved toward the aura, away from the ballroom.

A few doors down a room was closed off, but from inside it she heard voices—Roland's and King Dawson's but also a third voice she did not recognize.

"We should be patient, brother," Roland said.

"If we move now, their defenses will be low!" King Dawson said.

"No." Someone she didn't recognize joined the

conversation. "Roland is right. Give it time. Let them marry. Then Roland will be in a better position to seek help."

"I—," Roland started, but someone quieted him.

Silence.

Roanna's heart fluttered, and she hurried away from the door. Had they heard her? She didn't wait to find out. Hurrying back to the ballroom, she took care to slip in unnoticed. She danced with Father and then with Gregory before she spotted Roland reentering the ballroom. A moment later, he met her at the edge of the dance floor with a small glass in hand.

"Forgive me, my darling. I got caught up."

Her hand shook slightly as she took the drink, but she managed a smile. "I understand. I am glad you are back."

24

Roland acted normally for the rest of the night. He danced with her, introduced her to Dawsonian nobility, and smiled as if he hadn't participated in a secret meeting in the heart of the palace that very night.

At least she didn't have to worry that he knew she'd heard his whispered conversation with King Dawson. They hadn't heard her footsteps outside their door, in spite of their hushed whispers, or he would have confronted her.

She danced and laughed and ate, never letting on what she had heard. But she couldn't forget. They were waiting to make some type of move, but they thought it best to allow Roland to marry her first. What kind of move did they have in mind?

The idea filled her with unease, but more than that was the way she had found them. Without any knowledge of their palace, she'd been able to sense their exact whereabouts, as if she had seen their presence—their aura—like a physical shadow.

Sometime well after midnight, the party ended and Roanna was able to tell Roland good night. She left him at the top of the stairs and went directly to her room. Bette was there, waiting to help her undress, but she wasn't ready for bed yet. She was wound up. Tense. Confused.

She sat in front of the mirror at her vanity, staring

at the diamonds in her hair. This strange power—this anomaly—was why the Dawsonian doctor had warned Mother to keep her hair short. He had known.

But how? How could he predict that she—a brand new baby—would have some kind of strange power that came from her hair? Perhaps Mother had undergone the genetic testing after all. But if so, how had Dr. Presnell known the results? He wasn't even from Chester's Wake.

She rubbed her forehead and pressed her eyes closed.

"Are you all right, Miss?" Bette's voice pulled her around.

"Thank you, Bette. I'm fine. You can go to bed. I'll ask Mother to help me when I'm ready to undress."

Bette bit her lip, worry lining her eyes. "I don't mind waiting, Miss."

Bless her, Bette was the best friend she'd ever had. Besides Ben, of course. She smiled at Bette. "Very well. Let's go ahead and get me out of this dress, then." She wouldn't keep Bette up half the night because she was restless.

Bette took off the tiara, helped her out of the dress, and into her silky pajamas and dressing robe. But she shook her head when Bette moved to undo her hair.

She hadn't told Bette about the strange things happening to her. "I'm not ready to lose the look completely. I promise I'll return the diamonds to their pouch as soon as I'm ready."

Bette relented. "Good night, Miss."

"Good night, Bette."

Bette left her, and Roanna sighed. What strange plan was Roland and King Dawson involved in? It didn't sit well with her. What if they were planning an attack on Chester's Wake?

She moved to the window in her room and looked out. The moon was bright, illuminating the garden below. No one moved through the flowers. Most of the people had gone to bed.

She peeked into the sitting area of her family suite, but it was empty.

Maybe she shouldn't have sent Bette away. She wasn't ready to be alone. Sleep was as distant as Chester's Wake.

Moving to the door that led into the hallway, she considered her options. She couldn't very well go roaming the palace in her pajamas, dressing robe on or not. Still, she looked into the hallway.

A man rounded the corner into her hallways as she stuck her head out.

The color of his hair and the cut of his shoulders gave his identity away before she even saw his face. Their eyes met, and her breath caught.

Ben.

His eyes widened, and a smile spread across his face. "Roanna!"

She laughed softly as tears flooded her eyes and clogged her throat. "I can't believe you're here," she choked out.

He glanced around. They were alone. Emotions played across his face, and she knew him so well she could almost see what he was thinking; they shouldn't be talking. Not here, like this.

He grabbed her hand and pulled her into her room then closed the door. "I've missed you." His voice cracked.

She managed a small smile as she wiped tears. "It's only been a week and a half."

"Way too long." He shook his head, and her smile relaxed into a more natural one.

"I've missed you, too."

They stood in front of each other, staring. Roanna wanted to tell him a thousand things. About her hair, about the things she'd heard, about her wedding date.

But Ben spoke first. "I'm staying away from you on purpose. In retrospect, my coming into your room was a mistake." He said it in that deadpan way of his that always meant he was teasing.

She laughed quietly, cautious to keep her voice down, and she stepped to the door leading to her family suite and locked it from her side.

There were no couches in her room, but she sat on her bed and nodded for him to sit at her vanity. She needed to tell him all that had been going on. "It's not safe for you to be here with me," she said quietly.

He frowned. "What do you mean?"

She hesitated. She couldn't exactly say Roland had called Ben her lover. "I heard something Roland said. And it's not safe for us to be seen together."

He accepted her words with a slow nod. "It's why I didn't come tonight, though they offered an invitation." Silence hung between them. "I heard you've set a wedding date?"

Her throat tightened. Cursed tears. "Roland set it, yes. One month from today."

He nodded again. "They're throwing me a ball in two days to introduce me to the available women in the kingdom."

"Queen Katherine mentioned it." She looked down, suddenly unable to meet his eyes.

"Dr. Presnell is alive."

She jerked her gaze to his. "What?"

"I've been here nearly a week now. King Dawson and his brother, Prince Southerland, have been taking me all over the countryside. I mentioned him once, saying my father sometimes spoke of his visits between the kingdoms. They said he lives."

Roanna stood and paced. Did Dr. Presnell know what the length of her hair caused? Could he tell her more? "Have you met him?"

Ben joined her and shook his head. "I'll be here another week, at least. I plan to visit him. He lives further south, near the sea. I'll contact you once I learn more."

"My hair is doing strange things." She blurted it out, and it sounded ridiculous. "Dr. Presnell's warnings weren't foolishness."

He stopped pacing and stood in front of her. "What do you mean?"

She swallowed hard. "When I brush it vigorously, or when Roland or King Dawson are near, I get chills. They race down my arms and back, and sometimes I shiver."

His frowned deepened; he was thinking.

"That's all?" he finally asked.

She shook her head. "I also...hear...things."

He raised his brows. "You hear things?"

"Thoughts. Or I sense them, rather. Not everyone's thoughts, only Roland's and King Dawson's so far." He was looking at her as though she had lost her mind, so she looked away. "I don't know. Maybe I've imagined it all."

He stepped closer to her. "What have you sensed them thinking?" His gaze was dark. Worried.

"King Dawson said something about a rebellion." She whispered now. She was in Bartholomew

Dawson's castle. To speak against him would be seen as treasonous. "Roland," she glanced away, "I won't repeat what he said, but it was a warning against my relationship with you."

"Who was he warning if it was in his head?"

"That's just it." She looked back to him. "It was like they were speaking to each other, in their heads." Now only one of his eyebrows rose. He did think she was crazy.

"And you believe this is related to your hair?" His tone carried no mockery.

She relaxed a little.

"It didn't start until Roland came to Chester's Wake, and even then it was minor. I didn't know what to make of it until we saw that file in the dungeon. Then I began to put it together. Tonight, Roland was gone from our party, so I set out to find him. I sensed him, Ben. I found him because I could sense him. He was in some type of secret meeting with King Dawson and another man, and they were discussing a plan. I couldn't understand what the plot was, though."

He rubbed his hand across his face. "This is crazy."

He could be right. How could her story possibly be true? "What if it's an anomaly? What if I am one of the Rejected?" Voicing her true fear set her heart racing.

Ben watched her, his eyes soft and understanding. Finally, he sighed. "Let's not talk of this anymore. We'll wait until I find Dr. Presnell. For now, I want to know about you. How are you?"

Relief washed over her. He wouldn't turn her away just because something strange was happening to her. "I'm fine, mostly."

"How does Roland treat you?"

She smirked. "He is a peacock, as you so aptly dubbed him."

Ben grinned, and she relaxed even more.

"But he is kind," she went on. "He showers me with unnecessary compliments that make me uncomfortable, but overall he is kind." She paused, wanting to tell him one more thing. "He kissed me."

The happiness in Ben's eyes dimmed. His jaw flexed. "Oh?"

"I shoved him."

His eyebrows shot up. "What?"

She giggled and nodded. "He was quite surprised."

Ben laughed. "I'll bet." He grabbed her shoulders, still laughing. "You are unbelievable. It's why I love you."

The words slipped from his mouth and hovered in the air between them.

He dropped his hands from her shoulders like they had burned him. He backed away. "I should go now. It's dangerous for me to be here."

He would leave her now, and she wouldn't see him again for too long. They both knew what was at risk.

He took another step back and his jaw muscles flexed. "As I said earlier, it was a mistake."

Yes, a mistake. Immature. Foolish. Irresponsible.

"I don't want him." The statement came out like a cry. A painful, wretched cry. She'd felt this way from the beginning but had not been allowed to express it to anyone. But if she couldn't express these things to her best friend, to whom could she talk? "I didn't want him to kiss me."

Pain filled Ben's face, and he shook his head. "I have to go," he whispered.

She wanted to force him to stay, at least a moment longer. Force him to acknowledge the feelings running between them. She could push, she knew she could.

But he was so brave. So strong. How could she desire to break him?

He stepped toward the door, his back to her, his hand on the doorknob.

Tears burned her eyes and panic bubbled up her chest. She must keep calm. She could have her break down as soon as he was gone. A quiet sob escaped her mouth. Tears slipped from her eyes and ran down her cheeks.

Then, in a moment, he was in front of her. He cradled her face in his hands and wiped her tears. "Don't cry," he begged.

Roanna closed her eyes and willed the tears to stop. She didn't want to show puffy eyes to Roland the next day.

She froze.

She was engaged to Roland. Slept in his family's palace. Had agreed to a peace treaty with his kingdom.

Ben tensed as if he was having the same thoughts. His hands dropped away. He stepped back. "As much as it was a mistake, my words were true, Roanna. I love you. I love you with all of my heart and soul, and that will never stop, no matter the peace treaties between our kingdoms. I want you and only you."

His confession was wrenching, exactly what she'd hoped to hear, though she had barely realized it before this moment. Her tears came harder, and she pressed her fist to her mouth to keep the sound from reaching anyone else's ears. Her heart hurt as if it would explode with the joy of Ben's love and yet shrivel with the pain of his absence all at once.

"But," she spoke through her tears, "you would not start a war for us."

He looked at her, not speaking.

So, this was it.

He backed away. "I will be in touch about Dr. Presnell."

She nodded stiffly, not trusting her words to come.

"Will you check the hallway?"

She rushed forward. "Of course." The hallways were empty, and she nodded him forward. He left without another glance, and Roanna shut the door behind him, closing the door to her heart.

25

Ben

Ben paced his room, still dressed in his evening clothes.

When he had first arrived in Dawson's Edge, he had spent the first part of his week discussing politics with King Dawson. Then the last two days had been spent touring the kingdom with Prince Southerland. He had known Roanna was in Dawson's Edge, so he had tried his best to stay away.

When he walked around the hallway corner and saw her standing there, hair glittering with jewels, he'd reacted.

Act, don't react. Another of Father's favorites. Ben had known Roanna was there, and he'd created a plan to act. Still, when he'd seen her, he only reacted. Rushed into her room. Been utterly foolish.

The dead soldiers he'd seen with Father at the border danced across his mind's eye. He could have added to their number simply by entering Roanna's room.

Foolish.

He rubbed a hand over his face.

No matter how foolish, he couldn't bring himself to regret it. The way she had cried, the way her skin had felt beneath his fingers, swelled his heart with longing to protect her. To make her happy.

His heart clenched at the remembrance of her

painfully spoken words.

"I don't want him."

What if the girl he chose to marry loved someone else? Would she get a say in the matter, or would she be telling someone else the same thing Roanna had said? "I don't want Benjamin of Lox?"

This practice of marrying for peace wasn't right or fair. How could there be peace between the kingdoms when one or both sides was being forced into it? Wouldn't the peace be stabler if entered into with pureness of heart rather than manipulation via a marriage agreement?

Father would say Ben was using enlightened thinking, and they didn't live in an enlightened world.

Ben ripped off his tie and tossed it aside. Maybe Father was right. He was being a fool.

He finished dressing for bed, but sleep would not come. Every time he closed his eyes, he saw Roanna's tears. Heard her wrenching cries.

He rose early, showered, and dressed for his day. Hansen mentioned that Roanna and her Mother would be travelling with Queen Katherine and Roland to visit Roland's estate this day. Roanna wouldn't return until after his own ball, leaving Ben with the freedom to move about the palace.

Breakfast was served as usual in the large dining room. A few of the guests from the engagement party had stayed overnight, and they sat around the table with King Dawson. Ben took a chair beside an older woman and her husband. He had met them the night before and recognized them as the Duke and Duchess of Mayne, one of the southern provinces.

"Are you excited for your own ball, young man?" the woman asked.

"Excited to find a wife?" He winked. "What do you think?" He gave her his most charming smile, and she laughed.

"I think that's a yes! And I hear you've been touring the kingdom."

Ben nodded as he bit into a strawberry. "I have been, though I have yet to make it south."

The woman's eyes lit up. "We would love to host you."

Ben smiled, and they made plans for him to visit after the ball. Visiting the southern province would afford him the opportunity to seek out Dr. Presnell. This was good. Roanna's claims regarding her hair and her strange thought-hearing abilities needed to be explained. And they would be. Roanna, an anomaly? It was impossible. Especially the strength of her so-called abilities. Those types of anomalies had been bred out long ago.

The worry on her face when she'd spoken about being one of the Rejected was enough to spur him to action.

The day passed slowly, agonizingly. Families who had attended Roland and Roanna's engagement party readied to leave while families with eligible daughters stayed or arrived. It made little sense to him for the Dawsons to schedule two large events back to back. What was their rush after all these years?

The information Roanna had given him came back to him. She'd heard them talking about a big move they planned to make after Roland had married. She'd sensed King Dawson's worry over a rebellion.

Ben rubbed the back of his neck as he sat at the small desk in his guest room. Could Roanna be correct? No doubt she thought she was feeling these shivers she described. But this having anything to do with her hair was so farfetched it bordered on unbelievable. She could really read thoughts? Sense people across the palace?

But Roanna was not crazy—had never been crazy before. He had to trust her.

Dr. Presnell held the key. Hopefully, his new friends, the Duke and Duchess, would be able to help him find the good doctor.

Supper arrived at last, and Ben dressed slowly. He wasn't excited to mingle further with the Dawsonian royalty. He arrived to the dining room late.

King Dawson raised his glass as Ben entered. "Prince Benjamin! I'm pleased that you've joined us. Come sit! There are many people who would like to meet you."

Ben gave the room a smile and moved to King Dawson's side. An empty seat to his left stood waiting, and he sank into it. "Forgive my tardiness, Your Highness."

"Nonsense." King Dawson snapped his fingers and servers appeared to offer Ben a plate. "No forgiveness necessary. You know Baron Stern, I believe?"

The baron he'd met in Chester's Wake sat to his right, and next to him was his daughter, Lady Merry. He had met her at Chester's Wake as well. Ben smiled at the baron and nodded. "We've recently met, yes. How are you, Baron?"

The baron was regal, with wide shoulders and a head full of silver hair. "Quite well, Your Highness. My daughter is eager for the ball."

Ben managed to smile. He glanced at Merry, and she blushed prettily, but she seemed irritated at her father's words.

"I look forward to it, as well," he answered. "And it will be nice to already know a few of the ladies there." He gave them a friendly smile, and Merry seemed to relax.

They ate and talked for the next hour, and when they were finished King Dawson gripped Ben's forearm. "Come and mingle, Ben." His voice was light, but his grip was firm. This was not a request.

"Of course, Your Highness." Ben followed him from the dining room to a small sitting room with couches and chairs. Many from the table followed them, but not all. Ben met ladies his own age, ladies twice his age, and ladies somewhere in between. They came from the south, the west, the east, the north. And they all wanted one thing—to become the next Queen of Lox.

King Dawson stayed close to him, whispering footnotes in his ear. "Lady Clarice is the daughter of the Duke of Charlotte Town in the east. He has hefty connections across the ocean," or "Lady Britta hails from our southern coast. A lot of trouble makers down that way."

Ben took it all in stride, not letting on whether the king's comments had any effect on him. If he was to choose a wife from among these women, it wouldn't be the political match that would most benefit Dawson's Edge; it would have to benefit Lox as well, whether King Dawson liked it or not.

26

The night of the ball arrived. Clatter from the ballroom was so loud it carried to the top of the stairs as Ben moved from the guest wing toward the festivities. He kept his gaze straight ahead as he passed Roanna's room. She wasn't there, anyway.

He had prayed fervently over the last two days, asking that Roanna be kept safe and that if she must marry Roland that she be happy to do so.

The clatter drowned out his thoughts as he neared the ballroom. Music, laughing, talking.

He took a deep breath and straightened his shoulders. Hansen had dressed him in a black tuxedo with long tails, with a yellow rose pinned to his lapel. Yellow, the color of friendship. The color of peace, which was what his match would bring Lox and Dawson's Edge. Now all he had to do was find a woman he could have a genuine relationship with who would also be interested in fostering peace between their countries. Someone who could rise to the position as future queen of his kingdom.

"Ah, Prince Benjamin!" King Dawson waited for him outside the ballroom. Queen Katherine stood at his side, which surprised Ben. He'd heard she had travelled to the east with Roanna to tour Roland's palace. King Hamilton had returned to Chester's Wake, and Gregory stayed behind for the ball.

He greeted them with a smooth smile and a slight

bow. "Your Highnesses. I am quite honored to be here tonight."

"Come." King Dawson led him toward the ballroom. "We have many guests!"

Ben smiled again. This was it. The future Queen of Lox danced in the ballroom this night. He took another deep breath to calm his nerves, and a moment later, he was being announced alongside King and Queen Dawson.

The ballroom erupted in applause, and Ben bowed graciously beside the king and queen. As he rose, he took in the guests. So many girls. He was to be expected to dance with them all? He gulped.

Queen Kathrine leaned close. "You may dance with me first, if you need a moment."

His eyes widened, and he turned to her. "Is it so obvious?"

She gave him a knowing smile. "Only to the most observant." She laughed daintily and held out her hand. "I would be honored to dance with you, Your Highness."

He grinned and took her hand, and they danced. After a few moments, others joined them. Swirls of colors, fabrics, curls, and heels. Apparently, there were more men than he'd realized, because all the women had dancing partners.

"You will be a good leader," Queen Katherine said. "I can tell it in the way you carry yourself. You are always in deference to those around you."

"You're too kind, Your Highness."

Her eyes twinkled. "Not too kind. Quite truthful."

The music ended, and Ben bowed to the queen. "Thank you for saving me, Queen Katherine."

"You are most welcome. Now, mingle. Meet

someone spectacular."

He grinned and nodded, and Queen Katherine turned to dance with King Dawson.

He felt like a wounded antelope in a large pack of lions. He met several pairs of eager eyes. He had to ask one of them to dance.

"Prince Benjamin," Merry Stern's voice broke into his panicked thoughts. "Thank you for a lovely talk last night."

His panic lessened a fraction, and he stepped toward her. "It was my pleasure, my lady. Would you like to dance?"

She smiled and nodded. "That would be my pleasure."

Ben took her soft hand in his and they danced. "This is my second save of the night. I'm beginning to think all Dawsonian women must be saviors."

Merry laughed. "Not true at all. Some of us can see you need the charity." She gasped. "I'm sorry, Your Highness. I didn't mean it that way. You don't need charity in that you couldn't find a dancing partner. You certainly could. You're quite hands—"

"Stop." Ben chuckled. "You don't owe me an apology. I owe you more thanks. I have no idea with whom to dance or how to ask them. At least, not when they're all expecting me to ask them."

"Dance with my sister, Rachel, next. She's too shy to ever put herself in your path."

He raised an eyebrow. "If she is shy, I don't want to make her uncomfortable."

"Do you think that just because she is shy she wouldn't like to be danced with?"

He frowned. "I apologize. That was insensitive of me."

"Don't apologize." She smiled. "Just ask her to dance."

"I will. Thank you for the recommendation. Got any others?"

She grinned. "Britta Mayne is quite available."

"Mayne? Is she the daughter of Duke and Duchess Mayne of the southern province?"

"The granddaughter. She's very nice, though a little silly sometimes."

Merry never broke eye contact, and it seemed too good to be true that she'd be trying to introduce him to the family he needed to make connections with.

He also thought it interesting that it happened to be the family King Dawson had warned him against—the troublemakers from the southern province.

Finally, he nodded. "Thank you for the recommendation."

"As I said, this dance is my pleasure."

The song ended, and Ben bowed slightly to her. "I would like to dance again, Lady Merry."

She gave him a playful smile. "You have many suitors, Prince Ben. But if you've got the time, you may track me down." She disappeared into the crowd.

Tendrils of guilt toward Roanna worked into his conscience, but he shoved them away. He had no other choice but to be here. If he had to marry, it might as well be to someone who was as agreeable as Merry Stern. Roanna would not hold him accountable for actually liking the woman he was being forced to wed.

Would she?

He turned from staring after Merry and sought out the sister, Rachel. She stood with a few other girls, sipping from dainty glasses. As he made his way to them, their chatter ceased. He bowed to them. "Good evening, ladies. Lady Rachel, might I dance with you?"

Her cheeks reddened immediately, but she quickly handed her drink to a friend and stepped toward him. "It would be an honor, Your Highness."

He took her hand and led her onto the dance floor. He tried to pry a conversation from her, but when she wouldn't do more than give him a yes or no answer, he took pity on her. "You look lovely, Lady Rachel. Thank you for dancing with me."

She glanced at him and gave him a shy smile, and they finished their dance in peace.

27

Ben danced with over two dozen women before the night was over. He glided across the floor with all the grace he'd been taught, but his brain was fried. Too much smiling and forced conversation. He was ready for the night to end, and he hadn't found anyone he wanted to marry.

"Prince Ben." Merry held out a glass, saving him from the need to ask yet another woman to dance.

He took it gratefully. "I've grown tired and thirsty, and you're becoming a regular hero. Are you always so helpful?"

She smiled. "I try to be. How did you find the duke's granddaughter?" She cocked her head to the side, and again Ben's alarms sounded.

"Why so interested?"

"I'm simply trying to serve my king. He wants you to find a wife, and I'm trying to facilitate it."

"I don't buy it."

They kept eye contact another moment before she turned away. "As I said, I am simply trying to help you find a wife. However, I would prefer if it was someone rather than myself, and Britta Mayne is a pleasant girl."

He raised his eyebrows, surprised at her honesty.

Two pink spots appeared on her cheeks, but she did not bow her head in shame.

Ben narrowed his eyes. Merry Stern had an agenda, but what? She was pushing the Mayne girl on him when the Maynes were exactly the contacts he needed to make to find Dr. Presnell. Instead of calling her bluff, he nodded. "Lady Britta was quite pleasant." No Roanna—and no Merry—but pleasant. "I'm touring the southern provinces in the next couple days. Perhaps I'll get to spend a bit more time with her."

Merry's smile grew. "That sounds lovely." Their conversation lagged as they both drank.

The crowd began to dwindle as the next few dances passed, until only a handful of the guests still mingled.

"What about that second dance?" Ben turned to Merry expectantly.

Her eyes widened. "I thought you were tired."

He took the glass from her hand and set it on a nearby table. Then he held out his hand. "Dance with me?"

She blushed slightly once again, but took his hand. They moved to the dance floor as a slow song played. "Tell me why you aren't interested in marriage to me."

"I've never dreamed of being a queen."

Ben shook his head. "That's not what I'm asking. You're not even interested in trying to get to know me, and I would like to know why."

She opened her mouth, but he stopped her. "I realize it's not my business, but I'm curious. I feel we're on a friendly footing, so I thought you might like to confide in me."

Her eyes narrowed, and he chuckled softly. "That's all it is, I swear it."

She huffed. "Fine, if you must know, there is someone else I am more interested in marrying."

He quirked an eyebrow. "More interested in marrying? Does this mean it's not a done deal?"

The blush returned to her cheeks and she looked away. "No, it is certainly not a done deal."

So he was right—Merry Stern had an agenda, and it was keeping his interests at bay. Merry wasn't so different from him. Still, it didn't explain the coincidence that she happened to be pushing him onto the one family from whom he needed aid. He would let it go, for the time.

When the dance ended, he bowed slightly. "Thank you for your friendship, Lady Merry Stern. This night would have been quite unbearable without your help."

She gave him a playful shrug. "Only doing my royal duty, Prince."

Baron Stern approached. He gave Ben a slight bow, and Ben nodded to him. "Merry, your sister and I are ready to go."

"Thank you for coming and bringing your lovely daughters, Baron. It was nice to see your family again."

"We wouldn't have missed it, Your Highness. We'll be staying on for another day or so. Perhaps we will see you again before the whole thing is over."

Merry gave him one last look before leaving with her father, and Ben took the opportunity to find King Dawson and Queen Katherine.

"Ben!" King Dawson clapped him on the back like he was Ben's own father. The gesture didn't feel right—too familiar—but Ben let it go. "That seemed to go well. Anyone catch your eye?"

Ben glanced around. No women stood near them, but the question bordered on inappropriate. "There were a few women, yes. I will be spending some time with the Mayne family. Lady Britta was quite pleasant."

King Dawson's eyes narrowed, but in a moment,

the look vanished. "Good, good. And what of Lady Merry Stern? I spotted you talking with her quite a bit."

Ben couldn't deny the good feelings he felt toward Merry. "I enjoyed my time with her very much. In fact, I wouldn't mind spending more with her, as well."

"Done!" King Dawson beckoned a servant. "Send word to the Sterns to stay on for a few days."

"That's not necessary, Your Highness." Ben didn't want Merry to think he was pursuing her in spite of her feelings for another man.

"Nonsense. It's obvious you cared more for Merry than Lady Britta Mayne."

"Sir, I thought perhaps I might invite the Sterns to visit Lox."

Understanding dawned in King Dawson's eyes. "I see. That's a fine idea." He turned back to the servant. "Never mind. You may go."

That seemed to put an end to his meeting with King Dawson, so Ben said his good nights and made his way to his room. The halls were mostly empty as he moved through them. As he passed Roanna's room, he glanced away guiltily.

The urge to simply stop and knock was strong, but he forced his legs to keep moving. She wasn't there. He needed to get to his room and away from the possibility of her. It was the longest walk of his life.

28

Two days earlier
Roanna

Bright sunlight pierced the comfortable sleep Roanna had finally reached. She rolled over and pulled her comforter over her head. "Bette," she mumbled.

"I'm sorry, Miss. Her Highness says you must leave early. You're to travel to Ambassador Roland's estate."

Roanna took a deep breath and let it out slowly. Yes, of course. They must whisk her out of the palace before she could run into Ben. He'd be around as they prepared for his ball, and they wouldn't want her sneaking off with him.

She couldn't stop the slow smile that crept across her face at the thought of Ben, in her room, the night before. He'd said he loved her.

Of course, it had taken hours of lying in the dark to come to the conclusion that the memory was a happy one, and the pain of their doomed relationship still stung, but she would carry it as a good memory instead of a hurtful one.

With another sigh, she threw back her covers and made her way to the bathroom. The meeting might have been a mistake, but it was a lovely one. She could go on knowing he loved her. Knowing that, truly, if he could, he would marry her.

She showered and dressed in a white blouse and a plum colored, high-waisted skirt that fell just below her knees. Large brass buttons adorned the wide waistline.

Bette packed a suitcase for Roanna while Roanna worked on her hair. She kept her touch gentle, hoping her hair's tingles would stay in a slumber. Spending the next few days with Roland would likely be unpleasant. His nearness would awaken her hair, but she might be able to use the time to figure out how the shivers worked. If she could learn her hair's secrets, and Ben could find Dr. Presnell, they might be able to put the mystery to bed.

The thought gave her pause. Did she want to put it to bed? If she did that, what other reason would she have to stay in contact with Ben?

"Are you all right, Miss?" Bette stood behind her at the vanity, frowning into the mirror. "You look upset."

Roanna smiled and nodded. "Thank you, Bette. I'm fine. Just nervous."

Relief replaced Bette's worry lines, and she returned to packing.

"Bette."

Bette raised her eyebrows in answer.

"I saw Prince Ben last night."

Now both eyebrows shot up. She threw a look at the door separating Roanna's bedroom from the family suite.

"Don't worry," Roanna said. "Nothing happened. Ben and I know our fate. We ran into each other by accident."

Bette continued working, but she frowned. Her chipper morning attitude was replaced with tension. "Why are you telling me this, Miss?"

Roanna placed the final pin in her hair and sighed.

"I'm not sure. I suppose because I needed to tell someone." She turned in her seat. "You won't tell anyone?"

"No, of course not, Miss."

Roanna moved to the bed where Bette packed. "I don't want to marry Roland." She spoke softly. "But I will do it to keep peace. To keep people safe. That doesn't mean it's easy."

Bette's look softened. "I imagine it's not easy at all."

Roanna let out a rushing breath, and she laughed nervously. "I can't tell you how good it feels to get that off my chest and not be lectured for it."

Bette put down the nightgown she was folding. She wrapped Roanna in a hug. "I know I'm not old enough to be your mother and not quite young enough to be your friend, but I'm always honored to offer you any help you need, Miss."

Tears stung Roanna's eyes. "You are my friend, Bette. I lean on you." She thought for a moment, then hurried ahead. "I want you to lean on me, too. If you need help with anything, please tell me."

Bette pulled out of the hug, but she gripped Roanna's hands. "Thank you, Miss. That means a lot to me."

They finished packing. Then Bette topped off Roanna's look with a sleek, plum top hat. Mother knocked on the door between the rooms. Bette let her in then returned to the bed to gather the luggage. "We were just finishing up, Your Highness."

Mother smiled at Bette. "Thank you, Bette. Go ahead and take that down. We'll be there shortly."

Bette curtsied and left the room, pulling the luggage behind her.

"You did wonderfully last night." Mother moved to her and touched her hair. "You look beautiful, darling. Don't ever worry about the length of your hair. You are ravishing even with it kept short."

Roanna forced a smile, but she wanted to throw a dozen questions into the air. "Thank you, Mother. I look forward to seeing Roland's home. He called it a small palace."

"Yes, I've heard. I expect it will be nice." Mother took her arm and led her into the hall. "I'm sorry we have to leave so early. Roland says that even by train it takes a couple of hours."

Roanna considered stopping Mother. Telling her she knew Ben was here, and that was the reason for the immediate trip to Roland's estate. Instead, she continued walking. Bringing up Ben would only open herself up to another lecture, and it was one she didn't want to hear. If she wanted a lecture about anything, it would be concerning her hair. Perhaps by the end of the trip she would work up the courage to ask.

Roland stood with Queen Katherine at the front of the palace. The same white auto that had driven them from the air station waited now to take them to the train depot.

"Good morning." Queen Katherine practically sang. She pulled Roanna into a hug and kissed her cheek. "You'll love Roland's home. It's breathtaking."

"I look forward to it." At least she didn't have to lie about that part. She was curious about Roland's palace. He said he lived near the sea, and that made her happy. It would remind her of home, of their palace on the river.

Roland reached for her hand, and Roanna offered it slowly. She had no other choice, and she had to get used to the idea. "Good morning." He spoke softly.

"Good morning, Roland. It's a lovely start of the day."

"Made all the lovelier by your presence." He kissed her hand and smiled.

The gesture was sweet, yet it did nothing to endear him to her.

They climbed into the back seat of the auto while Mother and Katherine took the middle seat.

She clasped her hands in her lap, lest Roland think she wanted him to hold one of them. Time had come to take control of the situation. The drive to the train depot would be a short one followed by a much longer ride to Santa Rio. "So," she said, turning to him. "Tell me about the history of your home."

29

Roland told them all about his home—it had been built nearly one hundred years ago by a former king's second son. Roland had fallen in love with it as a child, and when his father had died, making Bartholomew the king, he had left it to Roland. Roland kept the entire place up and running year-round. He often entertained dignitaries, as he was an ambassador, and he employed most of the surrounding town. He also oversaw the farming of the local area. They grew tobacco and cotton.

The drive passed quickly, as Roland was a masterful story teller. Early on, Roanna's hair had started its shivering. She was able to keep her chills under wraps thanks to the gray sweater Bette had sent along with her.

"Who runs the place while you're gone?" Roanna asked. "You've been away for a great length of time."

Roland nodded. "It's true I am often away. I have a property manager who runs the place like a prince himself. Now, prepare yourself, for it's just over this hill!"

Roanna couldn't help the excitement at seeing what would become her next home. She leaned forward to get a better view out the window as the train topped the hill.

"Welcome to Santa Rio," Roland said.

Land stretched out on either side for as far as Roanna could see. In the middle sat a sprawling three-story palace, with some areas having four stories. The home was made of beige stones and coral tiles and might be called many things, but never modest. Bright green landscaping surrounded the palace, and behind the palace was the most beautiful sight.

"Is that the ocean?"

Roland grinned. "It's beautiful, isn't it?"

Roanna couldn't take her eyes from it. The waves crashed against the rocky shore, and to the right was a small beach. "Yes, it's beautiful."

When she finally pried her gaze away, she caught Mother and Queen Katherine smiling at her.

"I knew you would love it," Queen Katherine said. She gripped Mother's hand and turned to her. "Didn't I tell you she would love it?"

Seeing them so happy together filled Roanna with peace. She wanted to make them happy. Even if she'd only known Queen Katherine for a few short weeks, she had a desire to make her glad. She felt a kindred spirit in the queen.

A smile spread across her face. "I do love it. I can't wait to explore."

The railcar pulled to the small station near the palace, and from there an auto took them to the front door. Staff members greeted them, and Roland introduced her, Mother, and Queen Katherine to the property manager he'd mentioned earlier.

Mother and Queen Katherine wanted to be shown to their rooms to rest until supper, so servants took them to a staircase to their left. Despite not wanting to spend time with Roland, Roanna did want to explore the estate. He held out his arm. "Does it bother you to be alone with me?"

Roanna smiled nervously. "Not at all. Lead the

way." She held his arm, and they started with the ground floor. It boasted a grand staircase to the left, with a large sitting room behind the stairs. To the right was a small ballroom, the dining room, and the kitchens.

Near the kitchens was a staircase leading down. Roland explained that it led to the basements, which were used for storage.

The second floor held bedrooms, a library, and another more private sitting room. The third floor held offices and the staff's rooms.

Roland was a perfect gentleman throughout the tour, and Roanna was able to ignore, for a time, that she would be marrying him soon. For now, he was simply a fellow royal who was showing her around his home.

At last. it was time to see the outside of the palace. Roland wasted no time in taking her to see the view of the ocean. Waves roared and crashed, creating a glorious calm in the air.

Roanna stared in wander. "If this were my home I would never leave!" The words slipped out before she thought them through, and heat blazed her cheeks. She chanced a look at Roland, but he only grinned at her.

"I am pleased to hear you say so." He slipped her hand from the crook of his arm and gripped it between both of his. "I want you to be happy here, Roanna. I want you to love it as much as I do, and it is like a song to my heart to hear your appreciation for it."

He held onto her hands, and the shivers started gently. She pulled her hands away and smiled. "I do appreciate the beauty. Very much."

But his face showed his disappointment at her pulling away. She had to fix this.

She leaned up onto her tippy toes and kissed his cheek. She felt nothing—none of the love and excitement she'd felt the night before with Ben. "Thank you for showing me," she said to hide her feelings.

But the brief touch between them seemed to raise her strange powers to life. She shivered, but tried to play it off. "Can you feel the sea spray?"

"Are you cold?"

"My sweater is helping nicely."

He frowned but nodded. "Let's keep going then."

She had managed to ruin the nice atmosphere they had going. Now they were back to awkward. She sighed as they moved on.

Roland showed her the area where she might start her gardens, which was small, but he promised she could do with it as she wished. At last they made their way to the beach she had seen from the top of the hill.

"When it's particularly hot," Roland said, "this beach makes a perfect reprieve."

The waves were gentler here. They lapped at the shore instead of crashing into it. "It's lovely."

You are lovely.

Roanna tensed, but Roland seemed none the wiser. How had she done it? She hadn't heard his thoughts since that day at the Edge River. Hadn't seen his aura since the engagement ball.

"Do you swim here often?" It was a dumb question, but she had to say something lest he see she was upset.

He smiled. "No, almost never." He moved closer and took her hand. "But I'd be happy to change that once we're married."

Nerves shot through her at the idea. "We'd better get back. It must be nearing supper."

He nodded, but he seemed tenser than before. Unhappy, even.

Roanna excused herself to her room once back inside. She readied for the meal then made her way to the dining room. Mother and Queen Katherine waited for her, and Roland smiled as she entered. Roanna took the chair to his right, and Katherine sat directly across from her. Mother was at her other side.

The distance she had felt earlier from Roland was gone, and Roanna tried her best to enjoy the evening. Mother and Katherine kept it lively, and Roanna was grateful for their help. Perhaps sticking close to them would be the way to make it through these next few days unscathed.

30

Roland's distant attitude returned the next day. He touched her rarely, which suited Roanna just fine. Except she wondered what had set him off. Had she offended him by being too standoffish? What if he grew so frustrated with her that he called off the wedding?

That wouldn't be so terrible, unless it caused the peace treaty to fall through. But how could Dawson's Edge cancel out the peace treaty if they were the ones who broke it?

Roanna explored Santa Rio on her own throughout the day. Katherine had returned to the main palace to attend Ben's ball, and throughout the day, Mother joined her in exploring. The power of the ocean drew her, and she spent much of the time outside.

The future garden area was small, but she could expand it. Plant roses, marigolds, and maybe even poppies. She loved poppies.

No matter how she tried to occupy her thoughts with other things, her mind kept returning to the ball being held at Dawson's Edge that very night. Ben would be dancing with lots of girls. Girls who wanted to marry him, and would be allowed to do so.

She considered Santa Rio. This could be hers. Would be hers. The home was as beautiful as she had ever imagined. Was it really so terrible?

Roland was handsome and powerful. He could be

kind, albeit too complimentary.

Perhaps it was time to put forth more effort toward her betrothed.

Making the decision to be proactive, she hurried into the house. Roland would likely be in his office, working on relations between various countries. She rushed up the staircase, but as she reached the third floor, she slowed. She'd spent little time with Roland, overall. What if they had nothing in common? What if they held none of the same core values? Did she want to be married to someone who believed so differently than she did?

But maybe he held her same beliefs. He agreed with her on Termination. There were no orphanages full of the Rejected here in Dawson's Edge. That meant more to her now than ever.

She swallowed her nerves and moved forward.

A door clicked open to her right. "Roanna?" Roland seemed surprised to find her there.

Heat filled her cheeks, and she knew she couldn't turn back. "I was coming to find you."

His eyebrows rose in surprise. "Oh?"

Now even her neck burned with embarrassment. "I was in the gardens thinking of you. I just thought I'd say hello."

The frosty attitude he'd worn for the last day thawed a bit. "Come into my office."

She followed him inside. It was a large, airy room, with a wall of windows facing the ocean. "What a view!" she gasped.

He smiled and closed the door behind her. "Why do you think I chose this for my office?"

She sat in one of the chairs opposite his desk. "It's as lovely as everything else in Santa Rio."

He nodded and sat in the chair beside her. "You're enjoying it then?"

"Yes, very much." It was partly true. She gripped her hands together and barreled ahead. "I noticed you have no prayer chapel."

His eyebrows raised, but he nodded slowly. "I don't hold much to religion."

"I understand. However, I like to pray. Could—" She took a deep breath. "Could we build one?"

The rest of his cold visage melted away, and he took her hand. "If that will make you all the happier, I would be glad to do it."

She managed a smile. "Thank you. I would appreciate it very much."

He smiled, and she forced herself to stay put. They sat holding hands for another moment when Roland leaned forward and kissed her on the mouth. His kiss was gentle, and Roanna didn't shove him away.

But she couldn't hide the shiver that coursed through her.

Roland pulled back. His nostrils flared, and his eyes burned with—what? Irritation? Disappointment? Disbelief?

She forced out a shaky smile. "Perhaps I'm catching a bit of a cold."

He watched her. Evaluated her? He didn't believe her. Maybe he could see how his touch didn't turn her to putty in his hands. Or maybe he was noticing how she shivered every time he was near.

He leaned away from her. "You should rest until supper." His words were gentle.

Guilt jabbed her. She was toying with Roland's emotions. Whether she wanted to marry him or Ben, she had agreed to this marriage. She couldn't be cold toward him.

"I think I will." She stood and moved toward the door. "Thank you for seeing me."

He gripped her hand to stop her, and he stepped close to her. Much too close. "You never need to thank me for that, Roanna. I want to marry you. I want to see you always."

The guilt hit again, and she nodded quickly. "I'll see you at supper."

She hurried to her room but couldn't stop the shivering. Bette helped her into something more comfortable to rest in, and she climbed under the blankets and buried herself in the softness of her bed.

Roland had kissed her. It wasn't wonderful, but it wasn't horrible either. Her stomach rolled, and she pressed her eyes shut. How could she endure more than his simple kisses? And what of Ben? Who was he dancing with? Talking to? Romancing?

Tomorrow they would return to the palace at Dawson's Edge, and soon after that they would return to Chester's Wake. Then she would have time to gather her wits and come to terms with her fate. She would marry Roland Dawson, and she wouldn't turn him away.

31

The next morning, thunder woke Roanna. She glanced at the clock. Nearly seven, though still dark because of the storm blowing outside. They were to leave this morning to return to King Dawson and Queen Katherine's palace.

Roanna climbed from her bed. Bette hadn't come in yet, so she showered and began readying for the day. She had already chosen a travel dress and shoes, and sat down for her hair, when Bette slipped into the room. Her hair was askew, and her eyes were red rimmed.

Roanna frowned and went to her. "What's wrong, Bette?"

Lightning flashed and thunder rumbled in the distance.

"Bette," Roanna prodded. "What happened? Is there bad news?"

Bette glanced behind her at the door then shook her head. "No, Miss." But tears pooled in her eyes.

Roanna grabbed Bette's hands and pulled her to sit on the bed. "Tell me what's happened. Is it your brother?"

Bette shook her head. "I can't say, Miss."

"You must say, Bette. You can tell me!" Panic filled Roanna. If Bette wasn't willing to share what was happening, it must be something bad.

Bette took a shuddering breath. "It's Ambassador Roland."

Roanna gasped. Had Roland taken advantage of Bette?

But Bette shook her head. "Nothing like what you're thinking, Miss." She sniffed. "He cornered me. Asked me all sorts of questions about you and your family, and he threatened me."

"What sorts of questions and threats?" It didn't make any sense.

"He asked about your parents, and you. I don't understand what he was trying to dig out of me. I don't know any state secrets." She sniffed again.

Roanna huffed and leaned against the foot board. "Roland pressed you for family secrets? How strange."

If Roland was pressing for secrets about her family, it must mean he wanted something from them. When they'd been at Edge River, King Dawson had thought of quelling a rebellion. Perhaps Roland's actions had something to do with that plan.

Trepidation filled her. She could warn Father when they returned to the main palace, but what if she were wrong? If they started accusing Dawson's Edge of wrong doing and then found out they were mistaken, they would lose the Dawson family's trust and their peace treaty.

Then a different trepidation filled her. "You said he threatened you?"

Bette nodded and wiped at her tears. "He said he knew who my family was. Called them by name and town. He said he would kill them if I told." She gripped Roanna's hands. "I can trust you, can't I, Miss? You said I could lean on you."

Roanna nodded. "You did the right thing. You can definitely lean on me, and I will get to the bottom of this without bringing you into it. I can also have

Gregory check on your family."

Relief filled Bette's face, and she stood. "Thank you, Miss. That would mean so much to me."

"Of course."

"Let's pack, shall we?" Bette put on a brave smile, but it didn't reach her eyes. Roanna joined her at the closet and began pulling clothes out, but a moment later there was a knock at the door.

Roanna waved Bette away and answered it herself. Mother breezed into the room. "What a gloomy day to travel."

Thunder rumbled again, and Roanna nodded. "It's certainly gloomy."

"We'll be having breakfast in a half hour then leaving for the main palace."

"I'm not very hungry this morning, Mother."

"Well, you can eat like a bird then. But we must see Roland before we go, don't you agree?"

"Roland isn't coming with us?"

"No." Mother moved back toward the hallway. "I suppose he has much to do, and it won't matter since we will be leaving for home by tomorrow."

Home sounded so good. "I'll be ready in a moment." Mother left, and she moved back to Bette's side and helped her a few minutes more before taking Bette's hand. "Are you calm now?"

Bette took a shaky breath. "I'm much better now, Miss. You go ahead."

Roanna gave her hand another squeeze and smiled. "We'll be home soon."

She joined Mother, and they headed to breakfast.

Roland stood from his seat at the table when they entered. "Good morning, ladies." He bowed slightly.

Roanna worked to keep a calm smile on her face.

No reason to give him the impression she had spoken to Bette. "Good morning. I heard you won't be joining us for the return to the main palace." She moved to his side and kissed his cheek as if it were the most natural thing in the world.

He seemed pleased with the kiss, but he watched her closely afterward. She squirmed under his gaze and quickly took a seat.

"Unfortunately, I have much work to do here before the wedding. But I will see you again soon."

Roanna nodded. "I understand."

He gave her a tight smile and resumed his seat.

"I hope we will be safe," Mother said as she sat. "It's pouring buckets out there."

"You'll be quite safe," Roland said with a more natural smile.

They ate in comfortable silence with small talk between bites. The small talk was held mostly between Roland and Mother. He kept looking at Roanna, as if he were gauging her reaction to things he said.

She always gave him a small smile and hoped that would satisfy him. A few of his thoughts made it her way, but she was careful to keep her face neutral and her mind clear. She'd been thinking on her anomaly, and what it meant. She had even considered that Roland and King Dawson knew when the other one was speaking to each other's minds.

She wondered if he could hear her thoughts as well. Unlikely, but she determined to keep her mind blank. Roland mustn't suspect she could hear the things his mind thought. If she thought of nothing, it would help her keep her secret intact.

What's your favorite flower, Roanna? he thought once when Mother talked about flowers for the wedding.

Another time Mother mentioned taking a honeymoon trip and Roland thought *have you been across the ocean?*

They were questions any suitor would ask a future spouse. But why had he never actually asked her these things? After all, they'd spent the entire first day at Santa Rio together. He had said he would see her soon, though, so perhaps he would ask her then.

After breakfast, Roland accompanied them to the small train depot that would whisk them back toward the main palace. Mother kissed him on the cheek and bid him farewell, but Roanna hung back. She needed to mend this relationship that had somehow become broken. Having a moment alone with him might also allow her to gauge what was happening in his head, in regards to Bette's claims.

"I enjoyed our stay very much." She stood close to him, smiling up at him.

He returned her smile but didn't take her hand. "I'm glad to hear it, Roanna. We'll be very happy here."

But still he made no move toward her. It wasn't like him, who had taken her hand or offered his arm at every meeting.

The train whistle blew, and Roanna allowed her confusion to show. "I suppose I'll see you soon, then."

He kept her eye a moment longer, a slight frown on his face. But then he nodded once, took her hand, and kissed it. "Until then, Roanna."

She gave him the sincerest smile she could muster, and nodded. "Until then." She hurried onto the train and sighed in relief as they pulled away.

32

They rode for over an hour in the pouring rain. Wind blew the trees along the track until the trees bent sideways and the railcar shook. Mother frowned and gripped Roanna's hand. "Is this safe?" she muttered.

Roanna glanced out the window. Chester's Wake was small, with no rail system between the villages. She wasn't sure what was safe and what wasn't.

Only a moment passed when the door to their railcar opened, and a conductor stepped through. "We've just received word that the tracks ahead have been flooded. We're stopping at Lady Gretchen Dawson Ferguson's depot to ride out the storm and wait for the flooding to dissipate."

Roanna looked to Mother, frowning.

"Lady Gretchen is the king's sister," the conductor assured them. "We have already been in contact with her, and she welcomes you."

Mother nodded her agreement, but she gripped Roanna's hand more tightly. They were foreign royals trapped in a neighboring country. Not the most ideal situation.

Another half hour passed when the train rounded a bend. A modest estate rose in the distance. It wasn't as grand as Roland's home, but it was a quaint plantation home with acres of treed land surrounding it. The rain continued as they reached the station and pulled under the overhang. A servant greeted them and led them under a covered walk to the main house.

Once inside, an older woman met them. Her shoulders were hunched with age, and her gray hair was pinned into a thin bun. She introduced herself as Lady Gretchen Ferguson, sister to the king.

Roanna curtsied and thanked her for sharing her home.

"This cursed storm has been going since early this morning," Lady Gretchen said. "It's a big one. I see it lasting all night." She led them slowly to a sitting room to the right of the entrance. It was a small, cramped room, lit with gas lamps and candles. The house felt old. Antiquated. Dark.

"Surely it will pass soon," Mother said in a friendly voice.

"I am old, in case you haven't noticed." Lady Gretchen smiled. "I can feel a storm in my bones days before it hits. And this one has been brewing for a week. As I said, it's a big one." She called for tea, and a servant brought it a few moments later.

Roanna drank the hot liquid gratefully. She had a chill she couldn't shake. It could be from the rain, or maybe it was just her hair again. It might also be remnants from being with Roland...or perhaps there was something about the Dawson family itself, of which Lady Gretchen was a part. More pieces to the puzzle, and something she might explore later.

Lady Gretchen told them about her family, and how long they'd been at her estate. She had three grown children and two grandchildren. She laughed often and had a witty tongue, and she had Mother and Roanna laughing frequently.

"Supper will be soon, and the rain hasn't let up yet," she said at last. "I hope you will consider staying the night."

"Yes, of course," Mother said. "I am so grateful for your hospitality."

"Then I will have a servant show you to your rooms." She rang a bell and the same woman who brought the tea earlier returned. "Show Queen Charlotte and her daughter to the first guest rooms on the second floor."

The woman curtsied and waited for Mother and Roanna to follow. They stood to go when a man entered the room.

"My Lady." He spoke to Lady Gretchen. "An auto has arrived seeking shelter. It seems they are all getting rained out today."

"Oh." Lady Gretchen stood with a groan. "I'll greet them."

The man bowed and took Lady Gretchen's arm to help her, and the other servant led Mother and Roanna from the room. They reached the stairs and started up as Lady Gretchen greeted the new guests.

"May I present Prince Benjamin of Lox," a man said.

Roanna glanced at Mother, but Mother hadn't heard. She looked down the stairs just in time to see Ben bow over Lady Gretchen's hand. He didn't see her, which was just as well. They would likely have supper together, and Mother would overreact.

If she could talk to him before then, she could tell him what Bette said about Roland. Ben would help her figure out what it all meant. But would he be happy to see her? He had spent the last few days being spoiled by female attention.

She swallowed hard as she followed the servant to two rooms side by side. If she saw Ben, she would know—know if he was in love with someone else.

Someone he'd danced with last night.

Guilt filled her, but she didn't care. She wasn't necessarily betraying Roland, and she deserved to know what would become of Ben. If she could find a way to see him before Mother learned he was here, she needed to do it now.

She waited a few minutes then checked on Mother. Then she headed down the stairs and to the sitting room where voices met her ear. Ben's smooth, kind voice spoke to Lady Gretchen telling her about his thwarted trip to spend a week with the Maynes in the southern province of the kingdom. Roanna had almost reached the door when she heard a different voice. A woman's light, tinkling laugh.

She paused. Ben was here with someone else. If he was visiting the Maynes, it was likely the Maynes themselves.

She took a deep breath and stepped into the sitting room. "Prince Benjamin." She gave him a small curtsy. "How strange to run into you here."

Ben's eyes widened, and he stumbled to his feet. "Princess Roanna. Indeed." He bowed slightly.

She smiled, playing the royal part she was used to playing. "We were travelling to the main palace when the rain nearly washed us off the tracks. It was terrifying."

He nodded. "Same here, only we were travelling by auto from the main palace to the southern province. Please, meet Duke and Duchess Mayne and Lady Britta Mayne, their granddaughter."

Roanna turned to them and smiled brightly. "I met the duke and duchess briefly at the palace. How lovely to see you again, though I'm sorry your trip has been postponed."

"Postponed?" Lady Gretchen chuckled. "This is like a party for me. I haven't had guests in months."

Duchess Mayne took the older woman's hand. "That's terrible. Shame on us for not visiting you more often. You're right. We should make it a party."

As they jabbered about entertainment for the evening, Roanna chanced a look at Ben. She caught his eye and gave him a small smile. He nodded, almost imperceptibly, and she turned away in relief. He understood her need to speak with him.

"Lady Gretchen, I thought I might read while we wait for supper. Do you have a library?" Roanna asked.

Lady Gretchen looked up from Duchess Mayne. "Certainly. I wouldn't survive here without a few books. Two doors to the left."

Roanna smiled. "Thank you. I'll be there reading."

"Why don't I come with you?" Britta was a pretty girl, with big, blond curls adorning her head. She smiled sweetly, and Roanna worked to keep her disappointment off her face.

"That would be lovely." They left Ben with Duke and Duchess Mayne and Lady Gretchen.

33

"You're the princess of Chester's Wake?" Britta asked.

"That's right. And do you live with your grandparents?"

"I do. My parents took an exploration across the ocean when I was seven, but they never came home."

Roanna frowned as they reached the library. "I'm so sorry."

But Britta shook her head. "Grandfather and Grandmother are wonderful, but I thank you all the same."

Roanna had no interest in any books in this library, but she browsed the few shelves anyway. "I heard there was a ball. Did you attend?"

Britta blushed. "I did. I was rather surprised Prince Benjamin took any notice of me at all. There were so many girls!"

"It's no surprise, Miss Mayne. You're quite fetching."

Britta smiled gratefully. "That's very kind of you, but he danced more than once with Lady Merry Stern, and I spotted them talking multiple times throughout the night. I rather thought he fancied her."

The news stung. Merry Stern? The very woman Roanna had hoped to befriend. "But he chose to spend time with you, too, obviously."

Britta nodded. "You're right, and I don't mean to

sound ungrateful. I'm very excited."

Roanna smiled and went back to the bookshelves. To speak of romance when it involved the man she wanted to marry was too painful.

"You didn't come to the ball?" Britta asked.

"I was visiting Ambassador Dawson's estate, as we are engaged."

Britta's eyes widened. "That's right! I forgot. How exciting!"

Roanna managed another smile then plucked a book from the shelf just to have something to flip through. Maybe Britta would stop talking. As she settled onto a small couch, the library door opened and Ben entered.

He smiled sheepishly. "Mind if I join you?"

"Oh, I don't mind at all." Britta turned to Roanna. "Do you mind?"

Roanna put her emotions in check and gave a smile and nod. "Of course not." He moved to the shelves then grabbed a book and sat in a chair near her couch. Britta still looked at titles, seeming somewhat interested in what she was seeing.

"Is that one any good?" Ben nodded to the book in her hand and winked.

Roanna let out a small smile but didn't look up from the pages. Of course he saw through her ruse. She hadn't actually looked at the title, so she didn't know what the book was.

She flipped to the cover page for future reference.

Britta sat on the opposite end of Roanna's couch. "You know each other, I take it?" she asked.

Roanna glanced at Ben then smiled at Britta. "Our parents have been friends for many years, so we're well acquainted."

Britta returned the smile. "That's nice. And will you be staying in Dawson's Edge long?" She directed the question to Roanna.

"Not long, no. I'll be returning to Chester's Wake with my family by the week's end. What about you, Prince Benjamin? How long will you be visiting?"

"I'll be spending a week in the southern province of the kingdom with Lady Mayne's family. They have lived along the coastline for decades." He spoke casually, but instantly her heart lightened. Dr. Presnell lived along the coastline, or Ben thought he did, which meant Ben probably wasn't interested in Britta at all.

The girl's words from earlier came to mind. Ben had spent a good portion of his ball with Lady Merry Stern.

Her heart grew heavy again. "That sounds lovely. I love the water."

Britta nodded and smiled. "It's so warm along the coast, we've never had a visitor who didn't enjoy their trip."

"Then I'm sure Prince Benjamin will have a fantastic time."

"Tell us about Santa Rio." Britta leaned toward Roanna, her face congenial and happy. "I've heard Prince Roland's estate is the nicest of them all."

Roanna's eyebrows stretched upward. "Santa Rio? It was very nice, as you said. Every part of it was beautiful." At least she could say it truthfully.

"It's along the water as well, correct?" Britta had all but forgotten her book.

"That's right." Roanna laid her book aside. She didn't want to read it anyway, so they might as well talk instead. "There's even a small beach. Ambassador Dawson agreed to let me plant gardens and build a prayer chapel."

Britta's eyes widened. She looked between Roanna and Ben.

"What is it?" Roanna asked.

"Few have gardens, and no one has a prayer chapel. It seems so strange."

Roanna nodded. "I had heard about the lack of gardens, and I understand the belief system here. Thankfully, Ambassador Dawson is understanding of my own beliefs."

Britta nodded and smiled, but she still seemed confused.

Time for a subject change. "So," Roanna said with a smile, "what shall we do now? Do you play games, Prince Benjamin?"

He lowered his book and gave her a look, but laughter danced in his eyes. "I don't care for games, no. But if the ladies would like to play, I am open to the possibility."

"Oh yes!" Britta said. "Let's play. I love games."

Heavens, she definitely wasn't the right woman for Ben.

Roanna looked over the shelves and found a small wooden board and a bag of black and white circles. "What is it?" she asked.

Ben took the pieces and looked them over, but Britta saved the day. "It's Fanorona! I haven't played since I was a child, but I loved playing with my father before he died."

Ben's look softened. "Your father died?"

"When I was young. He died along with my mother, while they were out of the country. I was raised by my grandparents."

Ben set up the board on a small table. "I'm sorry to

hear it."

Britta smiled at him. "Thank you. It was a long time ago."

Roanna watched them interact. Ben was kind to her—Ben was always kind—and his actions were getting the poor girl's hopes up.

Roanna forced herself to stop analyzing them. Ben would choose whomever he willed, with no help from her. "Since you are the expert," she said with a smile, "you shall teach us what to do."

Britta sat on the floor near the short table. "I would be happy to."

They gathered around and listened to Britta's explanation, and soon they began a game between Britta and Roanna—Ben insisted ladies should go first, though Roanna knew it was only because he hated games.

The afternoon was fun. If Roanna couldn't have Ben to herself, at least she was still able to enjoy his company. It would be short lived once Mother found out he was here.

34

That night, Roanna readied for supper and paced her room. She needed to tell Mother about Ben's presence before they reached the dining room. If Mother found out Roanna had spent the afternoon with Ben and Britta Mayne, she would have Roanna's head.

Taking a deep breath, she pushed into the hallway and knocked on Mother's door. Mother's maid allowed Roanna entrance.

"Did you rest well?" Mother sat in front of a vanity mirror. She caught Roanna's eye in the mirror. "You look lovely, darling."

Roanna smiled. "I was restless, so I went downstairs instead. Mother, do you remember there are other visitors?"

Mother stood. "Of course, I remember. What about it?"

Roanna took a slow breath, willing herself to go on.

Mother raised an eyebrow. "Well?"

"It's Ben. He's travelling with a duke and duchess from a southern province, along with their granddaughter."

Mother's eyebrows rose higher, and her mouth fell slightly ajar. "Benjamin is here?"

Roanna nodded. "I saw him when I went downstairs. Britta Mayne is the duke's granddaughter. She and Ben met at the ball the Dawsons threw, and he's travelling to their home to spend more time with her."

That bit of news seemed to relax Mother, and she nodded. "What a strange coincidence. But I suppose all will be well." She gave Roanna a look, as if asking, "It will be well, won't it?"

Roanna smiled, relieved she took the news so well. "Yes, and Lady Gretchen has called it a party. After supper, she wants us to have dancing and fellowship in the small ballroom."

Mother laughed. "Lady Gretchen wishes to dance? I hope I can get around so well when I'm that old." She finished putting on her last piece of jewelry.

Roanna took her arm, and they headed toward the dining room.

Roanna's heart beat faster with every step they took. Putting on a show in front of Britta Mayne had been easy, but fooling Mother would be much harder. She would have to practically ignore Ben in order to keep Mother happy, and that wouldn't come without effort.

Lady Gretchen's home was much smaller than the main palace or even Roland's estate, and soon they were seated in a small but ornate dining area. A large, oval, mahogany table sat in the center of the room, and a long buffet had been set up along one wall. A medium sized rectangular window faced the forest on one side. Rain still washed against the glass, though no thunder rolled.

Lady Gretchen sat at the head of the table, and Ben spoke with her quietly. Britta and the duke and duchess hadn't arrived yet.

"Ah, here are more of our guests." Lady Gretchen's face beamed. "I haven't entertained in years."

Mother moved forward graciously and gripped Lady Gretchen's hand. "Thank you for having us. You're our savior." They spoke a moment longer, and it gave Roanna the chance to throw a look Ben's way.

He smiled at her, but the smile didn't reach his eyes.

Duke and Duchess Mayne, followed by Britta, entered at that moment, and Ben rose to greet them. He introduced them to Mother.

"Now," Lady Gretchen said. "We're all here. Let's begin, shall we?"

Mother sat at Lady Gretchen's right, and Roanna sat beside her. Duke Mayne took a chair on the other side of Lady Gretchen, and Duchess Mayne sat beside him, then Britta, then Ben. For a torturous moment, Roanna feared he would sit beside her so he could be across from Britta, but, of course, he had better sense than that.

Lady Gretchen called a server to begin the meal, and plates were set before them. Next, a second server joined the first, and the platters from the buffet were passed around the table.

Duke Mayne peppered Mother with questions, and Ben and Britta kept up a steady stream of small talk.

Duchess Mayne looked at Roanna. "Britta said you mentioned your engagement to Prince Roland Dawson. You must be very excited."

Roanna smiled. "Prince Roland is very gracious. We've just spent the last few days at his estate."

"It's beautiful, isn't it?" Duchess Mayne piled her plate with vegetables. "I haven't been there recently, but I remember the ocean view."

"I admit, it was breathtaking."

"So," Duchess Mayne asked as they began eating. "When will the wedding be held?"

A much less attractive subject to consider. "Just under four weeks, at the main palace here in Dawson's Edge. I do hope you will come."

"We would love to come." Duchess Mayne smiled.

Inviting guests was a factor Roanna hadn't considered before. Would Mother and Queen Katherine take care of it? Would nobles from Chester's Wake be invited? People from Lox?

She glanced at Ben, but then she felt a jolt from the opposite side of her body. Mother had kicked her.

She looked away from Ben. "Mother and Queen Katherine have been planning without end. It's sure to be lovely."

"Have you chosen a bridal gown?"

Curse Duchess Mayne and her questions. Bridal gowns were typically silky contraptions sewn in some shade of white, red, and black. Roanna hadn't thought of it once. "Not yet." She forced a smile. "But I'm sure we will commission one as soon as we return to Chester's Wake."

"It will be lovely," Duchess Mayne said. "And the wedding is sure to be better than his first one."

"Duchess!" Duke Mayne's face turned a putrid shade of purple, but Lady Gretchen laughed.

"That brother of mine never was good for much more than causing a splash. He was only a wee thing at my wedding, but even then, he spent the day tugging on the other girls' piggy tails."

Chills broke out across Roanna's skin, and she glanced between Mother's nervous face, Lady Gretchen's look of amusement, and the duchess's calm satisfaction.

Duchess Mayne had known Roanna knew nothing of Roland's first marriage?

And by the look on Mother's face, she had known.

Roanna forced a smile but didn't reply. Humiliation didn't begin to describe her feelings. How could something like this be kept from her? Her face burned, and she looked down at her plate. She couldn't bring herself to join another conversation for the rest of the meal.

35

Once the meal ended, the guests made their way to Lady Gretchen's small ballroom.

Roanna walked beside Mother. She wanted nothing more than to pull Mother aside and demand answers, but she knew better. They would discuss it later, when they were alone.

Still, Roanna's heart hurt. Mother and Father had kept this from her? It seemed obvious they must have known. Perhaps they'd even been invited to his first wedding. Why had they not mentioned it to her?

But worse than that was the thought of Roland being married previously. What had happened to his wife? Lady Gretchen obviously found the entire situation amusing. But how humiliating to be the man's betrothed and still know nothing about him. She felt like a fool. What had the people at their engagement party thought of her? Did they assume she knew? Or that she didn't care? Did they think he was all she could get, a used up fourth prince?

"Lady Roanna?" Duke Mayne's voice broke through her fog. "Would you care to dance?"

Lady Gretchen had started something she called a record, and it played soft music throughout the room. Ben was already dancing with Britta.

Roanna managed a smile and took his hand. "I would be honored."

Mother sat with Duchess Mayne and Lady Gretchen near the record player, and Roanna allowed the duke to sweep her out onto the dance floor.

"I am happy our kingdoms will have peace at last," Duke Mayne said. "It has never happened in the whole of the Dawsonian existence."

Roanna smiled, but his words brought to mind Roland's threatening of Bette. What kind of peace was that? She needed to tell Ben, ask his opinion on it. Were the Dawsons planning some type of attack? A takeover? An empire?

"Peace is so hard to come by," Duke Mayne said as the song ended. "Many times in the past, man has spoken for peace but had war in his heart."

Roanna frowned and Duke Mayne bowed slightly. "Thank you for the dance, Your Highness."

He left the small dance floor, and Roanna stared after him. His words left a gaping hole in her reasoning for marrying Roland Dawson. She was marrying him to bring peace to her kingdom. To keep the people safe. To keep Bette's brother safe.

But if Roland and King Dawson were planning something different, something sinister, her marriage to him would be for naught. She could not keep to herself what she had overheard any longer. She had to tell Father.

"Roanna, are you well?" Mother took Roanna's hand. "You're standing in a trance."

Roanna looked around. Ben was readying to dance with Lady Gretchen, and the duke had taken his wife's hand.

"I'm sorry, Mother. I was dizzy." She hurried to the cushioned seats Mother had been sitting at a moment before.

"You looked upset," Mother pressed.

Roanna threw her a scowl but quickly wiped the

telling look away before anyone else could catch it. "Upset it an understatement, Mother."

"We were going to tell you," Mother whispered.

"After the wedding?" Roanna found it hard to keep the venom from her voice.

Mother sighed. "It wasn't a wise plan, I know. But we were afraid you would refuse to marry him if you knew."

Roanna shook her head. "It is worse that Roland didn't tell me himself. How can you wish me to marry someone who respects me so little?"

Pain flashed behind Mother's eyes. "You are right, and I admit I don't relish the thought. But tell me you know the peace is necessary. You've heard your father's reports. There are more deaths each week."

Roanna's nostrils flared, and she looked again to the duke. Based on his cryptic remark the deaths might not stop with a simple marriage fulfillment. "I know the peace is necessary."

"Good." Mother sighed again. "Because Ben will ask you to dance next. It would only be polite. You must prepare yourself."

Roanna pressed her eyes closed. Of course he would ask her to dance. She had been so caught up in the news of Roland's previous marriage that she hadn't thought much of dancing. "Will you tell me more later? Please, Mother?"

"Yes, I will tell you what I know. What little that is."

The song ended, and the dancers took a break to refresh themselves.

Mother moved away to get a drink, and Roanna was left alone for a moment.

In no time at all, Ben stood in front of her.

"Dance with me?" he asked, his voice gentle.

She didn't look at him. Couldn't. He must pity her now. Poor little Roanna.

She took his hand, and he led her onto the floor as a servant started the next song. He put his arms around her, and they began to dance. She fought the chills racing through her, but these had nothing to do with her hair and everything to do with his nearness.

"You must meet me in the library later." The words were so low she barely heard them.

She looked at him at last. "You think this wise?"

"I don't care what's wise. You look as if you've seen a ghost."

She swallowed hard and looked away again. He knew her so well. "When everyone has gone to bed?"

"Yes."

They didn't speak more, but she relished every moment of being in his arms. Here she felt safe. Loved. Protected. All of the things she didn't feel with Roland.

36

Roanna allowed Bette to help her into her bed clothes, but as soon as she left, Roanna changed into a more casual day dress. Mother had left her with a promise to discuss the full Roland situation when they reached the safety and comfort of home. Roanna wanted to know more immediately, but she wanted Mother to go to bed so she could meet Ben in the library.

The clock passed midnight. Roanna peeked into the hallway. It was empty, and the house was quiet. She crept into the dim hallway and to the stairs. Nothing moved from the floor below, so she tiptoed down. Keeping her eyes peeled, she made her way to the library. A dim light shown under the closed door, and Roanna slipped inside.

Ben stood at the window, holding a book casually as if he'd simply been unable to sleep. But once she closed the door behind her, he tossed the book onto the couch and rushed to her. His arms closed around her, and Roanna breathed in the comforting scent of safety. She laid her head on his chest and imagined what it would feel like to be engaged to Ben. To be planning a wedding to him. She could almost imagine her dress.

"Did you know about Roland?" she finally croaked out.

"No. That's definitely something I would have told you." He pulled away and shook his head. "I can't believe he kept that from you."

Irritation pulsed behind her eyes. She reached up and rubbed her forehead. "This is insanity." She sat on the couch, and Ben sat beside her. He still wore his evening wear, but his dark blond hair was messy, as if he'd rubbed his hand through it.

"How was Santa Rio?"

"It was beautiful, really." She shook her head, remembering the beauty of the ocean and Roland's promise to build her a chapel. "But something happened just before we left. Bette came to me, clearly red-eyed. She claimed Roland cornered her for information on my family. He threatened her family if she told."

His eyes narrowed. "What could be his purpose in that?"

"I don't know, but then tonight Duke Mayne said the strangest thing. He mentioned the coming peace between Chester's Wake and Dawson's Edge, but then he said sometimes men speak of peace but have war in their hearts." She bit her lip before going on. "Do you think King Dawson plans to attack Chester's Wake?"

Ben sighed and leaned back against the couch. A frown turned his lips down. Lovely lips. Soft lips.

Roanna quickly looked away before her thoughts took over her actions.

"At the ball, I danced with Merry Stern."

That she'd heard was on the tip of Roanna's tongue, but she kept it to herself. Ben was here with her now.

"This pleased King Dawson, and he pushed me to spend more time with her. However, when I told him of my plans to travel and visit with the Maynes, he was clearly unhappy."

"Why travel with them, though?" The words

spilled out before she could stop them. What if he told her he was interested in Britta?

"It's my best chance at finding Dr. Presnell. But maybe the Maynes are causing disruption within the kingdom. This could be why King Dawson didn't like the idea."

Roanna considered his words then nodded. "It could explain his thoughts on a rebellion."

Ben cast a sideways glance her way. "Has that happened anymore?"

Hearing thoughts?

She swallowed the uneasy feelings swirling through her. "Yes. I heard Roland several times during the last few days." Chill bumps raced up her arms, and she rubbed them away. "What are the chances I'm simply insane?"

Insanity sounded better than having an anomaly. Of being Rejected.

He reached for her and pulled her against his chest. His hands rubbed her arms, warding off her chills. "I don't believe you're insane. I don't know what's going on, but you're not insane."

They sat quietly for a moment, but her fate weighed heavily on her. "What do you suppose happened with Roland's first wife? Could she have died?"

"Based on Lady Gretchen's reaction, something so serious is unlikely. Duchess Mayne mentioned your wedding going better than the last, not the marriage. Maybe she didn't show up."

That was somewhat comforting.

They sat in silence, Roanna in Ben's arms. Roanna had experienced Roland's unromantic kiss, but what would it feel like to kiss Ben? All she would need to do was raise her face to his; they were already so close.

"We shouldn't meet like this anymore." Ben broke into her thoughts. "It's too dangerous. If we happen to find ourselves in the same place at the same time again, we should limit ourselves to written correspondence."

Disappointment wormed its way through her, but she pushed it away. Kissing him wouldn't be the right thing to do, at least not right now. "You're the one who summoned me," she reminded him. She pulled from his embrace.

He sighed. It sounded more like a growl. "I shouldn't have asked you here. Stop looking at me."

She let out a small laugh. "Why on earth should I do that?"

"Because I'm going to do something we'd both regret later if you don't." He stood and paced away.

Roanna watched him, her heart melting inside her. He wanted so badly to be honorable. She would help him, as long as she could manage it. "What happens if we uncover something unpleasant regarding the Dawson family intentions?"

His gaze flew to hers, and surprisingly he seemed happy. "Then both of our agreements with their kingdom will be broken."

Realization trickled in slowly. If they discredited the Dawsonian's desire for peace, she and Ben would be free from their marriage contracts. Hope swelled in her chest, and her breaths came in short bursts. She dare not voice what it could mean.

"I should go back to my room now." She stood and moved to the door.

"Thank you for telling me about Bette and what Duke Mayne said. These are clues to the mystery. At some point, I hope we're able to put all the pieces together."

"Via our written correspondence?"

He chuckled and shook his head. "Go away."

"Good night, Ben."

He met her gaze one last time then whispered, "Good night, Roanna."

37

Ben

Ben forced himself to stay by the window as Roanna left the room. Every muscle in his body wanted to follow her. Stop her. Kiss her.

He closed his eyes and took slow breaths. If the Dawsons were planning an attack—if they planned to break the peace treaty—he might be able to stop Roanna's marriage to Roland. First, though, he had to prove it. What proof did he have but Roanna's crazy intuitions and the words of an ornery old duke?

Dr. Presnell would have more answers. Ben needed to find the doctor and press him for information.

His only regret with his entire mission was leading Lady Britta Mayne on. She thought he was coming south because he was interested in her. She was nice. Lovely, even. But he'd just as soon marry no one.

Once enough time had passed, and he wasn't likely to be seen with Roanna in the hallway, he moved to return to his room. He had reached the library door when a sneeze erupted from inside the room.

Ben froze. Slowly, he returned to the main part of the library. It was a small room, fitting for the small manor. There were a few couches, but no one crouched behind them. Then he saw a closet. If someone had heard his and Roanna's conversation, the peace treaty could be doomed already. He crept toward the door, his muscles tensed to attack.

In one swift motion, he jerked the door open.

Lady Britta gasped and shrank back. "I—I'm sorry. I didn't mean to spy. I only—"

"You what?" he demanded.

Yelling at her wasn't likely to endear her to his side. He had to get her to keep his secrets.

Ben stepped away to keep from cornering the poor girl in the closet. He took a deep breath and started again. "I'm sorry. I don't mean to yell. It's just that you startled me. What are you doing in the closet?"

She wrung her hands and stepped out. She looked toward the library door as if she would bolt at any moment. "I meant to retrieve the book I'd found earlier this afternoon. When I heard you coming in, it startled me. I hid. I don't know why." She looked down as her ears turned bright red.

"And you stayed there this whole time?"

She nodded, still looking down.

"And you heard everything I spoke of with Princess Roanna?"

She finally looked up. "You love her."

So much for his ruse. "I'm sorry, Lady Britta. I didn't mean to use you."

Her throat moved as she gulped. "It's all right. I wondered why you were even coming with us. I don't seem like your type." The red in her ears moved to her cheeks.

Guilt moved through him, and he ground his teeth. "I'm sorry."

She shook her head. "It's all right. I've never heard someone so in love before. It was quite romantic."

"Lady Britta, as you can imagine, the things you heard are very sensitive matters."

Now she looked up at him, her chin held proudly.

"I heard what you said about my family, and what Grandfather said to Princess Roanna."

"We meant no disrespect, Lady Britta. Strange things have been happening, and we're merely working to figure them out."

"You were absolutely correct."

The words hung in the air, and Ben finally frowned. "What?"

"King Dawson dislikes my family. He dislikes everyone in the southern province."

Was she giving him some sort of intelligence? "I don't understand why you're telling me this," he admitted.

"Because," she stepped closer and glanced again at the door, "King Dawson has threatened Grandfather. I overheard my grandparents talking before we came for the ball, and they mentioned they were surprised I had even received an invitation."

As the future King of Lox, Ben was sure the King of Dawson's Edge would not like him knowing this information. Yet, it was exactly the kind of information he needed. "Why would the king threaten them?"

"There are families in the southern province who don't believe in the Dawson family's use of—" She stopped, as if considering her words. Finally, she went on, "Their use of magic. Grandfather once called it a purging. I believe your country uses the word Termination."

Ben frowned. The Dawson family's use of magic? Termination of...the royal family? The girl wasn't making any sense.

"So, you're telling me this to help me what? Bring down the royals?" His stomach tightened. Speaking such words in the library of a royal family member

185

wasn't the smartest thing to do.

Lady Britta shook her head. "My family doesn't necessarily want to bring them down, but King Dawson threatened to take away my family's holdings if Grandfather didn't cooperate. I don't know what sort of strange things are going on, but if helping your cause will help my cause, I'm willing to work together."

"I can't guarantee that I will be helping your cause at all." In fact, he was fairly certain he couldn't help her in any way. If the Maynes wanted to change the nation's Termination practices, who was he to assist or stop them?

Lady Britta's face scrunched up. She shifted from foot to foot. "Perhaps I spoke too quickly, but above all, it sounded as if you and Princess Roanna are worried that your peace treaties will not be honored. I warn you that it's highly possible you are correct."

Her words sank in, and Ben gave a sharp nod. "I won't speak of the information you gave me. You have my word. And I thank you to do the same for me."

She nodded quickly. After a moment, she stepped away from him and toward the door to the hallway. Ben didn't stop her. He didn't need to pretend he had a reason to want her to stay.

As she reached the hallway, he called out. "Lady Britta."

She turned.

"Thank you for helping me. I do appreciate it."

She nodded solemnly and hurried away.

38

Ben finished dressing for the morning as Hansen packed his bags. The rain had stopped sometime in the night, and he and the Maynes would continue their drive south.

He strode toward the dining room where he would thank Lady Gretchen for her hospitality, say good-bye to Roanna, and meet the Maynes for the drive. Saying good-bye to Roanna was harder every time he had to do it, but seeing her unexpectedly was worth it.

Inside the dining room, Duke and Duchess Mayne sat on Lady Gretchen's right, and Lady Britta sat on her left. No Roanna, no Queen Charlotte.

"Good morning." He smiled, keeping his disappointment at bay.

"Good morning, young man." Lady Gretchen had already started eating, but she placed her fork down while he took a seat. "I wish I could talk you into staying a bit longer. It's been ages since I've had so much fun."

Ben smiled at the old woman. "I hope we are able to visit again someday."

She narrowed her eyes. "Do you jest?"

He held up his right hand. "I swear it."

Her face relaxed into a smile. "I will hope for it as well."

Ben dug into his food and forced himself to keep from looking at the door every few seconds. Roanna and Queen Charlotte never showed up, and disappointment spread over him as he realized they must have left early. It shouldn't matter to him, but it did. It always would.

They finished eating, and he bid farewell to Lady Gretchen.

She gripped his arm. "I hope to see you again soon, young man."

"I will look forward to it," Ben smiled. He leaned down, kissed her cheek, and then climbed into the Maynes' black day limo. Duke Mayne sat beside him, and Duchess Mayne and Lady Britta sat opposite him. They had a few hours of driving to reach the southern province. Making polite conversation for long hours didn't appeal to him, but he could use the time to dig for information on Dr. Presnell. He should have asked Lady Britta the night before, but he had been more focused on making sure she kept what she'd heard quiet.

"I'm so glad that horrid storm has passed." Duchess Mayne arranged her dress around her legs. "I am ready to return home."

The duke sighed. "We might have made more of an effort to get into Lady Gretchen's good graces."

Duchess Mayne huffed. "What for? She can't help our cause."

Ben glanced at Lady Britta. She raised an eyebrow as if they were proving her point from the night before—the Maynes weren't in the Dawsons' pocket.

Perhaps Britta had been right after all. Even if Ben couldn't promise to help the Maynes' cause, the knowledge of their relationship with the king could play in his favor. It meant he could gain an ally in Dawson's Edge. A seemingly powerful ally.

"So," he started, "your family has lived in the southern province since the beginning?"

Duke Mayne nodded and launched into a lengthy explanation of how his ancestors had followed the original Dawsons south. Half the time, he spoke in riddles, and he didn't seem to want to wind down anytime soon.

He spoke of the Maynes' long held loyalty to the royal family, and Ben frowned.

What had changed in the relationship between the Maynes and Dawsons of today? Lady Britta had said the Maynes wanted to purge the Dawsons of their use of magic.

True, the Dawsons had a reputation for being dark and untrusting. He had witnessed their behaviors on the Loxian border when he'd viewed the dead soldiers' bodies at the military base. But magic?

Could it be they spoke of anomalies? The same condition Roanna worried about for herself?

A dark foreboding worked its way through him.

"What about the current King Dawson? Do you believe he is called to rule?" A bold question to ask. Perhaps too bold.

Duke Mayne's eyebrows rose. He took his time in answering. "I believe the calling lies with the Dawsonian line, yes."

"I've heard of distaste for the royal conjurers. Is this a widely held sentiment?" He kept his tone light, but much hinged on the duke's reply. If the Dawsons felt their reign was being threatened, it might explain their intense and sudden desire to fulfill a peace treaty with their neighboring kingdoms. It might also explain Roanna's belief that King Dawson faced a rebellion—he was losing his kingdom, so he sought help from another.

"There are those in the south who believe the country should be as advanced as our neighbors, yourself included," Duke Mayne answered. "Dawson's Edge has been left behind technologically, because other kingdoms fear what they view as our lack of learning. It is time to end the anomalies in our country. The Dawsons refuse to release their hold to their dark magic, so it is time to alleviate them from their rule."

Lady Britta's mention of a purging made more sense now. Duke Mayne didn't necessarily wish to dethrone King Bartholomew Dawson, but he would if the king didn't stop his use of these magical powers.

Ben frowned. What were these powers the Maynes spoke of? Ben hadn't seen any magic since he'd arrived.

The duke continued his spill, but Ben's mind drifted to Roanna. How did her hair—and her thought-hearing abilities—play into this?

The hours passed quickly as the duke spoke, and Ben considered his words and what they could mean. Soon they had arrived along the southern border of Dawson's Edge. Blue sky met the ocean in the distance, and the shoreline held a grand and sprawling white manor.

Ben was ushered inside and shown to his room. Dinner would be served that evening. After the meal, Ben would ask after Dr. Presnell. His investigation had already begun.

39

Three days passed while Ben enjoyed the hospitality of the southern province. He rode horseback with Lady Britta, met local nobles, and asked after Dr. Presnell. The old man was alive, but unavailable, so far. The Maynes seemed to know him well and had given Ben a few pieces of information over the days they'd spent together. Dr. Presnell was adjoined to their cause and had been for years. Ben had pretended to be at least slightly interested in helping them achieve their goals in order for them to open up to him so easily, but the trade in information had been worth it.

The Maynes claimed the Dawsons could bewitch their subjects, forcing people to do things against their wills. He now knew they planned to demand the Dawsons give up use of their powers, and if the Dawsons refused there might be civil war. The rebel cause was seeking commitments from other countries to fight on the side of what they called the advancement of humanity. Duke Mayne hinted at help from Princess Isabella de Paul's family across the ocean, but it appeared the ties were weak and unreliable at best.

Now Ben sat for supper with the Maynes, who still believed him interested in marriage to Lady Britta. The Maynes' dining room was as grand as any of the others he'd dined at while in Dawson's Edge. Large windows faced the ocean, a grand table seated dozens of guests, and servers bustled through, dishing out the evening meal.

Ben would take a sandwich in his bedroom at Lox any day. It had been two weeks since he'd left home. Two weeks of touring Dawson's Edge and mingling with the Dawsonians.

He sat beside Lady Britta, who smiled when he spoke to her but had stopped making hopeful doe eyes.

"We've arranged another outing for you and Britta." Duchess Mayne smiled and took a drink from her glass. "A picnic along the beach."

It only made sense that the Maynes thought Britta was why he had come. He smiled and thanked the duchess, but worry churned inside him. What if his plan to expose a Dawsonian lie failed? What if Roanna's marriage to Roland moved forward, and he was still expected to choose a Dawsonian bride?

"Which beach, Grandmother?" Lady Britta's question pulled him back to the present.

Duchess Mayne leaned forward, a smile on her face. "The Keys. The most beautiful location in the south!"

Lady Britta's face lit with excitement.

Ben smiled and thanked her for setting it up, but the quicker this trip ended the better.

They finished supper, and Ben joined the family in Duke Mayne's study. Ben sat between Duchess Mayne and Lady Britta on a large sofa. He watched the clock, debating how long he had to stay before it would be appropriate to excuse himself.

"Maybe we should host a party while you're here," Duke Mayne said. He sat in a straight back chair, staring out the window into the dark night. "You're quite the prominent guest."

Ben's heart picked up speed. This could be his chance to learn more of Dr. Presnell. "Are there many more nobles in the area?" He had met a few but the more the better.

Mayne nodded. "Nobles and friends. It needn't be a large party, but something close and cozy."

"What of the doctor I mentioned a few days ago. Dr. Presnell? I would like to meet him."

"He doesn't go out much," Duke Mayne admitted. "But I can invite him. Leave it to us."

Ben smiled, keeping his face neutral. The Maynes might find it odd if he looked too relieved. "I look forward to it."

Lady Britta let out a huge yawn.

At last. An excuse to get away. "I'm afraid it's been a long day. I'm quite tired myself."

Duke Mayne nodded. "Agreed. Let's get you off to bed. It sounds like you and Britta have an exciting day tomorrow."

Ben smiled and stood, nodding to the duke and duchess. "I'll see you at breakfast, Lady Britta."

Britta smiled shyly. Her face lit up.

Something told him she wasn't giving up on him so easily. It wasn't an inviting thought. "Good night, everyone."

He retreated to his own room, looking forward to the solitude. He'd brought along his Messenger for keeping in touch with Mother since he'd been gone. He checked for a message from Gregory, but there was nothing. No surprise, since he'd seen Roanna just this week. Still, she should be home in Chester's Wake. He'd hoped she would contact him.

Trying to keep in touch with her was foolish. He would only cause himself more frustration, not to mention what he could do to Roanna and her future. His heart told him he should let her go. Allow her to marry Roland Dawson and work to fall in love with the peacock.

Ben ground his teeth. The thought of Roland holding Roanna's hand, kissing her, calling her beautiful—it turned his stomach.

He turned off the Messenger and readied for bed. By the end of this trip, he should have more answers. He should know by then whether a future with Roanna was possible. And if not, he would have to get serious about securing peace with Dawson's Edge. Maybe the right woman could help him forget about Roanna.

He closed his eyes and sighed. If Dawson's Edge did want peace, his mission was hopeless. No one would ever make him forget Roanna.

40

Ben awoke the next morning to Hansen's gentle shaking. "Your Highness, your mother needs to speak to you."

Ben groaned and rolled over. "Is she here?"

"No, sir. She is live on the Messenger."

Mother hadn't conferenced him once while he was gone, sticking to written messages instead. If she was live on the Messenger, it must be important.

Ben pulled himself from sleep and took the Messenger from Hansen. Mother's face peered at him from the small screen. She wasn't smiling.

A knot formed in the pit of Ben's stomach. "What is it, Mother?"

"There's been another attack, Ben."

Ben frowned. "An attack? What are you talking about?"

"Your father took you to see the base when a few of our soldiers died in an attack. There's been another."

Pieces clicked together in Ben's tired mind. "Dawson's Edge attacked us while I was here? After I'd already started meeting their women?"

Mother nodded solemnly, tears in her eyes.

"Mother, what aren't you telling me?" She was too upset for that to be her only news.

"Your father was visiting the base when the attack happened, and he was hurt."

Panic washed over him. "They attacked the base itself?"

"No, your father was out visiting the soldiers in the field. There was some type of remote controlled war bot. It attacked, and he was injured."

"It is serious?"

Mother gave him a wobbly smile. "No, not too serious. But we would like you to come home immediately. Your safety is in question."

His safety? What of Father's, the King of Lox? Why had he been foolish enough to leave the safety of Lox's borders and military base?

"Of course. I'll leave immediately."

His mind raced. He needed to leave quickly, but the only air travel came out of Dawson's capital. He would have to find a driver to return him to the main palace at once. Then what? If Dawson's Edge was behind this attack, and Ben ran into King Dawson during his departure, he would be faced with the choice of diplomacy or threats.

"Mother, was King Dawson behind the attack?"

"I don't know. We don't know yet. It's not clear."

Not clear?

"Thank you, Mother. I will be home as quickly as I can."

She nodded and gave him another teary smile. "I love you, son. Be safe."

"I love you too, Mother."

Hansen took the Messenger, and Ben hurried to dress. Leaving meant he wouldn't get to meet Dr. Presnell, but that would have to wait. For now, Mother needed him. Lox needed him.

Once he was ready, he hurried downstairs. Duke Mayne met him at the base of the staircase. His face was grave—pale as a ghost. "Your Highness, a message has arrived from King Dawson. He has sent for you immediately. I have an auto ready for you."

So, King Dawson knew of the attack. Now Ben needed to figure out whether the king had orchestrated it. "Thank you, Duke Mayne. Your kindness has been more than I could hope for. I'm sorry we have to cut our visit short. You will give my farewells to the ladies?"

The duke bowed slightly, and Ben hurried out the door without saying good-bye to Lady Britta or Duchess Mayne. A sleek black auto waited outside the Maynes' home. What he wouldn't give for his Black Widow bike right now.

A moment later, the driver finished putting his luggage into the auto's small trunk. Hansen sat in the front with the driver, and they sped away. The countryside flew past, and within minutes the ocean was no longer visible from the road.

Ben kept silent as they raced over the southern hills. At this speed, they would be in the capital in no time.

Guide me, he prayed. *Guide us all.*

Secrets were being kept within Dawson's Edge, and those secrets had bled north into Chester's Wake, at least where Roanna was concerned. How did Lox play into it all? He'd like to believe Mother and Father knew nothing of these troubles—the troubles with the Dawson's magic, a possible rebellion, and now Roanna's strange powers—but Father's intelligence agencies kept abreast of the movements between kingdoms. They had to be knowledgeable about some of it.

In spite of Father's injured state, it might be time to bring the questions to his attention. Mother would likely react badly, accusing Ben of trying to get out of the marriage agreement. She would be partly right, but it went deeper than that. There were too many mysteries, and Ben wanted answers. If they were ever to live in peace, the darkness needed to be brought to light.

41

Roanna

Roanna sat in the orphanage near the palace in Chester's Wake. The large orphanage had several floors of rooms. A girls' home, and now girls swarmed her as she passed out donations.

All these girls, Rejected. Failed by the system. Some of them exhibited anomalies already—a girl with a misshaped eye dropped a new bath set Roanna had brought. She retrieved it before Roanna had time to register it, so fast were her movements. The keepers of the orphanage told Roanna the child had mere months to live—her speed was too uncontrollable. It might turn out to be dangerous, they'd said. Her Termination was imminent.

Other girls were unhealthy, physically. While the Termination process was used to weed out anomalies, it had also been tweaked over the years to detect and eliminate those whose quality of life was in question—those with genetic mutations indicating future cancers, or those with extra chromosomes, or even those with major heart defects.

Roanna smiled at a child, no older than four or five, whose face lit up when she opened a package containing a doll. The child laughed with delight but then went into a coughing fit.

Roanna's stomach flipped as she considered herself and her own situation. Did it matter whether Mother had been tested while pregnant? These children were proof that the testing was wrong on occasion.

"Would you like me to hand out a few?" a young woman interrupted Roanna's thoughts. Gwendolyn was the same age as Roanna and had lived at the orphanage as long as Roanna had been visiting. She looked perfectly healthy, but she'd confided that it took much medication to keep her that way. Roanna wondered why Gwen hadn't yet been Terminated.

Roanna smiled and nodded in answer to Gwen's question, and Gwen took an armful of supplies to hand out. Roanna's mind continued to wander.

What about her? Her anomaly wasn't as loud and noticeable as any of these children's. Yet, if detected, she would have been Terminated.

Ben didn't always see her point when it came to Termination. He had come with her to visit the Rejected a few times in the past, and his heart always softened after the visits. But would he change his mind now that she herself might be considered Rejected? Failed by the system?

Or would he be repulsed by her? Convinced humanity had failed by not weeding her out and saving her from herself? Her stomach twisted at the thought.

Roanna finished her visit and prepared to return to the palace. Mother had commissioned three mock wedding gowns for Roanna to try. She had gone on and on about their beauty, but the idea of modeling wedding dresses for a marriage to Roland didn't fill her with excitement.

The palace was as busy as ever as Roanna made her way through it and to Mother's office. She pushed through the door, and her gaze fell to the mannequins holding the gowns. The first dress was billowing and white, with sleeves slightly off the shoulder and black flowers embroidered around the waistline and skirt. The second dress was a cream-colored gown, fitted and covered in lace, with strands of glittering diamonds sewn throughout. The final gown was red silk and sleeveless. The skirt billowed out in a full ball gown style, but the red silk was bunched at the hem to reveal thick, black lace.

"Roanna," Mother gushed. "They are even lovelier than I imagined."

Roanna managed a smile. "They are, indeed."

The seamstress was there to help her try them on, and Roanna allowed herself to be herded further into the room. Mother started in on topics of materials and dress styles, but Roanna couldn't stop thinking about the Rejected.

Mainly, her role among them.

Roland Dawson didn't believe in Termination. Would he hold her powers against her? It didn't appear so, but sometimes people believed in things because they'd never actually been faced with the issue personally. He might change his mind if he knew the truth.

She needed this marriage with Roland because she might not receive a better match. She might not find another husband willing to overlook her having an anomaly.

Mother gasped, and Roanna jumped.

"Roanna," Mother said. "This is the one."

Roanna turned toward a mirror the seamstress had set up. She wore the red silk gown with the black lace.

The seamstress stepped forward with a black top hat with a short black veil. "Here, my lady, try this on."

Roanna's hands shook slightly as she placed the hat on her head. Her image was beautiful. Certainly not what she would have chosen, but beautiful. She gave Mother a wobbly smile. Mother turned quickly to the seamstress.

"Thank you. We will take the red dress."

The seamstress went to work pinning and measuring for Roanna's exact fit, but Mother crossed her arms and gave Roanna a shrewd look.

Roanna forced herself to stand still for the seamstress, but she wanted to squirm under Mother's gaze. Mother knew something was wrong in Roanna's heart, and as soon as the seamstress left she would pelt Roanna with questions.

At last, she put her own clothes back on and the seamstress was gone. Roanna stood in front of Mother's desk, shifting like a naughty child. She scratched an itch at the nape of her neck, and her fingers slowly massaged their way into her pinned up hair. Asking Mother about her hair could be so simple. Or it could be disastrous.

What did she fear would happen? Surely, Mother wouldn't reveal Roanna had been cursed by the Dawsonian doctor. That was absurd.

As absurd as a person having magical hair?

She swallowed hard. "Mother, I have something I've been wanting to ask you."

Mother slipped into her office chair. "You obviously didn't enjoy any part of that. Please, speak your mind."

But Mother didn't understand what was bothering her. It wasn't the wedding or the dress. Roanna swallowed her fear. "Why have you always insisted I keep my hair short?"

Mother's eyes widened. Then she frowned. "What on earth brought this about? Is it because you wanted to grow it long for the wedding?"

"No, Mother. I've always wanted longer hair. It's just—" How did she say it? Telling Mother about her secret trip to the dungeon with Ben didn't seem like the best idea. Telling her about the strange bouts of mind reading seemed even worse.

She took a deep breath. "I found an old history. It mentioned a doctor who was visiting the palace on the night I was born." She watched Mother's face carefully, but Mother was a master at hiding her true feelings.

"It said he warned you to keep my hair short, and he was thrown in the dungeon for it."

Mother didn't speak. Only blinked, keeping silent for long seconds. Finally, she waved a hand dismissively. "I can't imagine what kind of history would have had that written in it, Roanna. There was a visitor to the palace when you were born, but he was thrown in the dungeon because he was suspected of stealing military secrets. He was from Dawson's Edge, and back then we had no hope of the peace we have now. Did your little history book mention that?" So, Mother was willing to lie to hide her secret.

"I saw the dungeon file myself. It didn't mention anything about military secrets."

Mother narrowed her eyes. "You what?"

Roanna paced to the window. She wasn't about to be thrown off because Mother tried changing the subject. "It doesn't matter how I know it. All that matters is that I saw the file, and I know the doctor warned you. It upset you, but what's worse is that you listened." She spun toward Mother. "Why did you listen?"

Again, Mother fell silent. At last, she sighed and looked to her lap. "He kept shouting it like a maniac. It frightened me."

"But after all these years, why stick to it?" Could Mother know about Roanna's strange abilities? This was the first she'd contemplated the idea. Perhaps Mother followed Dr. Presnell's direction because she knew of Roanna's capabilities.

Mother buried her face in her hands. After a moment, she looked up. "The law requires that all expecting mothers undergo Termination testing. I complied, but later I had the results destroyed before anyone could see them—including myself. I didn't want to know, and I didn't want my child Terminated no matter what a test said." She shook her head. "No one ever saw the results, I was sure of it. But then the doctor came, shouting his warnings. I thought, surely, he had somehow seen the results and he knew something. He believed you had an anomaly that would be set off by growing your hair."

Mother's words made no sense. How would a Dawsonian doctor know her Termination results? He didn't live in Chester's Wake and was only visiting for a short time. They did not practice Termination in Dawson's Edge. It would have been impossible for him to know the results of Mother's testing.

Yet, he knew Roanna would have an anomaly.

How?

"Roanna." Mother moved to her side. "I'm sorry I never told you. You obviously do not have an anomaly. It was the fearful actions of a loving mother." She hugged Roanna, and Roanna forced a smile.

You obviously do not have an anomaly.

If only Mother knew the truth.

"I understand, Mother. Thank you for answering my questions truthfully."

Mother smiled and kissed Roanna's forehead. "I love you, daughter of mine."

"I love you, too." She took a shuddering breath. "I think I'll go rest for a while."

Mother nodded, and Roanna left the office and headed toward her room. It was one of the only places she found refuge lately. As she walked through the palace, Gregory bounded around a corner and raced in the direction of Father's offices.

"Where's the fire, brother?" She smiled, teasing him.

But Gregory didn't return the smile. He barely slowed. "There's been an attack on Lox."

Roanna's smile fell. "What?"

Gregory didn't stop to explain, and Roanna hurried after him.

42

Roanna raced behind Gregory, her legs working to keep up with him. "What happened, Gregory?"

"I don't know for sure. I was sent a short briefing and told to report to Father."

"But you must know something!" She grabbed his arm. "Who attacked?"

He gave her a sympathetic look. "I don't know, Roanna. But you can come with me to see if Father knows."

He took off again, and she tagged along.

Father's offices buzzed with aides rushing around, talking into Messengers, typing on keyboards. Gregory bypassed them all and went straight into Father's main office.

Father sat behind his desk, looking into a Messenger screen. "I understand," he said. "Please keep me up to date."

As soon as he'd ended the call, one of his aides rushed forward. "Your Highness, a message from General Keefe."

Father held up a hand. "Give me a moment with Gregory."

The aide nodded and stepped aside, and Father waved them forward.

"What happened, Father?" Gregory's mouth was set in a firm line. His eyes were serious, his chin set, and his shoulders broad. He was all business. Roanna had seen him work with Father before, but never on something so important. This Gregory? He was the future king, and he would excel.

"An attack at the Loxian-Dawsonian border. Bartholomew Dawson is denying involvement or knowledge, but the responsible party has not been apprehended yet. So far, the Dawsonians are cooperating in the search."

"Casualties?" Again, Gregory's professionalism surprised her.

"Six that I know of. King Neville was among the wounded."

Gregory's eyes widened. "The king was on the front lines?"

Father gave a solemn nod. "He was visiting his troops when the attack was made. From initial reports, it appears a remote controlled war bot was used."

"What reason would the Dawsons have to attack the Loxians when they're in the middle of a marriage negotiation?" Gregory shook his head. "It doesn't make sense."

Roanna needed to tell them what she'd heard from the Dawsons. They needed to know King Dawson faced a rebellion and Roland was arguing on whether to enact a plan before or after their wedding.

Her mouth was dry, and words wouldn't form.

"I would like you to travel to Lox," Father said to Gregory. "Make a good will visit and offer our aid."

Gregory nodded immediately. "Of course."

"I want to go." The words were out before she could stop them. She needed to see for herself the damage and figure out if the Dawsons meant them all harm. She raised her chin so Father would know she meant it.

Father looked to her for the first time. "You will

certainly not be going to Lox."

"Why not? I'm the princess, aren't I? Gregory is the prince. We would be making a good will visit, as you said. It would not seem improper at all." But she knew she would lose the argument even as she spoke.

Father shook his head. "It's too risky. Gregory can handle things."

"Won't Dawson's Edge be sending an ambassador as well? It will be Roland, and you know it. Why shouldn't I go?" she broached with her last and best argument. How could it seem improper when Roland would be there as well?

Father wavered, and hope sprang up. "I can spend my time with Queen Frieda," she pushed.

Father sighed and nodded. "Very well. You will need to leave immediately."

Roanna nodded in relief, and she and Gregory hurried from the offices. Bette helped her pack quickly, and within the hour she met Gregory at an auto to take them to the air station. A few of Father's aides were coming along as well, and they boarded the airship together.

Gregory gave her a curious look as they settled into their seats. "Why did you want to come so badly?"

Her mouth went dry again. Ben was the only person she'd told about her secrets, but Gregory used to know them all.

"Do you remember I've been growing out my hair?" She spoke quietly so the aides surrounding them wouldn't overhear.

He frowned. "Yes. So?"

She licked her lips. "Sorry. Strange lead-in. Weird things have been happening over the last few weeks, and Ben and I have been working to figure them out."

His eyebrows rose. "You and Ben? I thought you weren't supposed to speak to each other. I sent the one message on your behalf, but that was weeks ago."

Roanna's cheeks warmed. How did Gregory know so much? Palace gossip must be alive and well. "Yes, well, the truth remains. Anyway, Ben and I discovered that Mother's rule to keep my hair short was a rule that came out of a warning from a Dawsonian doctor on the night I was born. We started investigating, and other strange things came to light." She couldn't bring herself to tell him about the shivers or mind reading.

"I overheard King Dawson and Roland. I don't know what they were talking about, but they mentioned something about a rebellion and a plan. They argued over whether they should begin their plan before or after the wedding."

Gregory stared at her, his eyes wide. Finally, he scoffed at her. "Why haven't you told Father this?"

Roanna shrank back, embarrassed. Why hadn't she told Father? She'd been so confused about her hair, about being able to hear people's thoughts, about being forced to marry Roland Dawson as she struggled to deal with her feelings for Ben.

She rubbed her forehead. "It's all happened so fast. I haven't had a chance to figure it all out."

His unsympathetic features melted away, and he took her hand. "Well, tell him now. He needs to know."

"But, Gregory." Telling Father would mean confessing the other strange things going on. Admitting she feared she had an anomaly. Her family might Reject her. Disown her. She would never be allowed to be with Ben, or anyone else.

"We don't know it meant anything. We don't

know the Dawsons are up to no good." And he spoke the truth.

She didn't want to marry Roland, but for the most part the Dawsons had been nothing but kind to her. Accusing them of this attack because of things she thought she'd heard in their minds seemed ludicrous, even to her.

"Father will know that, but he needs to be aware."

They fell silent, but the closer to Lox they travelled, the more her stomach churned. She should have kept her intel to herself, at least until she'd figured out how to tell Father.

43

Roanna and Gregory were met at the air station by a driver who took them to the Loxian palace. She had used the time on the airship to consider her options. If the attack had been ordered by King Dawson, it meant he had been using them all along.

But King Dawson was denying involvement. If Dawson's Edge wasn't responsible for the attacks on Lox, then who was it? The offense was a serious one because King Neville himself had been injured. If an enemy could attack Lox, they could certainly attack Chester's Wake.

Fear twisted in her stomach, and she took a deep breath. They would find whoever was responsible and punish them. In fact, it was unlikely Father even needed her extra intelligence. His network of informants would yield him all he needed to know in aiding Lox. Until then, she needed to be smart, stay away from Ben, and stick close to Queen Frieda. She would have time to tell Ben her thoughts later when King Neville was healed and the attackers had been identified and caught.

Roland would likely be arriving, and he would expect her full devotion. Until they knew more—until she found the words to tell Ben and her family the truth—she would give Roland the devotion he sought, but what about his words to King Dawson at Edge River? The words he'd only spoken in his mind? If Roland had communicated with King Dawson via his thoughts, and it appeared the king had done the same…did they also have an anomaly? Could it be why Dawson's Edge had rejected Termination for so long?

As the auto pulled into the rotunda in front of the palace, Roanna spotted Queen Frieda waiting for them. She pushed the thoughts away, climbed from the car, and greeted the queen.

"How kind of you to visit." Frieda kissed Roanna on the cheek then did the same with Gregory.

"What a terrible tragedy," Gregory said. "How could we not come?"

Queen Frieda smiled at him. "I've instructed Jeremiah to take you to your rooms. From there, you may see me in my offices. Benjamin will be leaving to see the king in the morning. You are welcome to go along."

Gregory nodded solemnly, and a moment later, the servant, Jeremiah, stepped forward to take them to their rooms. Roanna had always been fascinated by the Loxian palace. The waterfall against the mountains behind them filled the air with a calming, rushing sound. And the glass dome in the palace entryway filled the space with light and life.

The guest rooms were situated on the western side of the second floor, while the family's rooms were situated on the eastern side. The butler led Gregory to a room at the entrance of the guest hall, but he led Roanna deeper down the corridor. At the end of the hall was a wrought iron servants' elevator, and beside it was a fancier elevator used by the royal family.

As children, Roanna and Ben used to play on the elevators.

She smiled at the memory.

Jeremiah stopped at the door to the very last room, near the royals' elevator. "You may ask for me should you need anything. Do you know how to find Her Highness, the Queen?"

"Yes, thank you." Roanna had visited Queen Frieda's offices more than once.

Jeremiah bowed slightly, opened the door to her room, and then stepped away.

Roanna pushed through the door. Bette would be along shortly with her things. She would unpack for Roanna.

Roanna would hurry to see the queen. Getting more information on the attack was her main goal, but it was also always important to foster relationships between the kingdoms. That and the fact that she loved Queen Frieda and King Neville almost as much as she loved her own parents.

She closed her door, turned to take in the room, and then gasped. Ben stood near the window. He smiled at her. "We keep running into each other."

Roanna laughed nervously, her resolve to stay away from him melting into a puddle of nothingness. She rushed to him, and he enveloped her in a hug. She relished the feel of his arms around her. "I thought we were sticking to written correspondence."

He shrugged, but he didn't let her go. "That was the plan, wasn't it? I guess I changed my mind when my father was attacked. It changed my perspective, if you will. Made me want to tell all the people I love that I love them. When I heard Mother say you were coming, I couldn't stay away."

She pulled out of his embrace. "I'm sorry about your father, Ben. How terrible."

A shadow fell over his face, and he turned to the

window, which looked out at a forest on the mountainside. The sun was low in the sky. It was nearing sunset, and the forest would become a dark kingdom of its own soon. "I spoke with King Dawson. He swore to me he was not behind it." He looked to her. "I believe him."

Emotions warred inside her, and she turned to the window herself. If the Dawsons didn't order the attack, who did? They could all be in danger.

Ben gently took her chin and turned her toward him. "I did my own investigating while in Dawson's Edge, and I feel the Dawson family is genuine in their interests for peace. If anything, it is Dawsonian rebels who are working against our alliances with the royal family. I fear our mission is doomed." His voice cracked on the last word.

Roanna's stomach twisted. "Our mission?"

"We'll not be able to discredit their family. Not before you have to marry the peacock."

His words sent burning tears to her eyes. She swiped at them angrily but forced a smile. "It's the way we always knew it would be." And Ben still didn't realize the truth. Her truth.

He stroked her cheek with his thumb and leaned closer. Oh, so close. "Say the word, Roanna." He spoke in her ear, his hot breath tickling her skin. "Say it is worth it, and I will give it all up for you."

Roanna's breath caught in her throat. Say the word? "You would start a war for us?" It came out in a painful whisper.

Slowly, their eyes met. They knew the truth; whether or not the Dawsons had orchestrated the attack on Lox, they would retaliate if both Lox and Chester's Wake broke their marriage agreements with

Dawson's Edge. Especially if it was to create a union between themselves.

His gaze lowered from her eyes to her lips. Was that his answer? He would start a war?

He lowered his lips toward her and she held her breath. Ben's kiss was what she'd dreamed about for weeks.

But just before his lips brushed her skin, the door opened.

"My lady, Queen Frieda has—"

Roanna jerked away from Ben as Bette's voice stopped short. Dread filled her as she looked to the door. Bette wasn't alone.

44

Bette stood in the doorway, her mouth hanging open. Queen Frieda and Gregory stood behind her.

Roanna wanted to run from the room. Bury her head. Hide. But Ben stood calmly. He looked to Queen Frieda. "Did you need something, Mother?" His voice was soft.

Queen Frieda took a deep breath and then let it out slowly. "You may leave us, dear," she said to Bette.

Bette bowed quickly and bolted from the room. Queen Frieda and Gregory stepped into the room, and Queen Frieda closed the door.

"What are you doing in here, Benjamin? You would cause further harm to this kingdom?" Her words were spoken without anger. She sounded fatigued. Worn down.

Shame filled Roanna because for a single moment she had considered their relationship worth starting a war over. King Neville was already injured. Would she injure Gregory? Father?

She wanted to say something—anything. But what would she say? This was her room, and she hadn't invited Ben into it, but she hadn't sent him away either. She had welcomed him, relished his touch.

"I don't have an excuse for you, Mother." Ben stayed put, standing at her side. What was he thinking? He needed to get away from her, and somehow, she had to figure out how to make him stay away. Hadn't she just determined that very thing in the auto from the air station?

Queen Frieda studied him a moment longer. Then her gaze trailed to Roanna. "I love you as my own daughter as I suspect you know."

Roanna nodded. "Yes, Your Highness."

"Good. Then I want you to answer me truthfully. Is this why you came?"

Heat poured through her. Did she come because she thought she would see Ben?

Again, her resolution to be a diplomat came to mind. She stood tall. "No. I came as a friend. As family. And with Gregory, as an ambassador of good will between our kingdoms in this time of need."

Queen Frieda nodded. "Very well. Benjamin, you will stay away from her the rest of her visit. Do you understand me?"

"I'm a grown man, Mother."

"You are acting like a child, which is something you tend to do when Roanna is involved." He had finally pushed her to anger, but the Loxians were peaceful and her anger quickly faded. She looked between the two of them, then sighed. "This world is bigger than you are. You would both do well to remember that."

Roanna felt exactly like a child in that moment.

Gregory had stayed silent during the exchange, but he finally spoke up. "Perhaps it would be best if Roanna and I shared a family suite."

Now she needed a babysitter?

"No." Ben shook his head and finally stepped away from her. "I'll keep my distance. You have my word."

Queen Frieda watched him a moment then gave a single nod. "Good. You should prepare to see your father."

Ben glanced at Roanna then back to his mother. "Can we have a moment?"

Another flash of anger spread across Queen Frieda's face. She nodded, but she didn't leave or even turn away.

Ben stepped close to Roanna once again. He placed his hands on either side of her face, and leaned his forehead against hers. "I'm sorry, Roanna."

Sorry.

Sorry their short try at a relationship was over. Sorry he had embarrassed her in front of their families. Sorry he hadn't been able to save her from marrying Roland Dawson.

His voice told her he meant all of these things, and more.

Roanna pressed her eyes closed, the tears coming again. This was it. She would need to put Ben from her heart once and for all.

She didn't speak, and a moment later he stepped away and strode from the room.

Gregory glanced her way, but she waved him off. She would be fine. He followed Ben from the room.

Queen Frieda closed the door, and she crossed the room and took Roanna's hand. "There is nothing in this world that would have made me happier than Benjamin taking you as his wife. But that cannot happen, ever. I am sorry we allowed the friendship between you to grow so strong, but the time has come to put away childish things."

Tears slid down Roanna's face. It made her feel all the more ridiculous. Childish.

"Your own betrothed will be arriving soon from Dawson's Edge. You would do well to remember that."

Roanna managed a nod. "I didn't mean for any of this to happen." It came out in a whisper.

Frieda's face softened, and she wiped the tears from Roanna's cheek. "I know you didn't. Neither did Ben. It's simply the way of life, and sometimes we make hard choices for the benefit of others." She paused then went on. "When you're up to it, I would love your company in my office. I'm putting together care packages for the families of the soldiers who were killed in the attack."

Roanna's pain shrank a little at the thought of those families. Their world was bigger than her relationship with Ben. That's what Queen Frieda had said. "I will be down shortly."

Queen Frieda smiled and nodded. "I will see you then." She left Roanna standing alone.

As soon as the door closed, tears broke from Roanna's eyes like a rushing river. She fell onto the bed, sobbing.

Bette re-entered and hurried forward. "Oh, Miss!" She laid down beside Roanna and hugged her tightly. "It will be all right, Miss. I'm here."

Roanna cried harder and clung to Bette. "Oh, Bette, I'm such a fool."

"Shh," Bette soothed. "You aren't a fool. Cry your tears, and we will get you fixed up."

Roanna nodded, but her tears still flowed. This visit wasn't shaping up at all how she had expected it.

45

Ben

Ben jogged down the stairs to the first floor then took a hard left and headed toward the state offices.

"Ben, wait." Gregory's shoes pounded down the stairs after him, but Ben didn't slow. The last person he wanted to be lectured by was Roanna's brother. He was a good man—a friend, even—and one day they would rule neighboring kingdoms. But he didn't want love advice from him.

"Ben." Gregory caught up with him, grabbed his arm, and spun him around. "Tell me what happened."

Ben jerked his arm away. "I don't want to talk about it, Gregory." He hoped his tone and look conveyed how very much he didn't want to talk about it.

Gregory's gaze shot back its own fiery look. "I don't care about your relationship with Roanna. I want to know what happened in the attack. I need to know how I can keep my own people safe."

Ben drew back. An attack. Right here in Lox. Right. He rubbed his forehead. "I don't know." He turned back toward the state offices. "But you are welcome to come along and find out."

They marched through the palace together until they came to the marble-floored state offices. Kingdom officials dashed from office to office. Messengers chimed. Secretaries pounded letters on their keyboards.

"Where is King Neville?"

A pang of guilt shot through him. He'd been willing to sentence Mother's and Father's life's work to doom because he wanted Roanna for himself. It wasn't very kingly of him.

"He's in a secure location down south, being kept under medical care. I hope to see him tomorrow."

Gregory nodded and followed Ben to Father's eerily empty office, devoid of the rush going on outside. Ben stopped just inside the door and took a deep breath. Someday these offices would be his own. The weight of that realization felt like the world on his shoulders.

Once he'd composed himself, he stepped further inside. "I need to gather Father's technologies." He moved to the desk and grabbed the portable Messenger along with a few other items.

"Is he in contact with his aides?"

Ben stared, unsure what to say. Mother had been working round the clock, but what was Father doing in the medical center? He hadn't realized until now how little he knew. "I don't know." He shook his head. "But, again, we can find out."

"Wait." Gregory closed the office door then stepped closer to Ben. "There are a few things I want to tell you now, without prying ears."

Ben narrowed his eyes. "Go on."

"Roanna told me about the things she overheard from the Dawsons. Unfortunately, I have my own pieces of the puzzle to add."

Ben had looked King Dawson in the eyes as he'd sworn an oath that he had nothing to do with the attack. He'd promised all his resources to help find the responsible party. No matter what Roanna had felt from them—and no matter what Gregory had learned—it would take a lot of convincing to make Ben believe otherwise.

"What are you talking about?"

"The Dawsons grow restless. Their relations across the ocean are fizzling out, and there are rebels within the kingdom who want to use that against the royals."

"What about the prince's wife? King Dawson's eldest son married a princess from across the ocean."

"His wife has asked for a divorce."

Ben frowned and drew back. "How do you know this?"

"Merry Stern."

Ben froze. "You're in contact with Merry?"

Gregory didn't flinch, and realization dawned. Gregory was the one she was seeing. The reason she wasn't interested in any type of marriage proposal from him.

"The Sterns are in good graces with the king, but it doesn't mean they're loyal to him," Gregory went on. "The Dawsons' relationships across the globe are deteriorating, and they're fighting to keep their kingdom alive. Their allies across the ocean have stopped sharing intelligence, and they've cut off export between kingdoms."

Ben shook his head. "That doesn't explain anything. How would attacking Lox after they'd signed a marriage agreement with us help their cause?"

"That's where Roanna's intelligence comes into play. They face a rebellion. They need new resources, bigger armies, and more power."

Ben huffed and leaned against Father's desk. He put down the Messenger and rubbed his forehead again. "King Dawson swore the attacks were not under his orders."

"Then someone acting under his orders. Roland?"

The idea was an attractive one. Blame Roland Dawson, attack Dawson's Edge, and keep Roanna for himself.

But as much as he hated the idea of Roland Dawson, he didn't agree with Gregory's ideas. "I still say it doesn't make sense. They wouldn't attack us if they need our aid. Instead, they would do exactly as they've done. Seek our alliances. We need to speak with my mother and father, and their aides. They'll know what to do with this information."

Gregory studied him a moment longer, then he nodded solemnly. "So be it."

46

Roanna

Roanna allowed herself a single hour to revel in her embarrassment, shame, and disappointment. For years, she had lived with the knowledge that Ben's friendship was all she would ever have. It had been well with her soul.

How had things changed so quickly?

She brushed through her hair, and the shivers started, but she was doing well at keeping them under control these days. Over the last week, she had been practicing. Projecting her mind outward, feeling for auras—thoughts. She'd learned that while she could sense the auras, she never heard other people's thoughts. Except the Dawsons.

Her hair reached just past her shoulders now. It was growing much faster than she ever expected. Bette handed her a feathered, brass hair pin, and Roanna arranged it then gave herself a once over.

"I suppose I should go now."

Bette nodded. "I will help you dress before supper tonight, Miss."

Roanna smiled her thanks. She made her way to the empty hall and headed for Queen Frieda's offices. As she reached the bottom of the stairs and turned right, an entourage stepped into the main foyer of the palace.

Roland Dawson stood in the midst of them, and their gazes met across the short distance.

Roanna drew on the years of training and pasted on a smile. "Queen Frieda told me you would be coming."

One of the palace servants arrived to lead the rest of the entourage on their way. Roland and Roanna stood to the side in relative privacy.

Roland returned her smile. She expected a hug or at least a kiss on her hand. But he didn't reach for her.

The first shiver hit like a wave. Her smile faltered, and she struggled for control. It passed, but a moment later another shiver assaulted her.

Roland watched her curiously. At last, he stepped toward her. "Are you all right, Princess?"

She swallowed her panic and nodded. "I'm not feeling very well. Will you excuse me?"

His eyebrows lowered, and he nodded once. "Will I see you at supper?"

"I expect it, yes."

He nodded again, and she hurried back up the stairs and to her room. Right now, her strange hair was the least of her worries. She was stuck in the Loxian palace with the man who wanted to marry her and the man who couldn't marry her. All the while, the Loxian king lay injured from an attack.

Still, her hair. The shivers. It always grew worse when Roland came around.

The Dawsonian doctor had warned of her hair, and whenever she was around the Dawsonian royalty her hair went berserk. There was no coincidence there.

Where was Bette? Probably off working, as would be fit. But Roanna couldn't stand the thought of being alone.

She took a deep breath and composed herself. She could make it to Queen Frieda's office without running into Roland again. Slipping back into the hallway, Roanna headed toward the servants' elevator. It wouldn't be the first time she'd used it, and it probably wouldn't be the last.

Hurrying through the plain servants' halls, she dodged as many strange looks as she could. But most of them stopped her. "Can I help you, Miss?" Some of the older servers knew her—she'd been around a long time. Others didn't recognize her, and those were the ones who pushed harder. "You shouldn't be in here, Miss."

Roanna smiled at each of them. "I'm going to the queen's office." And she'd keep going.

She made a few wrong turns but finally slipped out of the servants' hall and into the main palace corridors. A few of Queen Frieda's aides gave her confused looks, but as with the servants, she gave them a smile and breezed past.

Queen Frieda glanced up from her work when Roanna entered. She was bent over a ledger, pen poised in one hand, Messenger in front of her. She used her empty hand to hold up a finger to Roanna— give her one moment.

Roanna perched on the edge of a chair as the person on the other end of the call gave details of the families affected by the attack. When the call finished, Roanna stood.

"How is King Neville?"

Queen Frieda managed a smile. "I haven't seen him yet, but we plan to travel there tomorrow. You may join us, of course, if you would like."

"I'll consider it. Ambassador Dawson arrived a little while ago. I suppose I should base my decision on his plans."

Frieda nodded again. "Not an unwise choice." She nodded to her desk. "Now, if you'd like, we can work on lining up help for these people."

Roanna hurried to the desk. "Yes, of course." She'd done benevolence work with Mother plenty of times. She hoped to continue the work when she was married to Roland, though Santa Rio was much smaller than an entire kingdom.

She pushed aside the unpleasant thoughts and threw herself into the work. Together, they lined up food deliveries, child care services, and personal assistants to help with burial preparations. Queen Frieda spoke to several families via the Messenger. She always spoke in the most pleasant of voices, and she cried with anyone who needed to cry. Roanna watched in awe. Queen Frieda loved her people—a trait Ben had inherited from his parents. How had he asked Roanna to allow him to give up that duty? He would have been miserable in the end, if he'd chosen her over the safety of his people.

They worked together for a few hours, but with the aides' help they finished well before supper.

"What will you do now?" Frieda asked. "We've planted a new plant in the gardens. It blooms the largest, brightest zinnias you've ever seen."

Flowers sounded nice. Roanna smiled her thanks. "That sounds lovely. I'll make sure to take a peek." She left the queen to finish up her work for the evening, and meandered through the halls on her way back to her room. As she walked, she passed the library. The lights were dim, which meant no one was inside.

She paused and looked in. The Loxian library was huge, much larger than their library in Chester's Wake. The Loxians held many of the old histories. They believed knowledge was power, and knowing the past was key to being successful in the future.

Considering Queen Frieda's love for her people and the Loxians' constant desire for peace, perhaps they were right in their obsession with books.

Besides, this library was where Ben had found the memoir mentioning Dr. Presnell.

Roanna glanced up and down the empty hallway. The zinnias in the garden would wait until later. For now, Roanna wanted to browse the library.

47

Lights came to life as Roanna passed through the library door. Books lined the walls from floor to ceiling. Large books, small books, red, green, and blue books. So many.

Roanna bit her lip. She spent so little time in the library at home. She had no idea where to start. Ben had mentioned studying here. She glanced around as though Ben's private spot would jump out at her.

Her gaze fell on a door in the back of the room, and she moved that way. A small plaque read *Special Collections*.

She wasn't even sure what she was looking for, but if the memoirs had mentioned Roanna's birth, then there was a good chance there were other books here that could help her solve the mystery of her hair and her connection to the Dawsons and their anomalies. The histories, perhaps.

She pushed inside the special collections room. It was much smaller than the main library, with a grouping of three chairs pushed together. Each chair had its own small table beside it, and a coffee table sat in the middle of the group. One chair was red, one navy, and the last was hunter green.

Was this where Ben studied?

Roanna sank into the red chair. Was this where he sat, reading, studying, thinking of her?

She pushed the thought aside. There was no more time for daydreams like that.

Standing from the seat, she looked at the shelves lining the smaller room. Each shelf was labeled, and she quickly found a collection of histories. She browsed for the history of Dawson's Edge and found it easily.

She wanted to start at the beginning. Find out why the original Dawson had left, when the Termination process had begun, and why the Dawsons didn't engage in it. She needed to know how a Dawsonian doctor might predict her anomaly at her birth and then warn Mother.

Roanna snatched the book from the shelf and sank into the red chair once again. Reading wasn't her favorite past time, but for now it was a necessary performance.

This is a documentation of the founding of Dawson's Edge, the third kingdom on the western isle. The original isle was a single kingdom but fell after the wars. Its inhabitants rebuilt in sections, founding a western kingdom and an eastern kingdom: Lox and Chester's Wake.

Dawson's Edge was formed after the rebellion in Chester's Wake. Dawson's Edge took the south, and Chester's Wake remained in the north. This is a history of those happenings.

Roanna read with interest. She'd learned history in her studies as a child, but she'd never studied the story out of her own interests. It took on its own life as she read it now. She could almost picture the former continent. It was hard to imagine as a single kingdom.

And then the rebellion. If she remembered, it had been a mostly peaceful one. How and why?

Chester's Wake lived in peace for nearly one hundred fifty years. The rebellion started in 163 P.W. (post wars). King Nathan Hamilton died, passing the kingdom to his sons, whom he'd left to rule in his stead. King Nathan had fathered non-identical twins, and he intended them to rule together—a feat that had never been attempted.

The brothers ruled peaceably at first. Soon enough tensions rose. One night, the elder—Dawson Hamilton— was caught with a badly mutilated girl. Dawson claimed the girl had attempted suicide, but he had stopped her.

The girl told a different story. She said the joint king had invaded her mind and forced her to hurt herself.

The younger king, Louis Hamilton, did not know whom to believe. It wasn't the first report he'd heard of his brother's strange abilities—though it was the first time a charge had been so severe.

Throughout this turmoil, the kings' supporters gathered behind the king of their choice. After months of hearings, arguments, and physical skirmishes, the brothers agreed to split the kingdom. Others who possessed strange gifts followed Dawson eagerly. Whether it was true that King Dawson held special powers was of no consequence to them, for they felt they would find greater freedom under his care.

Roanna re-read the words. Tiny chills broke out across her arms, but she didn't put the book down. King Dawson Hamilton might have possessed powers that allowed him into other peoples' minds?

She kept reading.

As more and more citizens fled to the south, King Louis Hamilton called the rebellion a tragedy. He assured his people that Dawson Hamilton possessed no special power, and that his subjects were safe under his care. Over time he was able to staunch the slow desertion of his people to Dawson's Edge, but much damage had already been done to the country's economy.

Under pressure from his council and nobles, King Louis Hamilton was forced to search for assurance that such a rebellion would never happen again. Louis worked closely with scientists and alchemists who discovered a test which would identify those with powers—later called anomalies—before birth.

After several years of testing, the Termination process was birthed.

King Dawson Hamilton was disgusted by his brother's choice to wipe out those who were different. Tensions grew between Dawson's Edge and Chester's Wake, and those in Dawson's Edge withdrew from the outside world, earning the country its reputation for secrecy and mistrust.

Over the centuries many of the special powers within the kingdom faded. Only the most powerful survived, and it grew to be known that those with more powerful anomalies were of the royal bloodline. The Dawson bloodline.

Roanna gasped and dropped the history book. Shivers washed over her, and this time she did not try to fight them. The Dawson bloodline?

With shaking hands, she retrieved the book and read on about the rumors that the Dawsons could read thoughts but also control the minds of others. There were even claims that the Dawsons possessed other strange gifts such as healing or the ability to hurt others with a simple touch.

The book broke into chapters. Many, many chapters. But Roanna's desire to read them had disappeared. Her shivers lessened, though she still shook slightly.

Only Dawsonian royalty had the power. Only descendants of Dawson Hamilton could read minds.

Roanna pressed her eyes closed and shook her head. Father could trace his line directly back to Louis Hamilton. Mother came from Lox.

This history had to be wrong. False.

She could hear thoughts, but that meant nothing.

She was not Dawsonian by birth. It was impossible.

Roanna's stomach rolled, and she dashed to a trash bin and vomited.

48

Bette laid out a conservative and modest evening gown for supper. Nothing too fancy or attention-grabbing. The palace was in mourning for their lost soldiers and injured king.

Roanna dressed quietly, her mind numb. She wanted—needed—to speak to Ben about what she'd read in the library, but how could she? He might be shocked over what she'd found. Unbelieving or even disgusted. Besides, he had promised his mother to stay away, and Roanna could not cause them more heartache than they were already going through.

Tonight, she would be forced to see Roland. The thought made her grow cold. If these Dawsonian powers were real—and she knew they were—it meant she was correct in her theory that Roland and King Dawson possessed her same anomaly. Could he hear her thoughts the way she had heard his and the king's?

"You're very quiet tonight," Bette commented. She laid out Roanna's shoes. "Is it what happened earlier with Prince Benjamin? You've had a long day."

Bette had no idea.

Roanna gave a small smile. "It has been a long day. I'll be glad to go to bed tonight."

"Will you go with the royal family tomorrow to see the king?"

Roanna hadn't given it much more thought, and she hadn't spoken to Roland.

Her stomach clenched again, but she managed to take a deep breath. If she was Dawsonian royalty — somehow — could she marry Roland? She certainly didn't want to, nor had she ever, but it seemed obvious now that the wedding would need to be called off. That, at least, brought some relief. Of course, that meant she'd need to admit what was happening to her.

"I don't know," she answered. "I'll need to speak with Ambassador Dawson as well as Gregory."

Gregory would likely be going. Roanna could confide in him, but she wouldn't. He would think her crazy, the way Louis Hamilton had thought Dawson Hamilton irrational.

What's happening to me?

She swallowed hard. The silent prayer was more a plea of desperation.

Tears formed at the corners of her eyes. Blasted tears, she would need more makeup.

How would her family react to this news?

I don't want to be Rejected. I just want to live and be happy.

She wiped her tears with minimal damage to her makeup. She wasn't even sure what she was asking.

What she needed most was to understand her heritage. One man could, perhaps, help with that. The man who had warned Mother.

Dr. Presnell.

Ben had intended to speak with the man. Had he accomplished his goal? In spite of Queen Frieda's warnings, Roanna had to speak to Ben. She had to have answers.

She left her room and made her way to the dining room. Others were arriving, and she sat beside Roland with a tentative smile. His return smile was tight.

"Good evening, Princess."

She'd seen him only a few days ago, but he'd grown colder toward her. She squirmed in her seat. If she could read his thoughts, could he read hers? Was he reading them now?

Servers placed baskets of rolls and breads on the table, but Roanna didn't reach for them. Her stomach was too queasy to eat. She might never eat again.

"How was your trip here?" Roanna asked. She needed to gain some semblance of normalcy and control, at least for now.

"Pleasant. And yours?"

"It was well."

"Roanna, I..." Roland paused, as if he were struggling with what to say. "We need to speak in private. Soon."

Her stomach clenched even tighter. "Of course. Tonight? I've been wanting to see the gardens."

His eyes narrowed. "You enjoy flowers very much, don't you?"

She nodded, confused at the change in subject. "I do."

His eyes grew distant for a moment, but then he nodded. "The gardens will do well. We can speak then."

Roanna forced a smile, but her mind raced. Roland could want to speak to her about anything—he might tell her he had heard of her relationship with Ben. He might tell her their peace treaty was over. Or he might say he could read her mind.

With a shaking hand, she reached for her water glass and took a sip. The room had slowly filled, and only a few places at the table remained empty. It seemed nobility and royalty from the entire isle had come to offer support to the Loxian royals.

Ben entered the dining room then. He scanned the room, but his gaze didn't slow as he passed her. He took his seat and made niceties with those around him.

Roland called out a greeting, and Ben replied in kind. Still he did not look at her. He was keeping his end of the bargain with Queen Frieda.

Roanna gripped her hands in her lap and willed the tears away. She could still remember the look in his eyes as he'd begged her to agree that she wanted him at any cost.

But she hadn't spoken. Hadn't given the word.

Was that why he'd given in to Queen Frieda's demand?

It didn't matter. Their relationship woes were small compared to the crisis she faced now. He sat across the table and three seats down. She watched him, trying to be inconspicuous. He never glanced her way.

Roanna finally gave up and turned to Roland. "Will you go to see the king tomorrow?"

Roland frowned slightly. "I'm not entirely sure that would be wise. I'm here to offer support, but Dawson's Edge is under suspicion, as you know. The attack happened at our border."

Roanna's heart picked up speed. In all the turmoil, she had almost forgotten they did not yet know from where the attack had come. "But Dawson's Edge is innocent. Prince Benjamin believes it vehemently."

Roland's frown grew, and his eyes narrowed. "You've spoken privately with him about it?"

Heavens, what a fool she was. She refrained from sighing at her own stupidity. "He spoke openly. I saw him when I arrived with my brother, Gregory, and in the presence of the queen."

His features cleared, and he nodded. "That gives me relief." But she didn't know if he meant Ben's confidence in Dawson's Edge or the fact that she hadn't spoken to Ben alone gave him relief.

She decided she didn't want to know.

49

Roland became caught up in a discussion going on at the table, and Roanna made small talk with the diners around her. After the meal, the crowd moved to a larger sitting room. Roanna had assumed she and Roland would retreat to the gardens immediately, but he continued his conversation from dinner with some duke or another.

Roanna spoke briefly with Gregory, but he was occupied with others in the room. Ben spoke intermittently with dignitaries who had come, but now he stood alone near a back window. Roanna threw a glance at Roland, but he was fully engaged. Queen Frieda was nowhere to be seen.

She slipped quietly through the crowd and made her way toward Ben. Sidling up to him would be foolish. so she stood at a short distance and looked out the window. "I need to speak with you," she said quietly. She chanced a glance at him, but he didn't look her way. His jaw tightened. "No. If you'll excuse me, Roanna." He stepped away.

Roanna stood frozen, a confused statue staring into the darkness.

No? He would not speak with her?

Tears burned her eyes and did not stop. She needed to leave the room quickly. Someone would surely see her and ask what was wrong. She couldn't very well tell them the truth.

She spun toward the door and hurried toward it.

She managed to bypass anyone who might stop her, but as she reached the hall Roland gripped her elbow. "Roanna?"

She turned to him and gave a terrible impression of a smile. "Roland," she said it too cheerfully.

He frowned. "What's upset you?"

She shook her head. "I'm just so tired. It's been a long day."

"Did you want to put off our talk?"

She met his gaze, and her confusion grew. This was not the ambassador who had followed her like a puppy around the palace at Chester's Wake. Nor was he the aloof prince she'd danced with in Dawson's Edge, or the demanding fiancé she'd spent time with at Santa Rio.

This Roland seemed attentive. Caring.

"No, I'm fine. We can go now if you're finished speaking."

He nodded and offered his arm. "You know the way?"

"I do." She watched his face, gauging if that news would upset him. But it didn't.

She led him through the palace and to the back where the gardens were located. The night air was warm and dry, and the moon was bright overhead.

"It's beautiful here," she said.

He nodded. "Is there a private spot?"

"This way." She'd played in the gardens enough to know the best hiding places. She led him to the right, to a bench near the palace. "Here?"

He nodded and sat. He took her hand and tugged her to sit beside him. "Roanna, this may seem strange to you. I am fairly certain of what's going to transpire, but if I'm wrong I do hope you'll forgive the oddity."

She frowned. "I will." She swallowed hard, anticipation building. Her heart thundered, and she waited.

Roland reached for her face. He placed both hands on her cheeks.

A shiver raced across her shoulders, but it was light.

Can you hear me?

Roanna gasped. She tried to hide her shock, but a small smile spread across Roland's face.

Say something back to me. In your mind.

Roanna shook, terror filling her. She watched his eyes, searching for malice or anger, but all she found was sympathy. He waited.

What could she say?

Then, it was like a door opened in her mind. She could feel his mind inside hers, and he had opened the door to his own as well.

I hear you.

His smile grew, and his hands slid from her face to her hands. "I suspected it when we were at Santa Rio, but I wasn't sure. Has this been happening your whole life?"

She shook her head but couldn't speak. How could this be real? Suspecting it and having it actually confirmed were two entirely different things.

"When did it start, Roanna?" His gentle speech was disconcerting; he was so different from who he'd been before.

"A few weeks ago," she choked out. "After we first met."

He considered her words. "Interesting." He released her hands, and she wrapped her arms around her waist.

"How is this possible?" She knew the answer in part—the Dawsons had powers. She amended her question. "How is it possible that I can do this?"

He looked back to her. This time his eyes were sad. "Only those of the Dawsonian line have this power, Roanna."

The shivers grew stronger, and then everything went black.

50

Ben

Ben turned from his bedroom window the moment Roland put his hands on Roanna's face. It was foolish to watch them in the gardens, he knew, but when he'd spotted them he didn't turn away. Now, however? He might have enough self-control to keep from interacting with her, but he definitely didn't have enough to watch her be romanced by another man.

He paced his room, his shoulders aching with tension and his head throbbing. He and Gregory had listened long into the afternoon as officials and aides discussed strategy with Father, and later Mother, over the Messenger screen. Intelligence suggested the attackers had definitely come from within Dawson's Edge, but because the war bot had been controlled remotely they were still working to trace the signal back to those responsible.

It meant someone within Dawson's Edge was acting on his own. Rogue. Someone wanted to start a war, but who? And why?

He thought he knew, yet he had no proof. He would wait to see to whom the war bot's signal traced back. Then he would know whether the rebels in Dawson's Edge truly meant to move forward with their plan to stomp out the Dawson line.

A moment of longing washed over him, and he moved to the window. All he needed was one last glimpse of her. He needed to know she was safe in

Roland's hands.

The bench was empty, and Ben sighed. Better this way. She had wanted to talk to him, but he couldn't. She hadn't spoken up when he'd defended seeing her, so he'd promised Mother to stay away. For now, he needed to focus. Roland was here to occupy her, and that would have to do. He needed to find the responsible party for Father's injuries, and whomever it was would have to pay.

The guests still mingled downstairs, but Ben couldn't stomach being around them. He needed to get to Father's side. See the damage for himself. He and Mother would leave first thing in the morning. Gregory was coming along but Ben hadn't heard if Roanna planned to join them. For both their sakes, he hoped not. He couldn't stay away from her if she was thrown in his face again and again. He barely had the willpower to stay away right now. He just wanted to see her. See her smile.

He dressed for bed and laid down, but it was many hours before sleep came. When he awoke in the morning, dull sunlight irritated his mood. He'd rather it be gray and rainy. Hansen helped him dress for travel, and he hurried to the garage where the auto was being loaded.

"Prince Benjamin." Victor greeted him at the door. "We expected to pick you up with Her Highness at the portico."

Ben pushed past Victor. "I didn't want to be around the palace guests."

Victor trailed him to the day limo that was being prepared.

"How long until we leave?"

"Less than an hour."

Ben nodded. He hadn't expected it to take so long, but he could wait it out in the garage. "Can I get some breakfast in here?"

Victor glanced toward his office. "I have some pastries, but if you'd rather have something else I can send word to the palace."

Victor's kindness was wearing him down. He finally gave the man a smile. "Pastries sound good. Thanks." He strode to the office and grabbed a few from a basket then made his way to the Black Widow he'd ridden a few weeks ago the day he'd come home from Chester's Wake. He climbed onto the seat. He could leave now, head south. He'd be there by the time Mother was ready to leave the palace.

The temptation was great, but Mother would scold him.

Ben bit into the pastry as his opposite hand beat fingers across the handle bar. The appeal of running away was strong, as it was every time he climbed onto this bike. Throwing it all away. Living free. Why shouldn't he do exactly what he wanted, whenever he wanted? Why shouldn't he make himself happy?

The image of the dead soldiers and the faces of their mourning wives reminded him. People needed protecting. They needed leadership.

He could offer that, and in his better moments he wanted to offer it.

Finishing off the pastry, he climbed off the bike. No sense wallowing in his self-pity. Instead he helped pile luggage into the trunk of the auto. Victor protested immediately, but Ben brushed him off.

"I can toss in a few bags." He smiled, and Victor relented. They weren't planning a long stay along the border. The area wasn't deemed safe, especially for

Mother and him. But Mother never travelled lightly, and they were bringing things Father had requested.

Some of the garage workers watched him from the corners of their eyes. They were nervous around him. Tense. But the regulars knew he spent all of his free time watching them rebuild long-forgotten auto engines as well as spiff up the newer models. Time passed slowly, but his departure arrived at last.

Ben rode to the front of the palace in the limo, where they parked in front of the family's personal portico. Mother and Gregory climbed inside.

No Roanna.

Ben glanced toward the palace entry. She might be running late, or she could show up to wave them off. But she didn't.

He clasped his hands in his lap and looked at his shoes to keep from asking Gregory about her. As they pulled away from the palace he repeated to himself, *It's better this way.*

51

Ben stared out the window as the landscape changed. For most of the trip, Mother kept a lively conversation going, though it did get strange when Mother told Gregory all about the Stern family and noted Ben had become well acquainted with Merry while in Dawson's Edge.

They finally arrived at the southern border, and Ben climbed from the auto and stretched his legs. More guards lined the premises than the last time he'd visited the military base. Large military bots rolled along the narrow roadways, and soldiers marched inside the gates.

"Why does it look as if they're preparing for war?"

Mother shot him a disapproving look. "Save those questions for the privacy of our quarters."

He frowned but kept quiet. One of their military generals greeted them at the auto. He escorted them inside what appeared to be the hospital. Ben's frown deepened.

"They're keeping Father here, on base?" He wasn't sure why it surprised him, but he'd expected Father to be in a nearby city hospital.

"It's well guarded," the general stated. He kept his focus forward, his broad shoulders guiding them through the halls like a sailing ship. "And we've called in the best in the medical world."

Mother was satisfied with the situation. She followed the general with her head held high and her chin firm. She'd never been one to shy away from trouble or to refrain from stepping in to take charge. As queen, it was expected and required.

Gregory stepped silently at Ben's side. They stopped in front of a door that was guarded on either side by armed soldiers. They both bowed to Mother.

She smiled and touched the nearest guard's shoulder. "Thank you. There is no need. Please let us in to see the king."

"Of course, Your Highness." The guard opened the door and stepped aside, and the general led them into Father's room.

Gregory stood back. "I'll wait until you've had your time with him."

Ben nodded his appreciation. He went into the room, and the guard closed the door behind him.

Father was sitting up in the hospital bed. One leg was wrapped heavily and suspended in a sling. The other leg was buried under the blankets. Mother rushed forward and kissed Father's cheek. He stared into her eyes, and Ben looked away.

He'd rarely seen an emotional scene between them. In front of others, they were always royal. Always in hiding.

Seeing Father lying in bed shook Ben's emotions. He'd never seen Father appear weak or vulnerable, but wearing a hospital gown and wrapped in bandages, he appeared to be both.

A moment passed, and Father waved him over. "Come here, Ben."

Ben stepped to the bedside. "It's good to see you, Father." Tears clogged his throat, and he tried to clear them.

Father reached up and hugged him. "Having you

here helps. There is much to be done."

"Who did this, Father?"

Ben wanted to find them. Needed to, even. The attacks had to stop.

Father glanced at the general then back to Ben. "There will be time for that later."

"There isn't time to wait, Father. We should be acting on our intelligence now if we have it."

But Mother shook her head. "That's not always the best way. We have intelligence and believe it's correct. We need to make sure and to formulate a plan."

The reply didn't ease the burning in Ben's gut. It didn't satisfy his hunger for retaliation and revenge. At this moment, so much anger boiled inside him—anger over these attacks, Father's injuries, and his relationship with Roanna. Nothing was as it should be. Everything was out of control.

"Your Mother is right, Ben." Father's calm demeanor took his anger down a notch. "Let's take a little time in being happy to be together, shall we?"

Ben ground his teeth. There would be time for retaliation later. He nodded once then pulled a chair to the bedside.

Mother propped herself on the edge of the bed.

"Tell me about your time in Dawson's Edge."

That adventure was the last thing he wanted to think about. "Their land is different from ours. Greener, hotter."

Father smiled and nodded. "Yes, it is different. What about the people? Did you find what you were looking for?"

Ben drew back. After a moment, he barked out a laugh. "If you meant did I find a wife, no."

But Father didn't laugh. "Then tell me who you

connected with."

He was being persistent. Why? "Two families above all others. The Sterns and the Maynes."

Father's eyes narrowed almost imperceptibly. The look cleared before Ben knew what to make of it. "Interesting. They both have women your age. You didn't find either of them acceptable?"

Acceptable? He spoke as if finding a wife were as inconsequential as finding the right tires for the Black Widow.

"Lady Britta was lovely, if not a bit daft." He paused and glanced toward the door where Gregory waited in the hallway. "Lady Merry Stern was a bit more—agreeable—but she let me know from the beginning that she wasn't sure she was interested."

He half-expected a lecture on how to change a woman's mind, but Father said nothing.

"Shall I show Prince Hamilton in?" the general asked.

Father raised his eyebrows. "Gregory is here? By all means, don't leave him out in the hallway."

Gregory stepped in a moment later. He bowed to Father and wished him well. Then he clasped his hands behind his back. "Chester's Wake promises all resources in helping bring your attackers to justice."

Father smiled. "Lox thanks you. In fact, I have been in contact with your father. Your own intelligence has been of great help already today."

Ben listened with interest. He hadn't heard of any of this intelligence. By the raised eyebrows on Gregory's face, he hadn't known, either.

Father laughed. "Pull up a chair. We can discuss it."

52

Roanna

The Night Before

Roanna woke to confusion. Darkness surrounded her, along with a sweet scent. Something held her. She blinked and searched her surroundings.

Roland. The garden at Lox.

Her eyes widened and she pulled from his grip. "What happened?"

"You fainted."

His words from earlier came rushing back. *Only those of the Dawsonian line have this power...*

She shook her head. He had to be wrong. "I'm not of the Dawsonian line."

His eyes were gentle, and he stayed silent.

This wasn't the Roland she had known over the last several weeks. The man she had come to understand was pompous and rude; uncaring and selfish. Only something very serious changed a person's demeanor so much.

She shook her head again, and tears gathered in the corner of her eye. "How could it possibly be true?"

"You've been hearing thoughts? My thoughts?"

She watched him. Gauged him. Ben was the only person she'd told about the strange phenomenon going on. He wouldn't have told a soul, let alone a Dawson.

So, if Ben hadn't told, how could Roland know that?

"And you've had cold chills, correct? It was the

shaking that first drew my attention at Santa Rio."

"How do you know this?" Her voice cracked, and she gulped in air.

"Because it happens to me, as well. As it happens to King Bartholomew, our other siblings, and our heirs."

"But I'm not a Dawson." She jutted her chin in the air and swiped away the tears. This conversation was surreal, to be sure, but ridiculous. "My father is a Hamilton, and my mother is Loxian."

Roland glanced up, and Roanna followed his gaze. The lights in Ben's room were on. Roland wouldn't know it was Ben's room, but perhaps he'd seen something in the window.

"I don't know what to make of that, either," Roland admitted, finally looking back to her. "But I've spoken to King Bartholomew. It's important that we see him. The sooner the better."

"I'm here as a goodwill ambassador. I can't leave right now."

"Then tomorrow. The queen will be leaving for the southern border anyway." He kept his gaze locked on her own.

Trepidation filled her. She began to run through possible scenarios in her mind, but she quickly shut them down. Could he hear her musings? She shut down the thoughts.

But something deeper pushed her to heed his words. A conviction in her belly said he could not know about her mind reading unless he knew from firsthand experience.

"What about my hair?" There was no doubt the instances were connected, as Dr. Presnell had warned years ago.

His eyes widened as his gaze travelled to her pinned up locks. "You put that together on your own?"

"Answer my question." If she was to go along with this, it would be on her own terms. Besides, his reaction told her that her suspicions were correct.

He glanced around then looked up at Ben's window again. "Can we speak somewhere else? I feel we're not alone here."

Roanna frowned and glanced up. Ben was nowhere to be seen, but she needed answers. "We can speak in my room." Inviting him in was a gamble. But at this point she had no choice but to trust him.

She stood, but he stopped her. "You can trust me, Roanna. I'll not hurt you."

Chills broke across her skin, but this time they had more to do with her fear than anything. "Do you hear everything I think?"

"No. I'll explain more inside." He stood and followed her into the palace. Sounds drifted toward them from the crowd in the sitting room. A few servers darted about inside the palace, but no one paid them any mind. She led him up the stairs and to the left then to the end of the hall.

"You know your way around the Loxian palace well."

She cut him a look, but his jealous behavior from the past seemed all but gone. "My family has spent much time here."

He didn't answer, and they slipped silently into her room.

Bette looked up from the clothes she was hanging. Her eyes widened. "Oh!"

Roanna hadn't counted on Bette being present. "Bette, you may leave us. Come back in an hour."

The timeframe seemed to give Bette a little comfort. She nodded quickly. "Of course, Miss." She left the room and closed the door behind her.

Roanna moved to the only seating in the room, a small couch in the dressing area. Roland joined her.

For weeks, she had been working to understand what was happening to her. To unravel the mystery of her past. She had thought Dr. Presnell was the only way to get answers. Perhaps she was wrong.

She took a deep breath. "You promised to tell me about my hair."

He nodded. "It isn't exactly a known science, but it is believed the power is tied closely to the length of the hair. The longer the hair, the more powerful the telepathy."

Her gaze moved to his own dark hair. It hung down his back, secured with a simple black tie.

"You said it has never happened before you met me? How long is your hair?"

Roanna fingered her hair, contemplating taking it down. Dare she mention why she'd always kept it short?

Dr. Presnell was a secret between her and Ben. For now, it would stay that way.

"Mother has kept it short for years. I've only recently been growing it out."

He took her statement at face value. "That might explain it in part, but it generally only works with others who hold the power. You have never travelled to Dawson's Edge before recently?"

She shook her head.

"Then the timing of your hair growth and meeting your first Dawsonian heir is coincidence. But it explains why you've never known of the power before."

She put his words together slowly, her mind like a foggy field. "You mean to say I can only hear the thoughts of others who have this power? Such as yourself and King Dawson?"

"That's right. And you can only hear things when we open our minds to being heard. I can't believe I've never been able to hear you before."

She considered her next words carefully. "I think I was working to keep my mind closed. I tried very hard to hide the shaking."

He offered an unexpected and confusing smile.

"Is that funny?"

"No. It's impressive. The shaking is part of the power, but it takes much work to control it. You must be very powerful."

Powerful or not, she knew almost nothing of what she was doing. She considered confessing that she'd been experimenting—reaching out for the auras of others—but decided against it. The less Roland knew about her for the time, the better. "So, the only time I can hear you is if you open your mind to me?"

"Not to you specifically, no. I can only open my mind in general. When that happens, anyone who is standing in range—the same way I'd speak with my voice—can hear me, so long as they have the power, of course."

That explained why she had heard both King Dawson and Roland the day they met at Edge River. The brothers had been speaking to each other, their minds open, so she had heard them.

"Can you sense each other, then? How do you know when someone's mind is open?"

He nodded as if considering the way it worked for

the first time in a long time. "I suppose you can feel it, if you are in tune. When my brothers wish to speak to me using the mind, I can feel the mental pull."

"I felt it, the night of..." she faltered. This information was too strange to be true. "The night of the engagement party, I felt a strange pull. I followed it, and I heard you speaking. You, King Dawson, and a third man I didn't recognize."

His eyes darkened. "What did you hear?"

Roanna froze. He had urged her to trust him, but perhaps she had made the wrong choice in doing so.

53

"I don't really know what I heard." She shook her head, remembering. "I heard an argument, but it was low. Something about waiting until after the wedding." The last few words came out painfully.

He leaned back on the couch, but his gaze never left her face. "That is all you heard?"

"Search my mind and tell me if I'm lying."

Roland smirked. "It doesn't work that way. I can only sense your presence, and hear your direct thoughts. You can lie inside your head just as well as out loud if you wanted." He slid his arm along the back of the couch. "It's amazing you've been able to figure all this out on your own. Were you taught about the Dawsons' powers in Chester's Wake?"

"No. We were only told you believed in some sort of magic. I didn't know you actually possessed anomalies."

His eyes penetrated hers. He was searching for the truth behind her words. Looking for anything she might not be saying out loud.

"It's the truth, Roland. I had no idea."

"You've told no one?"

"No." She fast made the decision to lie. She would not bring Ben into this, not until they were confident the attack on Lox hadn't come by a Dawson's command.

He removed his arm from the back of the couch and shook his head. "Astounding. Bartholomew will be fascinated to hear this story."

"I still don't understand how it's happening," she reasoned. "How can I inherit Dawsonian powers when I'm not a Dawson?"

"That is something I don't have an answer for, except to repeat what I've already told you. You would not have these powers unless you were of the Dawson line."

Roanna considered the implications of his words. If there were any possibility she was a Dawson...

Again, Dr. Presnell held the answers. He had known this would happen. Why else would he have demanded her hair be kept short?

"Could it be a curse?" It had been her first fear.

Roland's eyebrows shot up. "Doubtful. The power, or anomaly as you so aptly called it, comes by birth. It can't be thrown around as a curse." Roland's eyes narrowed and he leaned toward her. "Who would have cursed you, Roanna? What gave you such an idea?"

Stupid. She shouldn't have asked that. "I don't know." She thought fast. "It's a more pleasant possibility in my mind than the alternative."

"And what would be the alternative?"

She shifted, uncomfortable. "That my mother had an affair."

His eyes widened and he laughed. "You know, I hadn't even considered that."

She frowned and drew back. "Then what have you considered?"

His laughter faded away, and he shook his head. "That is something to be discussed later and not until I've consulted with my brother." He stood. "I have burdened you enough for one night. You will travel with me to Dawson's Edge?"

Roanna kept her seat. She looked up at him, standing confidently in her bedroom. What of their engagement? He had been cold toward her since the day she left Santa Rio.

"Yes, I'll go."

"Excellent. Then I'll see you at breakfast." He strode to the door.

She should ask him about their future. Their relationship. But she kept her mouth closed. Only heaven above knew what would become of them. If she truly were some relation to the Dawson line—and her mind-reading told her she was—it meant she was related in some way to Roland Dawson. However distantly, that fact would dictate their decision.

And if this turned out to be a misunderstanding, and she wasn't related at all, their marriage would likely go on as planned.

Roland disappeared from view a moment later, closing the door with a soft click behind him. Bette returned a while later and helped her into bed, but sleep would not come. Roanna laid in bed most of the night. She stared at the ceiling and considered all Roland had revealed.

Can it be true? I'm so confused.

She prayed silently, her prayers making no sense once again. She had powers, and they hadn't come about by magic. They had originated from somewhere. The question was where, and what was she to do with them? If Roland's words were to be believed, she was powerful. For the first time in her life, she felt as though she might be able to control some part of her future. It was a strange but not unwelcome feeling.

The original Dawson had been accused of going

into other people's minds and controlling them. So far, she had been unsuccessful in hearing anyone's thoughts besides Roland's and King Dawson's, but could she get inside someone else's mind without hearing their thoughts? Could she manipulate their decisions the way the old stories had said the original Dawson could? She hadn't tried that yet.

As the first fingers of light crept into her room, she climbed from bed and showered. She hadn't slept a single moment throughout the night.

What troubled her most was Ben. She needed to speak to him. He should know what she knew. They needed to speak to Dr. Presnell now more than ever before.

Once she'd dressed, she made the decision to find him. Most of the guests would not be up and about yet. She would go to Ben's room and knock on the door. Surely, he wouldn't turn her away again.

Her confidence waivered as she stepped into the hall and a servant came up from the stairway near her room.

"Can I help you, Miss?"

She smiled at the maid. "No, thank you. I want to enjoy the gardens in the early morning air."

The girl smiled, nodded, and then hurried down the hall.

Roanna followed at a much slower pace. No one stopped her as she approached the family wing. Noise came from inside Queen Frieda's room, and Roanna rushed past it to keep from being caught. She turned a corner to the left, and Ben's door loomed before her.

He had rejected her last night. Brushed past her without a second glance.

But she had new information. Taking a deep

breath, she knocked. No one answered, so she knocked again. He might still be asleep.

"Your Highness?" Hansen's voice interrupted her, and she spun around. Heat filled her cheeks.

"I was looking for Prince Ben."

Hansen had tended to her more than once over the years, but he watched her disapprovingly now. "The prince has gone to the garage, Your Highness. He is preparing to leave, to see his father."

So early? "Oh. I see."

"I suggest you speak with him when he returns in three days' time."

Roanna could try finding him at the garage, but Hansen was making it obvious he didn't intend to help. "Thank you. I'll do that."

She hurried back to her room, her heart heavy. Talking to Ben would have to wait, but how long? As she turned onto her own hallway, she paused at Gregory's door. Gregory was going with Ben!

She knocked on his door, and he opened it a moment later.

His eyes widened. "What are you doing up so early, sis?"

She pushed into his room. "I have something I need for you to do, Gregory."

54

Roanna sat beside Roland at breakfast. Her heart felt lighter after talking to Gregory, and she ate heartily because of it. Besides, it was good she had let someone know she was headed into Dawsonian territory. It would have been foolish to go without someone in her family knowing.

And Gregory had agreed to pass along a letter for Ben.

Once breakfast ended, Roland pulled her aside. "We leave in an hour."

"I'll be ready." She raced upstairs to give Bette the news.

Bette's eyes widened. "Do you think that's wise, Miss? We don't know who attacked King Neville, and Roland threatened me barely a week ago."

Roanna wasn't sure her plans were at all wise. She swallowed her fears and lifted her chin. "I believe the Dawsons are innocent, as does Prince Benjamin. I spoke with Gregory, and he approves. Besides," she fidgeted with her dress, hoping she was right. "I believe he was only asking you those questions to determine whether we were aiding the Dawsonian rebels." Or whether a hidden Dawson royal was coming to take their throne.

Gregory's approval seemed to satisfy Bette, and she got to work packing up all of Roanna's belongings. Roanna worked beside her, arranging hair brushes and makeup. In just under an hour, they had hauled

Roanna's bags downstairs. Roland's man was there to load the bags into an auto.

Roland eyed Bette. "You'll be bringing along your maid?"

Roanna shifted and glanced at Bette. She might be willing to risk herself, but she wasn't willing to risk her friend. "No. You'll be heading home, Bette."

Bette's eyes widened with fear, but she didn't argue.

Roanna bid her good-bye and promised to see her again. At last, they were on their way to the Loxian air station. They would arrive in Dawson's Edge within a few hours, and then she would meet with King Dawson. The king would have his own answers to her questions, and he would likely have several questions of his own.

That thought made her squirm. What would he want to know?

A wave of icy chill washed over her, and she shivered. She threw a look at Roland, and he grinned. She would have to be careful with her thoughts from now on.

"Did you need something?" she asked.

"Just trying to figure out what was causing that lovely frown."

She managed a small smile, but his use of the word lovely troubled her. "I see I'll have to be more careful to guard my privacy now."

"Nonsense. I was only teasing. We don't make a practice of spying on each other." His smile seemed genuine.

Roanna bit her lip. Should she ask what was on her mind? "Roland? May I ask you a question? It may offend you."

"Be my guest."

"You seem different now. Happier."

"I'm not hiding anything."

His answer was so simple. So honest. He wasn't hiding anything. He could be himself.

And that...made him happy? Sudden pity washed over her. "I'm sorry, Roland."

"You don't need to be. It's always been this way, and I'm neither ashamed nor embarrassed."

That made sense. "One more question?"

He nodded, so she went on. "What does this mean for our engagement?"

He took in her words and looked away. Finally, he sighed. "That is a harder question to answer." He took her hand. "I do find you lovely. And I felt a pull for you from the moment I laid eyes on you."

His words did nothing but fill her with discomfort, but she didn't dare pull her hand away.

"But now I realize that pull may have been from the powers. If you are, indeed, Dawsonian, we will need to find out how close to the line you fall."

"And what if I am Dawsonian? What does that mean for my parents? And for our peace treaty?"

Roland shook his head. "Those are questions for my brother, the king. He will decide."

Roanna accepted his answer, but as they boarded the airship and headed toward Dawson's Edge, her shoulders grew tense. Her kingdom's fate rested in her hands. She'd thought of it half the night as she laid sleepless in bed.

But how could Dawson's Edge attack Chester's Wake if one of their own daughters worked peaceably between them? On the other hand, they might accuse Chester's Wake of taking her as an infant.

Stealing? Mother and Father had record of her birth. They couldn't have stolen her.

The knots in her stomach tightened further, and she prayed for the flight to pass quickly.

At last, they reached Dawson's Edge. The auto met them at the air station and drove them to the palace. The trip was long and uneventful.

King Dawson met them at the palace entrance. Queen Katherine was not at his side. Did she not know Roland and Roanna were arriving?

"Ah, the mysterious Princess Roanna." King Dawson kissed her hand. "Lovely to see you again so soon."

Warmth spread through her at his words. Trust, the same feeling she'd had from him the first time she'd met him. Perhaps their powers drew them together as Roland had mentioned.

"Come." King Dawson took her arm and urged her forward. "We have much to discuss."

Roland trailed them as they maneuvered through the palace, which was such a stark contrast to the Loxian palace. It took a moment for her eyes to adjust to the darkness. Where Lox was bright, Dawson's Edge was dim. Where Lox had windows, Dawson's Edge had tapestries. Lanterns. Paintings.

The state offices, however, were alive with activity. The kingdoms truly did seem to be working together to figure out who was responsible for King Neville's attack.

Inside King Dawson's office, Roland shut the door behind them and they all sat. "I'm going to try speaking to your mind now," King Dawson said.

Roanna shifted in her seat. So soon?

But she nodded. "I'm ready."

I'm sorry you're going through this. It must be quite the shock.

His words took her by surprise, but drawing on her royal training, she recouped quickly.

Thank you. It is very gracious of you to help me.

King Dawson smiled and looked to Roland.

Roland chuckled. "What did I tell you?"

King Dawson looked back to Roanna. "I am stunned. I've never heard of a lost family member being found. I wonder if there are more." He raised an eyebrow, lost in thought for a moment. "Never mind that. We need to trace your origins. Figure out where you come from."

Roanna frowned. "I come from Chester's Wake, as a princess, no less. I will not be treated like some science experiment."

"I apologize, Princess. You are right. We should treat this in a different manner."

She nodded, accepting his apology. And she was very interested to know what manner that would be.

55

"Would you allow a genetic test?" King Dawson sat close to her in a chair at her side. Roland sat directly beside her on the opposite side of the couch.

Genetic testing. It was part of the technology that allowed scientists to test for anomalies. To see the threads of a person's make up. The tests that determined if a fetus was to go through the Termination process.

"That will tell you how I'm able to do these things?"

"In a manner of speaking, yes." But his eyes said there was more.

She narrowed her eyes. "Is there something you're not telling me?"

"Well, the test will tell us whose line you hail from. Our father had four sons, with I being the eldest and Roland being the youngest. Then, there is our grandfather's line which included our father and his siblings."

"And don't forget our own sister," Roland said.

Realization dawned on Roanna. "Lady Gretchen."

"That's correct, though it's more likely you hail from a male line rather than female. If you were Gretchen's heir, she would surely be aware of it." He smiled as if this were funny, but Roanna didn't join him in the mirth.

They were speaking against Mother and Father, discrediting her upbringing with them. Couldn't it be just as likely that Father was the one who hailed from the Dawsonian line?

But no, it had to be her alone. She was the one with the magical hair.

"Fine." She nodded. "I will do the test, but I want to know my family will be safe from any form of attack."

King Dawson's demeanor changed. He leaned away from her, and his gaze became lofty. "I will make no such promise, Princess. You must watch yourself as it sounds as if you mean to accuse me of something."

Roanna's insides twisted, but she held her ground. "I accuse you of nothing, Your Highness. Prince Benjamin assured me that he believed in your innocence regarding the attack at the Loxian border. I believe in it as well. But if my genetic test gives you some sort of unfavorable result, I mean to protect those I love against retaliation without explanation." Mainly, if they got it in their minds that her parents had kidnapped her from them.

Her words seemed to satisfy him. "Very well. You have my word, at least until we get to the bottom of things."

She couldn't ask for more than that. "When do we start?"

King Dawson stood and walked to his desk. "There is nothing to it. You stay put." He pressed a button on his Messenger, and a woman's face filled the screen.

"Yes, Your Highness?"

"Send for Dr. Jacobs."

"Right away, Your Highness."

King Dawson dropped into his desk chair and propped his feet up. "Roland tells me you overheard us the night of the engagement party."

Roanna studied his face, which was decidedly neutral. What was he asking? "I sensed you." She stumbled over the word *sensed*. "I had a strange sensation, something I'd never felt. When I found you, I heard a few words. Nothing that made sense to me. I had only realized that it was your voices I was hearing, when a third voice warned you to be quiet. I was afraid someone had heard my footsteps, and I hurried away. The entire thing was very confusing."

Roland and King Dawson looked to each other. "Stefan." They said it in unison.

Prince Stefan Dawson? He had been the third voice?

"He must have sensed your mind," King Dawson said. "We didn't think to include him in this conversation."

"No need." Roland shook his head. "It's not as if she could be from his line."

"True." They spoke of her as if she weren't sitting in front of them.

When the door opened, relief filled her.

A short man hurried inside.

"Ah, Dr. Jacobs. Princess Roanna needs a genetic test."

The doctor's eyes popped. "Of course, Your Highness." He glanced at Roland then finally to her. "If you'll follow me."

Roanna swallowed her nerves and stood. She looked to King Dawson for instruction.

"Roland will accompany you. He can show you to your room when you're finished."

Roanna nodded, and Roland joined her. She had no idea what to expect.

Dr. Jacobs led them through the halls of the palace. Roanna leaned close to Roland. "What will this entail?"

"A simple cheek swab." Roland squeezed her hand. "Perhaps a few drops of blood. The test goes quickly, though it takes a bit longer to get the results."

The doctor's office was a clean, simple room. White walls, with silver countertops, tables, and instruments. Shelves along one wall held colorful vials and bottles of liquids and herbs.

Dr. Jacobs nodded toward a cushioned patient's bed in the middle of the room. "If you'll have a seat there, we will begin."

He used a long cotton swab to wipe the inside of her cheek. Then he pricked her finger with a sharp instrument and collected the blood drops in a small medical tube. He took the swab and blood sample to a contraption on the metal countertop. There were beakers, tubes, and burners.

"How does it work?" she asked.

Dr. Jacobs gave her a tight smile. He was a nervous sort of fellow. "Leave the science to us, my dear." He turned to Roland. "Against whom I am running these samples?" He sounded scared. Timid.

"The males of the royal family for the last two generations."

Dr. Jacob's eyes widened even further, but he didn't comment on it. "We're finished here. I'll message King Dawson when I have results."

Roland had taken a seat but now he stood. "Thank you, Dr. Jacobs."

Roanna stood from the patient table, but she hesitated in joining Roland. "How long until you have results?" Her whole world hung on the balance of this test.

"A few days." The doctor offered a kind smile.

Roanna nodded then moved to Roland's side. He led her back to the main palace entrance then up a grand staircase. "You will be comfortable here, Princess. We'll call for you as soon as we get the results."

She smiled her thanks, and he led her to the same room she'd used the last time she had been here. He opened the door to let her in, and a wave of memories hit her. Memories of seeing Ben come around the corner and him pushing his way into her room. Holding her. Saying he loved her.

"Did you hear me, Princess?" Roland frowned at her.

She pushed away the memories. "I'm sorry. I'm so overwhelmed by everything."

He smiled. "It's fine. I said you shouldn't use your powers here. There are others of the royal line who could overhear, and we don't want them to know what's happening just yet."

"Of course." But as he left her standing in her doorway, her mind worked. Who else was in the palace who could hear her? Stefan, perhaps. But his bride couldn't hear thoughts, nor could Queen Katherine. As far as she knew, the other brothers were not at the palace.

King Dawson and Roland might want to communicate without Roanna hearing. In that case, she would be sure to listen.

56

Ben

Ben focused on Father's words. They confirmed what he'd already begun to suspect; Dawsonian rebels were working against the Dawson royal family. "Do you mean to say the attacks have been orchestrated by the Maynes?"

Father glanced at Gregory then back to Ben. "The intelligence gathered by Chester's Wake was very strong. The signal for the remote-controlled war bot originated from their estate. Perhaps they've been working with someone else, as well."

Working with someone? Gregory had mentioned that the Sterns were not loyal to the Dawson family. It was likely they were the Maynes' accomplices.

Fury boiled inside him. While he dined with the Maynes, they were sending a war bot to attack his people. He clenched his fists, willing himself to stay calm.

Gregory shook his head. "Why did Father not mention this to me?" He stood and paced the small hospital room. "Why would rebels start a war and blame the Dawsons?" He didn't mention the Sterns, but he had to be thinking about his relationship with Merry.

Ben took in Father's weakened form then shot from his seat and joined Gregory's pacing. Heat washed over him. He would seek his revenge on the Dawsonians who would do such a thing. And to think he'd considered marrying one of them.

"We need to renounce our marriage agreement with these people. I do not wish to marry any of their noble women."

Mother took in a sharp breath. "Ben, you're being too hasty in this. It isn't the Dawsons who attacked, only a handful of their people."

"I will not marry into a line that might later turn out to be rebellious. We can never know the depth of the traitors." How could he trust any of them after this?

Mother stood and hurried to him. "Roanna is still engaged to Roland Dawson. She will not be yours simply because you break your marriage agreement."

Ben shook his head and focused on Father. "You would have me marry someone whose countrymen would do such a thing as this?"

Father watched him, his eyes sad. Finally, he shook his head. "I won't ask you to do it if your conscious is seared against them. The choice is yours, but please don't make it hastily."

His softly spoken speech calmed Ben, but only slightly.

"Don't forget, the Dawsons could hold it against us if you break the agreement." Mother returned to her seat at Father's side, but she was clearly unhappy.

"We are helping to clear their name after rebels in their own country attacked us and wounded our king," Ben said. "They cannot hold it against us if we break the betrothal." He knew it was true.

"Calm down." Father's voice barely reached through the ringing in his ears. "The intelligence is not yet complete. We are working to uncover everyone involved before we react."

Ben threw a look Gregory's way. His face was guarded, but he must be thinking of Merry's family's involvement. The Maynes and the Sterns were rebels. Who else in Dawson's Edge?

His hands clenched and unclenched. "Let us retaliate, Father. Sometimes a fight is the only way to keep the peace. How many more should die?"

Mother frowned and her brow creased. "This is not the Loxian way."

Anger boiled over. "Look at Father!" he shouted. "Is the Loxian way to roll over and die?" His entire life he had played along, followed the laws, and kept the peace in order to maintain freedom. Lox lived in happiness because of it. But bowing to the enemy in order to keep the peace was not freedom at all. He would not stand idly by and let the Dawsonian dissenters destroy his kingdom in order to purge their own.

Mother's eyes widened at his tone, and he took a deep breath. "I apologize, Mother. But I've done everything you've asked. You even wanted me to marry a Dawsonian—against my wishes—and I played along. Now two of those women I danced with are a part of my father's injuries."

Father frowned. "Two women? You know the other rebels?"

Ben glanced at Gregory again. He stood near the window now, a pained look on his face.

"The Sterns are involved, I'm almost certain of it. They want the royal family gone. Apparently, they will stop at nothing."

Father grunted as he shifted in the bed, the news distressing him. "Gregory, what do you say to all of this?"

Gregory's jaw worked as he tightened his bite. But then his face changed, and panic lingered in his eyes. "Roanna."

Ben frowned. "What about her?"

"She left with Roland. She's in Dawson's Edge now. What if the rebels attack the royals, and she's put in danger?" He marched toward the door.

"What do you mean?" Ben grabbed his arm. "We left her in Lox this morning."

Gregory shook his head. "No." He dug in his inside jacket pocket and pulled out an envelope. "She asked me to give this to you. She was leaving with Roland Dawson, and she said this would explain everything."

Hot dread washed over Ben. He tore open the letter.

My Dearest Ben,

I've tried to reach you twice now. I understand why you would not speak to me last night, though it hurt me deeply. I tried again this morning, but you had already gone. Roland Dawson has shed light on the search we've been on these last few months. He promises answers, but only if I see King Bartholomew, whom he claims has the answers. We leave this morning for Dawson's Edge. I hope I am not walking into a trap, but because you vehemently explained your trust toward King Dawson, I believe I am acting wisely. Gregory knows my whereabouts, as I didn't feel fully comfortable leaving without any word to anyone.

I am sorry to leave your family in your time of need. I sincerely pray for King Neville's recovery, and for the attackers to be caught. I do not know when we will see each other again, or if either of us will be married when that happens. But please know I will always love you even if we are never more than the dearest of friends.

I will try to send word again, just as soon as I acquire the answers we have so desperately sought.

All my love,

Roanna

Ben crumpled the letter in his hands, closed his eyes, and sucked in a deep breath. What if the Maynes and Sterns learned she was in the Dawsons' palace? They could stir up war with Lox and Chester's Wake all at once by attacking.

"Ben, you must let us in on what is happening." Mother spoke softly as she pried the letter from his hands. As she read it, confusion replaced concern.

"What does this mean, son? What answers have you been seeking?"

Gregory shook his head. "You can stay and explain if you like, but I am going to retrieve her."

Ben gripped his arm again. "Wait for me. Give me a half hour, and we will go together."

Gregory's nostrils flared, but he nodded.

Ben returned to Father's side, with Mother beside him. "I will explain all in time, but Roanna is in danger. If the rebels wish to start a war, then harming Roanna while in Dawson's Edge is the perfect way to do it. Will you allow me to go?"

Mother didn't look happy, but she nodded.

"Father?"

Father seemed a mix of awe and irritation. "Go, but you must communicate with us. Give us an idea of these answers you've been seeking."

Ben's mind raced. What could he say without sounding absurd? "Roanna and I discovered—a plan, if you will—to cover up strange happenings on the night of Roanna's birth."

The frown lines on Mother's forehead deepened.

"What on earth? You are speaking in riddles."

"We don't have time for this." Gregory gripped the door handle.

Ben turned back to Mother and Father. "Please, I will explain all in time."

Father and Mother nodded, and he raced to the door to join Gregory.

Please give us speed to save her.

If the rebels harmed her, he would never forgive himself. And the Dawsonians would pay.

57

Roanna

Roanna sneaked from her room. She crept along the dark halls of the palace, working out her brain muscles as she went. Stretching her ability to sense without being sensed.

Powerful was what Roland had called her. She hadn't considered it until now, but if he called her powerful, did that mean she was better at controlling the power than he was? More powerful than King Dawson?

She paused at a corner and swallowed hard. Could she truly be related to King Bartholomew Dawson? To Roland Dawson?

At least it appeared she wouldn't have to marry Roland. But what then? Would Mother and Father disown her—a child they'd raised but who held an anomaly, a condition they actively worked to stomp out in their own kingdom? And how would the Bellevues see her? Lox practiced Termination as well.

She moved quietly around the corner and toward King Dawson's offices. Tiny chills washed over her as she drew closer. She worked to control them but only barely so that maybe she could hear them without being detected herself.

But as she worked her mind, she heard nothing.

The palace's office area was busy. Were they all working on the Loxian attack intelligence? Was Ben already at his father's side? Had Gregory given him the note she wrote?

He'd only agreed to deliver the note after she pressured him. He even reminded her that Ben had promised Queen Frieda to leave Roanna alone. He said she was torturing Ben by continuing to throw herself at him.

Roanna had nearly slapped him for that remark, and he'd finally agreed to take the letter when she'd assured him it had nothing to do with their relationship and everything to do with their kingdoms' safety.

She watched the Dawsonian officials bustle about. She could inch her way to King Dawson's office, but that was likely to get her noticed.

With the office's preoccupation, no one seemed to notice either way. She hurried through the hustle and stopped outside his door. Voices came from inside, but she couldn't make out what was being said.

Footsteps drew closer, and Roanna turned to a desk on her left. She shuffled papers, pretending to be busy as an aide rushed inside the king's office. Roanna turned quickly and stuck a pen in the door so it wouldn't close all the way. Her ploy worked, and the door stayed open a crack.

"What do you intend to do with her?" Roland asked.

"You can't marry her, obviously," the king answered.

"I've told her as much. Do you think Chester's Wake will break the peace treaty?"

A pause and then, "We will have to ensure they don't. We need them now more than ever, especially if Lox believes we orchestrated the attack."

A chill raced down Roanna's spine. What would

they do to her family? To her? And what did they mean about needing Chester's Wake now more than ever?

The memory of King Dawson's fear of rebellion filled her mind. It must be rebels who were responsible for the attacks against Lox. What about the skirmishes along the border with Chester's Wake? Perhaps it was all rebel activity, and King Dawson hadn't been able to stop it.

They sought to fulfill peace treaties with Lox and Chester's Wake in order to keep their kingdom from falling apart. And now she was one of them.

She backed from the door just as it flew open and the same aide as before came rushing out. He stopped short, giving her an odd look. But he kept moving without ratting her out.

She turned to hurry back to her room, but it was too late. Roland and King Dawson stepped from the office. Their gazes fell on her immediately, and King Dawson's eyes narrowed.

Roanna refused to cower under his fierceness.

"You should have heeded my advice to stay put, princess." Roland took her arm, but still the action was gentle.

"You'll forgive me if I don't trust you." She silently congratulated herself at keeping her voice from shaking.

Roland still held her arm as he guided her away from the offices. He sighed. "I do forgive you, and I understand. But you must take my word. We wish you no harm."

"And what will King Dawson do if my family wishes to break the peace treaty? If we are not to marry?"

"I cannot say, as I am not the king. But we wish you and your family no harm."

No use arguing, but Roanna wanted to press him further. Icy fingers wrapped around her throat, and she struggled to breathe deeply.

Family. Who was her family? The Dawsons or the Hamiltons?

He returned her to her room. "I do not wish to lock you in, but you've left me no choice." He pulled the door closed behind her, and a lock clicked into place.

Roanna laid her forehead against the door and sighed. Coming had been foolish, but the genetic testing wouldn't have happened otherwise. It had been her only choice. She looked around, contemplating her options. They were limited.

She fell to her knees and bowed her head.

Let me escape this Dawsonian prison, and keep my family safe. My Chester's Wake family.

58

Hours passed and no one came to let her out. Nor did Roland or King Dawson return for her. She paced, her mind racing with thoughts. She'd been over the information a dozen times: the doctor at her birth, the warning, her long hair, and the information Roland had given her.

How had Dr. Presnell known she would be of the Dawsonian line? He had obviously known she would have powers, and those in Dawson's Edge knew that only the royal family had these powerful abilities. It stood to reason that the doctor knew where she came from.

But how could she come from anywhere other than Mother's womb? Mother was present at Roanna's birth, after all. The whole thing was much too confusing.

A knock sounded, and Roanna bolted toward the door. "Please let me out!" she pleaded.

A lock slid out of place, and Roland stepped inside. He closed the door softly behind him. "I am sorry to have kept you waiting so long. Are you hungry?"

"You lock me in my room as I await news of my lineage, and you propose I eat first?"

"We have initial reports back from Dr. Jacobs, it is true. But they are not entirely conclusive at the moment. We must await the full report."

"What? Why?"

Roland seemed...uncomfortable.

"What are you holding back? I came here voluntarily, and now you keep me captive." She lifted her chin, hoping her royal indignation might sway him. Apparently, she was correct.

Roland's throat moved as he swallowed. "Your genetic testing assured us you are a part of the Dawsonian line, which we already knew based on your powers. However, the testing hasn't concluded paternal results."

Paternal results? Cold wrapped around her once again, and her stomach churned. "Tell me what that means."

But Roland wouldn't be swayed further. "It means you are definitely a Dawson, but we don't know by whom. If you won't eat, I will leave you in peace."

She grabbed his arm. "Please! Don't keep me locked here. Allow me to roam freely. There are gardens here. Can't I go there?"

Roland paused once again. Finally, he gave a single nod. "I will assign you a guard. You may visit the gardens, the library, or the dining room. That is all, for now. You shouldn't have gone sneaking around." He shook his head and sighed. "Wait for the guard's knock. It will come shortly." He pulled away from her grasp and relocked her inside her room.

Tears sprang to Roanna's eyes but did not spill over. How could she sit still knowing one of the Dawson men was her father? What of her real father? The one who now ruled over Chester's Wake?

She realized her hands were shaking, and she clasped them tightly and sat on the edge of her bed. This was worse than any nightmare she could ever imagine.

The tears burned her eyelids and threatened to race down her cheeks.

A knock sounded, and she jumped.

The guard. She hurried to open the door. A large man stood in front of her. "I am to escort you to the gardens, Your Highness."

She swallowed her nerves and wiped away the tears that hadn't made it out. "Thank you." Her voice warbled. She stepped into the hallway and made her way to the Dawsonian royal gardens.

59

Ben

"You should have given me the letter as soon as you saw me." Ben fumed as they boarded the airship for Dawson's Edge. Gregory had been in contact with his father, and King Hamilton had contacted Dawson's Edge, who had confirmed Roanna's presence and safety.

"I had no idea of the letter's contents. Roanna assured me it wasn't a personal letter, but after your display yesterday morning, I had reason to doubt." He shot his own scathing look Ben's way.

Ben brushed off the rebuke. He should have refused to leave Roanna's side, ever. He should have defied Mother. Now Roanna was in danger simply by association with the Dawson family.

"You're one to speak," he said. "You've been in contact with Merry Stern and never realized she was the enemy."

Gregory stayed silent, as he should.

Merry Stern. If he could see her now he would wring her neck.

"We will retrieve Roanna and be on our way," Gregory said. "If Dawson's Edge refuses to cooperate, we will consider the marriage agreement void."

Unless the marriage had already taken place.

The thought turned his stomach. Dawson's Edge couldn't be so foolish as to think a quick marriage would assure their safety if they were suspected of the attack.

And surely Roanna wasn't so foolish as to think getting her answers was worth a shoddy marriage. Unless, of course, she wasn't given a choice.

They arrived in Dawson's Edge mid-afternoon. Neither King Dawson nor Queen Katherine greeted them at the palace. Roland Dawson was also mysteriously absent.

A palace aide met them. "Your Highnesses, if you'll follow me."

"Where is the king?" Gregory asked.

The aide glanced over her shoulder at them. "He is busy at the moment, but he will see you shortly. He asked that I bring you to his office."

"We would speak with him now," Gregory insisted.

She shook her head. "I apologize for the wait. An unexpected matter has arisen."

"What unexpected matter?" Ben demanded. He couldn't bear not knowing if Roanna was safe, but he knew they walked on thin ice. Two royal heirs in a foreign kingdom, demanding their way? Not likely to be favored.

They entered the palace. "Again, I apologize. King Dawson will be with you as soon as he can."

"Then show me to my sister," Gregory said. "We would see her before we go to King Dawson's office."

"Please wait in the office suite. I will see what I can do."

She'd apparently been coached to hold her ground, no matter what.

Ben followed behind her silently, seething. Roanna could be anywhere in the large palace, with its many places to hide an unwilling princess.

They followed the aide to the offices, but they needn't have worried. Roland Dawson waited for them.

"Where is Roanna?" Gregory demanded.

Roland bowed slightly to Gregory. "Prince of Chester's Wake. Welcome." He turned to Ben and his eyes narrowed slightly. He did not greet him.

"I want to see her. You took her, and I would know she is safe."

"I did not take her, as you say. She left with me completely of her own will."

"But under what intentions on your part?" Ben could not keep the contempt from his voice.

Roland's nostrils flared, and he turned on Ben. "You are most unwelcome at this meeting, Prince Benjamin of Lox. What right do you have to be here? Were you to maintain your love affair even after my wedding to Roanna?"

Hot anger spread through Ben. His muscles tightened and he readied himself to fight. "The royal families of Chester's Wake and Lox have long been friends. I come on behalf of that friendship, as a gesture of good will."

"Enough." Gregory stood even taller. "Where is she?"

"She is in the gardens, at present. Unharmed, I might add."

"Why is she here?"

Roland's eyebrows rose. "That is something you will have to discuss with her."

"Then you will take us to her."

"I'm afraid you will have to wait a bit longer for that."

Ben wanted to explode at the man's insolence.

Why the secrecy? "Talk plainly, Ambassador Dawson." He worked to keep his voice calm. "You say Roanna is safe, yet you won't prove it. What has happened since Roanna arrived here?"

"That is for my brother, the king, to divulge. As it is, he will be along shortly."

Roanna had come for answers, and it appeared King Dawson had given them to her. Roanna wouldn't keep him in the dark. They'd been on this mission together for the last few months. She would tell him.

But one thing he knew for sure, his marriage agreement with Dawson's Edge was null and void. The Dawsonians were not to be trusted, ever, and if he had his way, he would dissolve the entire kingdom.

60

Ben fumed as he waited outside King Bartholomew's office. They sat in a small waiting area, alone. What was taking the king so long? "If they harmed her…" he left the sentence hanging.

Gregory didn't acknowledge the statement. He moved to lean against a corner wall, clenching and unclenching one fist with the other shoved in his pocket.

Roland Dawson rounded a corner and met them. "The king is still attending to other matters. If you'd be more comfortable waiting in a private setting, I'd be happy to show you to one of my brother's personal relaxation rooms."

What Ben wanted was information, but bullying Roland Dawson wouldn't get him anywhere. It hadn't done any good so far, and Roland was many years his senior. Perhaps it was time to start acting like a prince again.

Gregory had pulled himself off the wall he'd been leaning against. He nodded solemnly. "That would be acceptable. Can you please let my sister know we are here?"

Roland led them away from the busy office area. "Right now Roanna is with King Dawson and Queen Katherine. I will let them know you're waiting for them as soon as they finish."

Ben didn't question Roland's statement, but his mind raced. Roanna had come to Dawson's Edge for answers regarding her birth. What answers could the Dawsons have on that subject? Perhaps they knew about Dr. Presnell. But it was hard to believe Roanna would confide in Roland Dawson. The whole thing made no sense.

Roland left them in a small sitting room. One wall looked out over a large green field. The other three walls were lined with bookshelves. A piano sat in one corner, and several couches and chairs were nestled in small sitting areas.

Gregory moved to the windows as Roland closed them into the room.

"Why would Roanna leave with Roland?" Ben asked. "She must have said something to you."

Gregory looked at him at last. "She told me what she overheard between the Dawsons." His eyes narrowed. "I have a feeling she didn't tell me everything, so I'm guessing you know more than I do." Gregory scowled, his eyes practically shooting fire. "Regardless," he went on. "I have no clue why she would seek Roland's help." He turned to the bookshelves. "I will be glad to be done with Dawson's Edge when this is over." Gregory went back to silence.

They stood like statues for long moments. Occasionally, Ben moved to the window to see if anything was happening outside. But from his vantage point, he saw no one. He watched Gregory from the corner of his eye. Tension emanated from the other crowned prince.

It didn't matter to Ben how Gregory saw him, but as Roanna was his sister and they would be neighboring kings, it would be better to stay on good terms.

"You blame me for this."

Gregory took a few moments to answer. "You practically forced her away. What do you suppose your mother said to her when we left the room yesterday?" The loathing was back.

Ben turned toward the rolling field out the window. Was Gregory right? Had he chased Roanna away?

No. Roanna was on a mission for answers. He had to believe it, and he did believe it. "You're wrong. You don't understand what Roanna has been going through these last few months."

"And you've made it all the harder on her, no doubt."

"No." He shook his head. "Roanna's troubles have nothing to do with our relationship. On the contrary, it is most likely that your own parents know the answers to her questions but have been keeping them from her."

Gregory stepped close to him, anger radiating from him. "You speak ill of the King and Queen of Chester's Wake?"

All Ben's anger over the last weeks—all his frustrations over the last years—boiled to the surface. He could take it out on Gregory in one moment of violence. Gregory wanted to fight as badly as Ben did. The anger was written all over his face, and in his body language. He was angry over Merry Stern's betrayal and because the Dawsons kept Roanna from him.

But Gregory wasn't his enemy. Rather, he was the ally.

Ben ground his teeth and took a deep breath. "No, I don't mean to speak ill of your parents. I only ask that you trust me. This has nothing to do with my relationship with Roanna. She can explain it all when we see her, if she wishes to."

The fire left Gregory's eyes, and he stepped away.

A moment later, the door opened and King Dawson strode in. He did not smile but stood with straight shoulders and his chin raised. "Two princes in one visit. To what do I owe the honor?"

"I've come for Roanna," Gregory said. He stepped toward the king. "She left with little notice, and given the recent Loxian attack, I felt it safer for her at home."

"You do not feel Roanna is safe in Dawson's Edge?"

"I do not feel her safe when we still do not know who ordered the attack. Can I see her?"

King Dawson kept eye contact with Gregory for long, torturous moments. "Roanna came to me of her own will. While we are investigating the strange circumstances surrounding her arrival, it is best she has no contact with you."

The earlier anger shot to the surface. Ben stormed past Gregory. "Where is Roanna? She would not willingly refuse her own brother."

King Dawson's eyebrows shot up. "You mean to imply Gregory Hamilton is her brother? On the contrary, he is not."

Ben sat on the precipice. He could allow his anger to overtake him. He wouldn't get far pummeling King Dawson before guards would overtake him. Maybe kill him. Then where would Roanna be?

He forced himself to calm down. "Then Roanna found the answers she sought," he stated it simply, letting King Dawson know he knew the quest Roanna was on.

King Dawson's expression did not change. "Roanna is safe, and that is all you need know for the time being."

"No." Gregory shook his head. "You're playing word games. She is my sister, and I am her brother. I would see her now."

"You are welcome to stay and wait, but it is most likely your own fathers require your assistance in locating those behind the Loxian attacks. Roanna will see you when all of our questions have been answered. Until then, you are welcome to stay and dine with us for supper."

Ben looked to Gregory. He saw the same resolve on Gregory's face. They would stay, as long as it took.

61

Ben's knee bounced up and down as he waited for King Dawson to pore over Gregory's notes on the intelligence Chester's Wake had uncovered. It had been two nights since they'd arrived in Dawson's Edge, and so far, the Dawsons had come up with one excuse or another as to why Roanna was not available.

Gregory had been in contact with his father, who was demanding King Dawson allow Gregory to see Roanna immediately.

King Dawson smiled kindly and assured King Hamilton his compliance.

Ben didn't trust the man. He ground his teeth and forced his leg to stop bouncing. What could Roland Dawson have told Roanna in the first place to make her think following him to Dawson's Edge would be a good idea? Roanna was no fool. It must have been something important, or she wouldn't have come.

King Dawson sat back in his chair with a huff, holding the reports in his hands. "The Maynes and Sterns are the rebels? That is your big conclusion?" He quirked an eyebrow and frowned.

"You see the evidence for yourself," Gregory insisted as his jaw worked. It must be hard for him to indicate the Sterns when he'd only just started a relationship with Merry.

King Dawson sighed. "I do see the evidence, but it seems so unlikely. The Sterns in cahoots with the Maynes?" He shook his head. "My sources have told me nothing of it."

"Perhaps your sources aren't to be trusted," Ben spat out.

The king turned venomous eyes toward Ben. "What business do you have here, again?"

"My father was attacked." Ben worked to keep his voice steady. In this moment, he would go to war with Dawson's Edge in a heartbeat—whether the king himself or simply the subjects were the culprits behind the attack.

"Yes, well," King Dawson stood. "You did not come to discuss these attacks. Prince Hamilton came to retrieve his sister, and the reason for your presence is still in question." He marched to the door. "My people can bring in the Sterns." He still spoke to Ben. "If you are the ambassador in place for this mission, you may assist in questioning them and deciding on their innocence or guilt."

Gregory stood, too. "We will see Roanna now."

King Dawson's eyes narrowed. What was the man hiding? "Because I respect your father, I will have her brought to the palace gardens at once."

After all the fuss he'd made, it seemed unlikely the king would make it that easy. But Ben would not complain.

Gregory nodded once. Then they followed him to the elevators. The king's entourage of guards and aides followed as well. The elevator took them downstairs. Then a servant led Ben and Gregory outside.

"I don't trust him," Ben said as soon as they were alone.

Gregory shook his head. "I don't trust any of this. What secrets of Roanna's could the Dawsons have the answers to? It is foolishness."

It was foolishness, but again Ben knew there had to be a reason. Roanna had acted impulsively lately— her life had been stressful—but she wouldn't put herself in danger without good reason.

They waited long minutes, and Ben stopped and fingered a soft, green leaf. Where was she? He looked up to the palace, searching the windows, but he saw no one.

"Gregory!" Roanna's voice drew him back. He hurried to Gregory's side as Roanna reached her brother and hugged him.

"Why did you come here, Roanna?" Gregory chided. "Whatever answers you seek could have waited. It was foolish to seek after these mysterious answers when things were so dangerous." He shook his head. "I should have stopped you. We need to go home today."

Roanna's face paled. She glanced behind her, as if someone watched from the shadows.

Ben searched the area she'd come from, but he saw no one.

"I won't be returning with you today," Roanna said. "I hope to go home soon, but I cannot go yet."

"Roanna." Gregory's face contorted with irritation. "You can't stay here. It isn't safe."

She swallowed hard, and her gaze flitted to Ben's face. "There are things you don't understand."

Ben stepped forward. He reached for her hands, but she stepped back. He frowned but let it go. "If we don't understand them, then explain. Please?"

She didn't look behind her, but her body language told him someone was monitoring her.

He didn't wait for her answer. He marched to the doorframe where she'd come from and looked around.

No one was there.

He growled and returned to her side. He lowered his voice. "Is someone watching you?"

She met his gaze, her eyes wide and her nostrils flared. "No, no one is watching me."

She emphasized watching.

They were...listening? The Dawsons were listening to her. Forcing her.

"Roanna." His voice cracked, and he tried again. "Roanna, your family needs you. We can keep you safe. The people of Dawson's Edge aren't honorable. No one here can be trusted."

Pain danced behind her eyes. She bit her lip. "I need to stay, for now. I promise you will understand more, later."

Ben reached for her hands again, and this time she didn't pull away. "Has Roland done something to you?" he pleaded. "Have you been hurt, or forced into an early marriage?"

She frowned, but the fear was still plain on her face. "No, nothing like that."

When she didn't pull her hands away, he stepped closer. "We are in this together, Roanna. What did they tell you? Do they know about Dr. Presnell?"

She gnawed on her lip another moment, then nodded almost imperceptibly. "I promise you will learn the truth soon." She squeezed his hands but still didn't pull away.

His heart ached to pull her into a hug, but something held him back. She would not welcome the hug, maybe because the Dawsons were monitoring her.

"Have your feelings changed?" he asked as softly as he could.

Again, the smallest of head movements. A shake.

Relief and determination poured through him. He released her hands and turned to Gregory. "I won't go until she is ready to return."

Gregory's face showed his irritation with his sister, but he nodded. "I will stay, as well. But Roanna, you need to tell us what is going on. Lox has been attacked. It isn't safe here, and Father and Mother need us."

Tears filled her eyes, but she blinked them away. "I should go back inside now."

Instinct told Ben to grab her and not let go. The Dawsons had some kind of hold on her, but what? If they knew of Dr. Presnell, then they might know more. They might know of the curse—or whatever it was—that the doctor put on her hair. Did they know she had heard their thoughts?

She went inside without another glance.

Ben growled, then stomped back to his own room.

62

Ben attempted to pass the time by checking in with Mother and Father. He assured them of his own safety and relayed the conversations he'd had with King Dawson over the last few days. Father had been sent home to heal at the hospital, and he was interested in Ben's reports.

Ben left out Roanna's strange behavior, but the pain and confusion in her eyes played fresh in his mind. He shouldn't have rejected her in Lox. He'd been trying to keep his promise to Mother, but he should have followed his heart, and his instincts. He and Roanna belonged together, regardless of anything keeping them apart.

He finished his communication with Father and Mother then closed down his Messenger. A groan escaped his lips as he let his forehead fall forward and hit the desk. Gregory hadn't spoken to Ben since Ben had stomped off after seeing Roanna earlier. He wondered what the prince might be up to.

A knock sounded on the door. Ben waited a split second before remembering Hansen wasn't there to open it for him, so he rushed to the door and quickly opened it.

A servant stood on the other side. He bowed slightly. "Dinner is being served downstairs, Your Highness."

Dinner. Why hadn't he thought of that? Roanna would likely be there. Now that he and Gregory had seen her, the Dawsons should have no reason to keep her away from them as long as they were all being monitored.

"Thank you. I'll be down soon."

The servant bowed again, and Ben closed the door. He had brought very little in the way of luggage, but he found something suitable and changed as quickly as he could. As he stared at himself in the mirror, his mind reeled.

This whole thing had started because he'd wanted more time alone with Roanna. Because he'd dragged her to the dungeon to search imprisonment records.

He should have left off the records and simply told her how he felt. Told her he loved her.

He growled and headed into the hall. Telling her he loved her wouldn't have changed anything. It probably would have made things worse—perhaps thrust their countries into war with Dawson's Edge proper, rather than a small militia of people within the country.

The palace buzzed with activity, and several guests sat at the table as he entered the dining room. Relief poured through him when he spotted Roanna sitting between Queen Katherine and Gregory. Roland sat across from her.

Ben took the seat beside Gregory.

"Good evening, Prince Ben." King Dawson nodded his way as if he hadn't insulted him earlier in the day. "I trust you are having a fine visit."

"It is quite well. Thank you for your hospitality." Ben kept his voice steady, but he wondered what trick the king was up to now.

He managed a smile for Queen Katherine then glanced casually at a few of the other guests, including

Roanna.

Her gaze was glued to him, and when he met her large, round eyes she did not look away. Still fearful but she wasn't even trying to hide it.

He ground his teeth as anger burned in his gut. If only he could speak to her privately. But how? King Dawson barely wanted her own brother to see her; it was unlikely he would let Ben have a few moments alone. And with the way Roanna was behaving, it was equally unlikely she would agree to meet him without the king's permission.

Servants brought out platters of food, and conversation died away as guests filled their plates.

While others ate, Ben wracked his brain for ways to get a message to Roanna. If only he'd thought ahead, he could have passed a scrap of paper via Gregory who sat between them.

Gregory spoke in tense tones whenever anyone asked him a question, but he mostly spoke in low tones to Roanna. The stern wrinkle on his forehead never eased up. He was hammering her hard about her choices.

"How is your father today, Prince Benjamin?" Roland asked, pulling Ben's attention away from Gregory and Roanna.

"He was well when I messaged him and my mother earlier. Thank you for asking."

"That's good to hear." Roland's eyes blazed with something Ben didn't quite recognize. Anger? Irritation? "It seems your efforts would be needed more at home than here in Dawson's Edge at the moment."

"Apprehending whoever is responsible for Father's injuries, as well as the injuries to Lox, is where my efforts are most needed."

Roland didn't reply. Instead, he looked away and began speaking to another guest.

Ben's irritation tightened in his chest. Dinner couldn't end soon enough.

At last, King Dawson stood. "Let us continue the festivities in the banquet hall."

The other few palace guests agreed with smiling faces.

They wouldn't be so happy if their country had been attacked as Lox had. Their merriment spoke of their ignorance.

He followed the others out, but Gregory grabbed his arm from behind. A piece of paper was shoved into his hand as Gregory passed him. Roanna was several feet ahead, clinging to the arm of Queen Katherine.

A note? Roanna had thought ahead where he had not. He almost smiled but caught himself just in time. He would have to wait to look at the note.

He quickly slipped it into his pocket.

King Dawson and the others congregated in the banquet hall.

Ben had just stepped through the doorway when the world shook.

63

Ben caught himself on the doorframe before he crashed to the ground, but others weren't so lucky. Guards rushed forward, grabbing the king and queen to rush them to safety.

"Get Roanna!" King Dawson shouted as he was prodded toward a sliding panel in the wall. "Keep her safe!"

Another guard took Roanna's arm and herded her behind the queen.

Ben barely had time to register the king's comment as the ground still shook.

"What's happening?" someone shouted.

One guest suggested an earthquake, but that was foolishness. They were under attack.

A vase slipped from a high shelf and knocked a guard unconscious.

Gregory made his way to Ben. "This is the rebels' doing."

"I agree."

"We have to get Roanna." He looked at the wall panel that had already closed.

Gregory had to have heard the king's words about Roanna, but he said nothing. Ben wouldn't bring it up, but his mind worked to understand the king's concern.

Why was Dawson working so hard to protect her?

The shaking stopped. Guards raced in the corridors outside the banquet hall. Window glass was shattered on the plush carpeting, and parts of the ceiling hung down.

"It has to be war bots," Ben said. "This is too much damage for a single bomb."

Ben moved to the wall where Roanna had disappeared. He slid his hands along the panel, searching for a secret entrance. "There's nothing."

Gregory squatted beside him. "It must be a remote entry. We don't have access."

They stood, and Ben searched Gregory's eyes. "Did you hear the king's words about Roanna?"

Gregory's gaze darkened and his frown blanketed his entire face. "We need to find her."

Ben nodded and moved from the room, pushing past the hysterical guests. He had known almost nothing of the Dawsonian palace a month ago, but because he'd recently spent several weeks being wooed by them he had a better understanding of his whereabouts. He led Gregory to the guest hallway, and to the elevator that would take them to an underground bunker.

"The hidden pathway they took must lead below ground," he said. "Where else would they take the family?"

Gregory kept silent as Ben worked on the keypad at the elevator entrance. "We don't have a code," Ben said. "Or an entry card."

Gregory's eyes widened for a moment. "I'll be right back." He raced back down the hall, and a moment later returned with a key card. "The guard knocked unconscious in the blast," he explained.

Ben should have thought of it himself.

Gregory scanned the card, and the elevator door slid open. They stepped inside. The door closed, and the elevator moved of its own volition. They sank into the lower parts of the earth. Once they reached the bunker, they would likely be greeted by guards with guns—after all, they were uninvited guests, in this instance. But hopefully the king would see them and allow them entrance before they ended up casualties of war.

Ben readied himself as the elevator came to a stop. He wanted to be prepared in case they were attacked as soon as the door opened, but the bunker was a madhouse. Aides rushed around the room, people shouted, and guards stood with guns at their sides, watching the chaos.

Gregory and Ben weren't noticed until they stepped from the elevator. A guard stopped them. "Your Highnesses, this is a restricted area."

"We've been collaborating with the king on these attacks." Ben stood rigidly, his chin lifted, using his most authoritative voice. This wasn't his kingdom, but he hoped the guard would stand down.

The guard paused only a moment. "Wait here while I verify." He stepped away and used some type of radio device. When he finished, he turned back to Ben and Gregory. "The king will see you. Follow me."

Ben kept his relief inside as they pushed their way through the crowd. They passed a door as it opened and a guard stepped out. Roanna sat at a couch inside the room, but the door shut again before Ben could make eye contact.

The king paced inside a room labeled War Room. He turned furious eyes on Ben and Gregory. "What are you doing down here? The guard tells me you came without escort."

Ben was tired of being treated as if his presence in Dawson's Edge were of no importance. He stepped forward. "You left your guests to die, so yes we took it upon ourselves to steal a key from an unconscious guard. Now, do you have any intelligence on these attacks?"

King Dawson sneered then turned away. "We have nothing. The grounds have been patrolled heavily since the latest attack on Lox. We don't know how someone got through."

"Maybe someone on the inside is working with the enemy," Ben stated.

Again, the king turned with a sneer. "You think we haven't thought of this? Boy, you aren't a king yet. You'd do well to remember it."

Heat burned Ben's cheeks, but he refused to stand down. He took a deep breath and worked to calm his nerves. "We aren't enemies," he said. "We both want our people to succeed, and our countries to be safe. The same enemy attacks us both. Let us work together."

"Prince Benjamin speaks truth." Gregory stepped forward. "Let us work together."

The fire in King Dawson's eyes dimmed, but only slightly. "Very well. See what you can learn."

Aides brought Messenger devices to Ben and Gregory, and they each worked to contact their kingdoms. Ben waited while Mother spoke with her own people. His foot tapped the floor under the table in the war room, and his mind roamed back to Roanna. He wanted to see her. Needed to speak with her.

What information could Dawson have possibly given her that would make him treat her so protectively? And why would she let him?

A communication came through the Messenger. It was Mother with a barrage of information. Loxian intelligence had picked up on chatter from a unit near the border stating that three guards had been placed in the Dawsonian palace as double agents.

"Your Highness," he spoke, calling the king over. King Dawson read the brief report and growled.

"We need a check on all palace guards," he barked. An aide rushed from the room.

King Dawson turned to Ben, his dark eyebrows lowered. "This had better not lead us down a mole's tunnel."

Ben kept back any retort as a different aide stepped to King Dawson's side. "The queen wishes to see you, Your Highness."

"I would like to see my sister." Gregory spoke up quickly, stepping forward.

King Dawson scowled but nodded his consent.

Ben didn't wait for permission. He followed the men toward the room where Roanna and Queen Katherine were being kept.

64

Roanna

King Dawson strode into the room. Gregory and Ben followed him.

Roanna's heart squeezed at the sight of Ben. He had asked if her feelings had changed. She'd wanted to laugh at the question—as if her feelings for him could ever change. The problem wasn't her own feelings but his, once he learned her secret. Memories from earlier in the week assaulted her, memories from when King Dawson had come for her with the results from Dr. Jacobs.

Roanna had been wandering the gardens, not really seeing anything in front of her. Two days had passed since she'd arrived. She spent as much time outside as she could manage while considering ways to contact her family. She had rounded a corner and saw King Dawson striding toward her. The look on his face—he practically glowed.

He had answers from the test.

The king did not hold back. "The genetic test revealed that you are—well, it revealed you are my child. Mine and Queen Katherine's."

Initially, she'd believed he lied. Dawson's Edge was known for their lies and deceit and distrust, and now she was witnessing it firsthand. She shook her head, tears spilling from her eyes unchecked. "That is impossible. I've been given the account of my birth by my own mother."

But her heart had told her it was truth. How else could she explain the anomaly of her hair, the shivers, and her ability to hear Roland's and King Dawson's thoughts? She wasn't Mother's child.

"Maybe the test was wrong." Her words came out in a whisper. "The Dawsons and Hamiltons used to be related. Perhaps the power has crossed lines."

Sympathy danced in King Dawson's eyes. "The test was very clear. You were a match to myself as well as Queen Katherine. There is only one explanation, and that is that you are the princess whom we were told died during birth eighteen years ago..."

The Dawsonian princess. Not the daughter of King Hamilton and Queen Charlotte of Chester's Wake, as she had always believed, but someone altogether different. Someone with strange magical powers— powers which may or may not have gotten her killed if detected at birth.

She watched Ben now, across the room in the small, cramped bunker. How would he see her once he learned she was King Dawson's daughter? She'd considered the story a thousand times, and while they had no definitive answers, she could only assume that she was stolen by Dr. Presnell and stowed away until Mother went into labor. Perhaps he had even caused Mother's early labor. The questions she wrestled with now was the fate of the true Chester's Wake princess. What had become of her?

And how could she ever tell her family?

Gregory moved to her side and sat on the sofa. "Are you unharmed?"

"I'm fine, Gregory. Ready to go home."

He shook his head. "We shouldn't be here at all. It

isn't safe."

After an attack at the palace, she was apt to agree. But how could she leave? It was unlikely King Dawson would agree to such a thing. He and Katherine still didn't know how she had ended up in Chester's Wake—she hadn't told them about Dr. Presnell—and he wanted answers.

"Roanna, did Roland threaten you?" He glanced a few feet away at the king and queen, then lowered his voice. "Why did King Dawson insist they keep you safe?"

Her stomach tightened. Gregory had heard King Dawson's panicked cry?

Her gaze flitted to Ben's. Had he heard? His lowered brows and pained expression told her he had. But there was something else in his eyes—a tenderness. He wanted to speak with her.

That might change once he learned the truth.

"Roland has been nothing but kind," she defended. She was surprised to feel it was true. Roland had been the key to all her questions.

"Can I speak with you, Roanna?" Ben's voice was choked, and her heart squeezed again.

"Of course."

His look pleaded with her for privacy. She stood and went to his side. They were only a few feet from everyone else in the room, but it was all he needed. He gripped her hands.

"Please tell me what's going on."

She swallowed hard and glanced at King Dawson. He watched them, frowning, but not stopping their conversation.

Roanna's stomach tightened and twisted. She couldn't tell him the truth. Couldn't let him know what she'd learned. There was too much tension. Too much unrest and hatred between the countries.

"Roland knew things," she whispered. "He knew about my hair, and he had answers."

Ben frowned. "How?"

"I can't explain right now. Not here," she choked out.

Ben's frown deepened, but he didn't challenge her. Was he angry?

"Roanna, I—"

An aide rushed into the room. "Your Highness," she spoke to King Dawson.

Ben turned to the aide, his sentence left unfinished. "The guards have been checked. Three have been missing for several days."

King Dawson's nostrils flared. "Why have their absences not been brought to my attention sooner? It is as the Loxian intelligence predicted. Track them down!" His voice had escalated to a bellow. "Back to the war room." He marched from the room, and Gregory moved to follow him.

Ben turned to her even as he stepped away. "We will speak more. I promise."

Tears filled her eyes. Would things ever be the same?

"Roanna, I promise it."

She managed a nod. Then he was gone.

Moving back to the couch, she caught Queen Katherine's watchful eye. The queen patted the seat beside her, and Roanna sat.

"You are close to the Prince of Lox?"

Close? That was an understatement. She nodded.

Queen Katherine gave her a small smile. "He seems a nice, reliable boy."

Roanna had no reply, so she changed the subject. "Queen Katherine, I would very much like to see my Chester's Wake family. I wish to hear their explanations if they have any. And I wish to tell them the things I've learned."

Fear danced behind Katherine's eyes. "I understand your longings. You were raised by them. You will be allowed to see them, but first we must ensure they will not prevent you from returning to Dawson's Edge. We must also secure our borders and be sure you will be safe in Chester's Wake."

It was as she suspected, but it was harder to hear when it was said out loud. She stood and paced the room.

"Roanna," Queen Katherine spoke. "Come sit beside me. Please."

"I want to do something. To help."

"It is not your place to help."

Roanna spun toward Katherine. "Not my place? And why not! I'm still a princess, aren't I? I want to help, not cower in an underground bunker."

Katherine frowned at her but didn't speak. Anger bubbled inside Roanna, and she rubbed her temples to break the tension. At least in Chester's Wake she was allowed to work for the people. Participate in decisions. She was even allowed to travel to Lox, against her parents' better judgment.

Here in Dawson's Edge? Apparently, she would be treated differently. She should have known, based on the way Roland had treated her.

Katherine stood and came to her side. She took Roanna's hands, stopping her from pacing. "I am sure there is something you can do to help, but it won't be at this moment. No one will let you out of this bunker until the threat is gone."

Something she could do?

The words ran through her mind as an idea formed.

Is this possible?

The idea solidified in her heart. She could do it, if someone would let her.

"I want to speak with King Dawson."

Katherine's frown deepened. "He is strategizing."

"I have an idea, and I want to speak to him."

Uncertainty danced in Katherine's eyes. She glanced at the door guard. "Will you ask King Dawson if he will see Princess Roanna?"

The guard bowed slightly and stepped from the room.

Excitement and nerves twirled in her stomach as her heart picked up speed. He would likely say no, but what if he didn't? Her idea could work, after all.

The guard returned a moment later, King Dawson behind him. The king was alone.

65

"I won't hear of it." King Dawson turned from her and paced to the other side of the room, as if distance would settle the matter.

"I won't be in any danger." At least, she likely wouldn't be in any danger. "The Sterns don't know the things we've only just discovered. They don't know we're on to them, and they haven't attacked Chester's Wake that we know of. If I come to them as an ally, they will have no reason to doubt it. Merry and I were already building a friendship before this started."

King Dawson growled and didn't look at her. Was he thinking over her suggestion? Merry Stern would have no reason to doubt her if she showed up wishing to join forces. She could mention that Chester's Wake was tired of the tensions with Dawson's Edge, and that she couldn't bear the idea of being married into the royal family. Both of these statements would be true, though taken out of context.

"It could work," Ben said.

Roanna spun toward the door where Ben and Gregory now stood.

King Dawson's face turned red. "Get out of this room."

But Ben stepped further inside. "Roanna met Merry Stern while Ambassador Roland was in Chester's Wake. It wouldn't be unthinkable for Roanna to call on Merry while here in Dawson's Edge. For all Merry Stern knows, Roanna is simply here with her fiancé."

Ben stumbled over those last words. His gaze shifted from Roanna to the king.

King Dawson shook his head. "I will not put you in harm's way."

"Roanna," Katherine spoke. "Please don't ask us to allow this." Her voice broke, and tears pooled in her eyes.

Defeat washed over Roanna. They wouldn't allow her to help. "But I know I can do it." One last plea. "I have come this far, haven't I? I am no weakling."

"Roanna, don't be a fool!"

Gregory?

She turned to him, tears burning her own eyes now. "What?"

"You followed Roland here, which was foolish of me to allow, and for a reason I still don't understand. I stand with King Dawson on this matter. I cannot allow you to be put in any further danger." His nostrils flared and his cheeks reddened.

Tears started down her face. How could he? Hadn't they always been each other's confidant? Each other's ally?

"I love you, sister," Gregory said. "And that is why I must insist your mission is foolish."

"It is settled," King Dawson said. "I will hear no more of it." He stormed from the room without another word, leaving Roanna, Katherine, Gregory, and Ben behind.

"I'm sorry, Roanna." Gregory reached for her shoulder, but she pulled away from him.

He kept her gaze for a moment longer, sighed, and left the room.

"I know you're disappointed," Katherine said. She

didn't wait for Roanna's rejection. She returned to her seat on the sofa.

Ben grabbed her hands and pulled her to a secluded corner. "You can do this," he whispered.

She pulled one hand away and swiped at the tears running down her cheeks. "This is ridiculous. As if I haven't been conniving and investigating on my own for the last few months." She looked into his eyes and saw the truth in them—he believed in her. Trusted her. At least for now.

"When we leave this bunker, I can help you."

She frowned. "It will never work." They spoke in low whispers. "They haven't let me out of the guards' sights."

"Leave distracting the guards to me. Once we're out, I'll get you to Merry Stern."

She bit her lip. "I don't know, Ben. Surely the Sterns know I'm here. They will wonder how I got out of the palace for a leisure visit when it's just been attacked."

Ben frowned. "But haven't you been away, visiting Roland's estate? You probably haven't had time to hear of the attack." He asked it so innocently, his eyes wide. For a moment, she almost believed they were back in Chester's Wake, and Ben was trying to lure her to the dungeon to scour old prison records.

She couldn't help the smile that spread over her lips. "The ocean is lovely this time of year."

His smile grew when she played along, but then it faltered. He stepped closer to her and lowered his voice again. "I still don't understand what is going on here." His jaw worked as he paused. "Are you still engaged to Roland Dawson?"

The intensity in his eyes bored into her. For a

moment, the attack didn't matter. The Sterns didn't matter, and her Dawsonian lineage didn't matter. She swallowed hard. Her throat constricted. "No."

His gaze danced away, and he nodded. But red filled his cheeks.

What was he thinking?

"Will you do it if I help you?"

Hadn't this been her idea? "Yes."

"Then wait for me in your room. We'll go first thing in the morning."

She nodded. "I swear it."

He gave her one last devilish grin. "I'll see you around, then." He released her hands and left the room.

Roanna sighed. She would do it, but she could only pray she was making the right decision.

66

Roanna paced her room. They had returned upstairs sometime after midnight. She'd slept fitfully and been awake since dawn waiting for Ben. A guard stood outside her door, and soft pink had enveloped the sky.

She had reached with her mind several times, feeling for hidden plans between King Dawson and Roland, but if they were speaking with their minds they were too far away for her to hear. The longer she waited, the more hopeless this mission seemed. Surely the Sterns would have heard she was in the palace at the time of the attack. Then again, the Dawsons had kept her presence in the kingdom quiet. They didn't want anyone knowing the things they had discovered about her heritage. There was a good chance the rebels had no idea she was there.

A knock sounded, and she gasped. She was too jumpy. Too tired. Too everything. Taking a deep breath, she opened the door as if it would be the queen, but she found Ben. Her eyes widened, and she quickly pulled him into the room and closed the door. "How did you get rid of the guard?"

He grinned. "Gregory helped."

"Gregory?" That was hard to believe considering he was against the idea of contacting the Sterns.

"Well, first he gave me a lecture on risking your life and your reputation. He reminded me that we are royals, and we cannot go traipsing around the country side unprotected. As if either of us could ever forget that." He sighed and sat on the foot of her bed. "But I reminded him that the king of Dawson's Edge was keeping his sister captive, and if we wanted you away from here at all, we had to take matters into our own hands."

The pit of Roanna's stomach twisted. "It's not as simple as that, Ben. I don't want to leave Dawson's Edge behind."

The excited light in his eyes dulled, and he watched her cautiously. Curiously. "Can you tell me about it?"

She swallowed and wiped her hands on her dress. Why were her nerves so tight? This was Ben. She could tell him anything.

"Shouldn't we go?" she said instead. "What, exactly, is your plan?"

He clenched his jaw, not masking his hurt very well. He stood. "I've been doing a little investigating. The Sterns live north of here. You will be leaving on the train. Gregory helped me with that plan as well."

He paused, and she waited. But his tone wasn't as open and friendly. Guilt washed over her. Why was she keeping her secret from him?

"Anyway," he went on, "Gregory is speaking with the king now, convincing him you would be safer at Santa Rio for the time being. Along with the queen, most likely. That will get you out of the palace, and from there, it should be easy to make a detour to the Sterns."

Roanna raised her eyebrows. "Easy? I don't see how."

His grin returned. "You have so little faith."

She smiled back and rolled her eyes. "Fine. I trust you." But did she? She was keeping secrets.

He shifted toward the door as if he were about to leave.

"How is your father?" She blurted it out, hoping to keep him another few moments.

A softer look came over him. "He's doing well. I spoke with him while we were in the bunker, and he was out of his bed and sitting in an office chair. His injuries will take a few weeks to heal, but at least he will heal."

"I'm glad."

He kept her gaze another moment then moved closer to her. "Thank you for coming to Lox to check on us. I'm sorry things happened the way they did."

She swallowed and offered a shaky smile. "I forgive you."

He raised his brows and chuckled. "Well I'm glad that's settled. I should go." He paused. "What's wrong, Roanna?"

She forced out a laugh. "Nothing. I'm being ridiculous. Thinking as if we are still young and wishing you could stay with me longer."

"I have a feeling King Dawson would not take kindly to that."

"No," she agreed, looking away. "I doubt he would." Right now, King Dawson was acting as if Ben were the devil himself.

Ben hesitated another moment then moved toward the door. "Gregory can be very convincing. I suspect you'll be leaving on the train as soon as breakfast is finished."

She nodded, and he opened the door. He had so much confidence, but she worried things wouldn't go

so easily. She hurried to get ready.
It was likely to be a long day.

67

Roanna entered the dining room as King Dawson leaned toward Katherine and took her hand. "You will be safer there," he said to her. "Roanna is travelling with you, and Santa Rio will be a haven until this is blown over."

Katherine gave him a shaky smile. "I know. I worry for your safety, though."

"I will be fine," King Dawson assured her.

Roanna watched them with part fascination, part embarrassment. These were her parents. Her parents?

Her stomach tightened once again at the thought, but she couldn't deny the connection she'd felt to them when they'd first met. Breakfast passed in tense whispers, and as soon as they'd finished eating they were taken to the train depot where their bags were waiting along with an unmarked train car.

A conductor urged them to board the train that would take them to Santa Rio. Roanna scanned the platform for Ben, but he was nowhere in sight. What did he have up his sleeve?

The plush rail car offered little comfort when Roanna's insides quivered at the idea of the act she would need to pull off with Merry Stern.

Roanna wore a deep purple velvet dress that fell in ruffles just below her knees. Her knee-high black boots laced up the backs, and she wore a smart, black, top hat. A bit fancy for simple travel to Santa Rio, but as Ben assured her last night to trust him, she'd dressed as if she were making a social call to the Sterns. When Katherine had commented on how lovely she looked, Roanna had thanked her and offered an excuse about only bringing a small amount of luggage in her travel from Lox.

The train whistle pierced her ears. Out the window, a plume of steam burst into the sky as the train lurched forward.

Katherine smiled at her from her seat on the leather couch across the car. "The men will have this sorted out soon."

Roanna considered returning the smile and leaving it at that, but she decided against it. "Queen Katherine, don't you ever want to take action yourself? Don't you want to participate, rather than leaving it to the men?" She spoke cautiously, not wanting to put Katherine off by insulting her.

But Katherine smiled knowingly. "Not at all, sweet Roanna. I want to do nothing more than the things I already do. While I understand the desire of some women to make their way in the world, I am quite content with my role as queen. I have always wished to help the poor, raise my children, and stand by my husband's side. I assure you, there is nothing dishonorable in that."

Roanna studied the Queen of Dawson's Edge and had to concede the point. The queen was happy—and successful—in her place as queen. There was nothing dishonorable, indeed.

Roanna turned to the window and watched the land roll by. Leaving the state affairs for the men was fine for the queen and other women, but Roanna was not that kind of girl. She wanted to be at the heart of the action. And she could be. She was tired of being told what to do and expected to do it. She had a choice, and she had decided to start exercising it.

No doubt, she would be able to pull information from Merry Stern. The Sterns didn't know she had been at the castle during the attack.

They had ridden for nearly a half hour when the train began to slow. Queen Katherine frowned. "What on earth?"

Roanna tensed as she searched out the window. Surely Ben wasn't thinking to hijack the train.

A loud clanging rang out as the tracks were shifted to a different line. A line headed north.

The train restarted, and Katherine sighed. "Thank goodness. I was worried for a moment."

Roanna kept silent. Katherine hadn't even checked to see if there was a problem. She had no idea they were headed north rather than west.

A few minutes later, a servant entered with a tea service. He offered a cup to the queen, and one to Roanna.

"Thank you," Katherine said, smiling up at the servant. She sipped from her tea as the servant exited.

Roanna looked at the cup, but her nerves were too tight to drink it. She placed her tea on the side table and watched Katherine instead. After a few minutes, Katherine yawned.

"The lull of the train always makes me sleepy," she said. She set her tea down. "I believe I'll rest my eyes. It won't be much longer now." A moment later Katherine was breathing gently in sleep.

Roanna watched, wide eyed. She'd fallen asleep much too fast. Had Katherine been drugged? She turned toward the window, looking for hints from Ben. He'd said to trust him, so she would try. But her stomach wasn't cooperating with her brain, and it twisted with nerves.

After long minutes, the train topped a hill. The Sterns' estate rose in the distance. To the left of the estate was a small village, and to the right a wide forest.

The train slowed as it neared a station close to the estate. They chugged to a stop, and a moment later the door hissed open, steam billowing around the platform.

Ben waited for her outside.

68

Ben stood, smiling up at her.

"How did you manage this?" She climbed from the railcar and glanced around. The platform was mostly deserted.

"I know a few people." He left it at that and took her arm. They walked toward the front of the train where an auto waited. "The driver will take you to the estate. You can tell them whatever you want, but some form of being at Santa Rio would work best. This morning, after King Dawson approved your trip, I made sure the servants were buzzing about you and the queen travelling. If the Sterns heard about it at all, it won't seem a stretch that the gossips have their days mixed up."

Roanna nodded. "I can do that."

They reached the car, and Ben paused. "Be careful in there. I don't believe it will be dangerous for you, but I can't promise anything."

"I'm not afraid." She mostly meant it. Only a tiny wiggle in her stomach spoke of her nerves.

A slow smile spread across his face, and he let go of her arm and opened the auto's door. "I'll see you back here soon. Try to not linger more than a couple hours. I don't want to have to drug the queen again. With any luck, we'll be pulling up to Santa Rio as she awakens."

Roanna nodded again. She could do this. She climbed into the sleek, white auto and in a moment, the driver had whisked her down the gravely road on their way to the Sterns' estate. The house was large, made of whitewashed wood and only a few windows. It had a rippling roof made of some type of green clay, and various contraptions hung from a large porch.

The driver stopped the car outside the house, and Roanna eyed the strange hanging creations as she ascended the stairs to the door. They looked like weather devices—a barometer, a thermometer, a rain gauge. But they had tubes jutting out from all sides, weighted balls hanging from the ends, and strange number combinations.

The door opened before she reached it, and a butler met her at the door. "Can I help you, Miss?"

Roanna's driver stood behind her. At the butler's words, he huffed. "Sir, this is the Princess Roanna Hamilton of Chester's Wake."

The butler's eyes widened, but he quickly bowed. "Do come in, Your Highness."

Roanna smiled and breezed past him. "I've come to visit Lady Merry Stern if she is in. We met in Chester's Wake, and I thought it nice to make a friend here in Dawson's Edge as I've been engaged to marry Ambassador Roland Dawson." She worded her speech carefully so as not to lie outright.

The butler bowed slightly. "Allow me to show you to the sitting room. I will see if Lady Merry is available."

The house looked large on the outside, but the inside was small and cramped. The foyer area was tight, and the butler led her through a series of small hallways. Rooms branched off every few feet, but each room was equally small. At last, he deposited her in a sitting room with a few chairs, a chaise lounge, and a sofa. A round table sat in the middle of the room, and a vase decorated the table. The vase had no flowers.

"If you'll wait just a moment, Your Highness." He bowed again then lumbered away.

Roanna took a deep breath the moment he was gone. She had considered all night what to say to Merry. Before she could think another moment, Merry stormed in. Her eyes wide, she evaluated Roanna.

"My lady," she said, curtsying slightly, and out of breath. "I heard there was an attack at the palace. You are uninjured?"

Roanna raised her eyebrows. "An attack? Oh my. We've been to Santa Rio. I hadn't realized—that is, I heard of it but didn't realize it was serious. Was it serious, then?"

Merry watched her silently for another beat then took a seat beside her on the couch. "I'm not sure how serious it was, to tell the truth. But I'm glad you weren't harmed."

"I'm sure it was nothing." Roanna waved her hand. "King Dawson would have informed us otherwise." So much for not lying.

Merry smiled, though it didn't reach her eyes. "What brings you to Stern Estate? How is Gregory?"

Gregory? Roanna had nearly forgotten Gregory had shown Merry around the palace in Chester's Wake. Had they become friends then? "Well, if you remember, I became betrothed to Roland Dawson. I've been worried about knowing no one, but then I remembered you. I thought we might visit and become friends, though my time is short."

"Wonderful!" Merry called for the butler and ordered tea and finger foods to be brought at once. "Did you say how Gregory fares?"

"He's well. Worried over the escalating problems, no doubt, but well." That was true, at least. "He takes things very seriously, whether he wants to or not."

A flash of something like pain passed behind Merry's eyes. It came and went so fast that Roanna had no chance to decipher it.

"He was very kind to me when we met. I hope the attacks haven't caused too much distress."

"Yes, well," Roanna paused for effect, drawing on all her courage to go on. "He's worried because he wonders where the attacks could be coming from. Across the ocean? Might they attack Chester's Wake next?" She shook her head. "And he wonders if someone isn't up to a nasty trick." Sha paused again then leaned close to Merry, keeping her voice low. "He worries over the integrity of the Dawson family."

Merry's expression changed, from one of rapt attention to delighted understanding. She straightened and took a long sip of her tea. "If you want my honest opinion, he has right to worry over the royal family. The Sterns have long suspected evil on their part."

Roanna wasn't raised in Dawson's Edge, and she realized things might be worse than she ever saw. But the king and queen never struck her as evil. Misguided, perhaps, and sometimes too conniving. But not evil, so far. She kept her face neutral. "Oh?"

"They use their power only to benefit themselves. I could see them attacking Lox then staging an attack on themselves in order to cast blame on someone else."

Disgust filled Roanna. Disgust over Merry's overt lies. She channeled it into her own performance. "How could they be so cold hearted? Men and women in Lox have died. It feels wrong to marry into such a family."

Merry sat back and sighed. "The Sterns long to do

something about it, but we have no allies. Father and a few other families have been in touch with the countries across the ocean, but we need more. We need an ally here on our own continent."

Roanna raised her eyebrows. "Oh?"

Merry studied her another moment then leaned forward. "Would Chester's Wake be interested in an alliance?"

"I couldn't make such promises, but it doesn't seem unlikely. Especially where Gregory is concerned. He could convince Father, I'm sure."

Merry's face lit up at the mention of Gregory.

Roanna bit her lip. What was Merry's relationship with him?

"You say they use their power for themselves," Roanna said. "How so?"

Merry frowned, seeming to weigh her words. "It is said the royal family possesses some type of strange powers. Do you remember I told you about the conjurers?" She shook her head. "I don't understand it all myself, but they force their thoughts on others. They take choice away from people."

Based on the things Roanna had seen herself this seemed unlikely. She'd been stretching her mind all week and hadn't detected them using their powers at all. It was doubtful they would—or could—force anyone to do anything.

Merry took a bite of her small pastry. "The Sterns are partnered with the Maynes from the south," she went on in a low tone. "Our families have been working together for years to make a change in Dawson's Edge. In fact, the Maynes are expected here for lunch today. Could you stay? I'm sure they would be thrilled to hear of a possible alliance with Chester's

Wake."

How long had she been in the house already? Ben said they were pressed for time.

When she paused, Merry went on. "Don't feel pressured into it. Speak to Gregory, if you feel the need. You can always meet the Maynes and Dr. Presnell later."

Roanna's body tensed up. Every nerve seemed to buzz. "Dr. Presnell will be here?"

Merry waved a hand dismissively. "He's a close family friend. He's very old, and a bit senile, but he often tells the cleverest of jokes."

"I would love to stay and meet him." Ben would have to understand. What more could they do? She'd been trying to meet the doctor for months, as had Ben.

Yes, Ben would understand. She would stay for lunch, and he would have to wait.

69

Merry led Roanna onto the porch. They sat in rocking chairs facing a winding drive. It was a beautiful home, if old and small. Different from the palaces Roanna was used to, as she'd never even seen a rocking chair, let alone sat in one.

"Can you expound on what the Dawsons do, exactly, that the Sterns feel the need to call them evil?" Roanna asked.

Merry looked out across the estate, her eyes straying toward the train station.

Roanna glanced that way. Was Ben watching? Wondering what she was up to?

Finally, Merry looked back to her. "There are times when the nobles want to move the country in a certain direction, but somehow the majority always changes their mind. We believe it's because the royal family changes it for them."

It was absurd, but discomfort spread through Roanna. The Dawsons were hated by the other noble families because of their powers? They sat in silence for a while as Roanna digested the information.

"What about others throughout Dawson's Edge who have powers? Would you stop them as well?"

Merry frowned as if she hadn't ever considered it. But a moment later, the look cleared. "Few have powers as strong as those of the royal family. We are mostly concerned with being controlled by them unfairly, rather than the powers themselves."

Roanna let the words sink in, but they didn't ring true. The rebels were making excuses to fuel their own selfish desires.

"How will Chester's Wake aid us if you are still betrothed to Roland?" Merry asked now. "You have already signed a peace treaty, haven't you?"

"The question I am more concerned with is how the Sterns and Maynes will assist Chester's Wake." She said it softly, trying to change the subject. "The arrangement should be mutually beneficial."

Silence seeped between them again. Had Roanna gone too far?

Merry took a deep breath. "Forgive me. You're right, of course. My father will need to discuss the matter with your father, I suspect."

Roanna let out a nervous breath. "Yes. We're speaking much too deeply, aren't we?"

Merry smiled, but something caught her eye and she looked toward the gravel drive. A black auto approached. "Here are the Maynes and the doctor now."

Tension returned to Roanna's shoulders. She rolled her neck slightly and took another deep breath. Meeting Dr. Presnell was something she'd been trying to do ever since she'd learned of his existence. She needed to speak to him, but also to woo answers out of him. He would know who she was, of course, if he was the one who took her from her rightful parents in the first place. Would he reveal her secret?

The tension moved to her stomach, and she willed her butterflies away. The auto approached at a steady pace until it reached the circular drive at the front portico where Roanna and Merry sat.

They stood as the auto came to a stop, and within

a moment Baron Stern came from the house, followed by the butler and a few other servants.

They stood in an informal greeting line as Duke and Duchess Mayne climbed from the auto, followed by an even older man. Dr. Presnell.

He was shorter than she'd expected, and hunched over. His white hair was thinned out of existence, but the few wisps he had left floated around in disarray. He wore thick glasses and walked with a cane.

Baron Stern greeted the guests, followed by Merry and her mother. So far, no one had questioned Roanna's presence. What did Merry's father think of her being here?

Her plan was solid, but she needed to be cautious. If they discovered her betrayal, she could be in great danger.

When the Maynes reached her, Roanna smiled and held out her hands to them. Lady Mayne's eyes widened. "Princess Roanna," she exclaimed. "I didn't expect to see you again so soon after Lady Gretchen's."

"Indeed," Roanna said. "Good fortune. I was visiting Santa Rio when I decided to stop by and see Merry. I do hope we will be fast friends."

"Of course," Merry smiled. "We already are."

Lady Mayne seemed appeased. "It is wonderful to see you here."

At last Merry presented her to Baron Stern, and then came Dr. Presnell. She watched him closely to see how he would react. Did he realize who she was? That she was the very baby he'd yelled warnings over more than eighteen years ago?

Dr. Presnell approached her. He peered up at her, frowning slightly. "How do you do, young lady?"

"This is the Princess Roanna Hamilton, of

Chester's Wake." Lady Mayne placed her hand on the doctor's shoulder.

His frown didn't let up, nor did his expression change. "Ah, how nice."

He moved on, and Roanna let out a pent-up breath. Either he had no idea who she was—and had never kidnapped her—or he was senile indeed.

In either instance, she wouldn't be getting her questions answered.

Before entering the house for lunch, she threw a look toward the train station. Queen Katherine could be close to awaking. Ben was probably pacing, waiting for her return.

The butler led them through the tight hallways into the house. He brought them to the dining room, which was larger than the other rooms. Still, it was only large enough for the table and chairs. The servers barely had room to maneuver around the diners.

Roanna sat beside Merry, who sat to the left of her father. Merry leaned close to Baron Stern, whispering with him. Whispering about Roanna? Merry and her father seemed very close, and a quick glance around showed no presence of Merry's mother. What had happened to the woman?

The other diners took their seats, and Dr. Presnell sat directly across from Roanna. At this smaller table, she would be able to converse with him easily. What should she say? What would Ben tell her to say? What did she most want from him?

Answers.

The thought was more like a desperate prayer.

"Dr. Presnell," she said only loudly enough to catch his attention. Perhaps being direct would be the easiest way. "I recall hearing your name in the past.

You used to travel between the kingdoms, didn't you?"

He raised bushy eyebrows as he focused on her. "I did. I travelled between Dawson's Edge, Chester's Wake, and Lox. That was many years ago, though."

"Why did you stop?" It might be unsafe to ask, but Dr. Presnell took the question in stride.

"I'm an old man, Princess. Travel upsets my humors." He smiled, and she couldn't help smiling back. He seemed a nice enough old man.

Did you steal me as a baby? She wanted to ask. *Did you take me to Chester's Wake and pass me off as their princess?*

Her heart pounded as she considered voicing the questions. Instead, she nodded. "I understand." If he did know her, he was skilled at hiding his feelings.

The diners made small talk as the servers dished out the appetizers.

Roanna spoke when spoken to, keeping a pleasant look on her face. But her mind worked. Dr. Presnell was at lunch with the Sterns and the Maynes, two families bent on dethroning the Dawsons. Two families who felt jilted, somehow.

Dr. Presnell was a part of that movement. He had to be, or why else would he be here?

What if he was a part of the movement even when she was born? What if he stole her away from the Dawsons in order to aid that cause?

Somehow, she knew it was true.

"Let us speak freely." Her words surprised even herself, but she had years of experience at hiding her true feelings so she went on smoothly. "Lady Merry spoke of an alliance between your families and Chester's Wake. My father, the king, is uneasy with the loyalties of the Dawson family. What should I tell him in regards to a possible alliance?"

The chatter ceased, and Merry stared at her, her mouth dangling open.

Baron Stern took a moment to answer, but when he did, his voice was firm. "We would welcome Chester's Wake's alliance. Perhaps my daughter was hasty in her manner of recruitment," he shot a look Merry's way, "but make no mistake, we are happy to make negotiations. You may pass these words on to your father."

"What of your engagement to Ambassador Dawson?" Lady Mayne asked. She leaned forward eagerly.

Roanna remembered Lady Mayne's unthoughtful words at Lady Gretchen's estate—letting Roanna know about Roland's former engagement. Mother had later confided what little she knew; Roland had been engaged but left his own fiancé standing at the altar all those years ago.

"Roland will never hear of these tidings from my mouth," she said without hesitation. No, he would likely hear it from King Dawson himself.

Baron Stern nodded gravely. "Then I will look forward to hearing from King Hamilton."

"I hope it will be as soon as possible." She pretended to prepare for a bite of food then paused. "Has your resistance already begun? Merry tells me there was an attack at the palace."

Baron Stern kept her gaze, unwavering. He seemed to be measuring her loyalty. At last, he nodded once. "I would be more comfortable discussing such matters with your father, but our efforts have intensified of late."

"And what is the meaning behind all of this? Why

attack at all?" Something inside her pressed for answers. She needed to know more, if these might be the types of people behind her disappearance as a baby.

Baron Stern straightened his shoulders. He sat tall and proud. Intimidating.

Roanna refused to shrink.

"Dawson's Edge has long been held back from advancement by the Dawson family. We would join the rest of the civilized world in stomping out anomalies. Chester's Wake practices Termination, does it not?"

Chills spread across Roanna's arms. Termination? Then they truly did mean to destroy the royal family.

"We do." She worked to keep her voice calm. "Though I must admit, I don't care for the practice myself. I work closely with the orphanages that house the Rejected."

Baron Stern's eyebrows rose, but he didn't take her words as a challenge. He nodded. "We would be happy to join with Chester's Wake in this endeavor."

She forced a smile and took a bite, and the meal resumed.

Dr. Presnell seemed unfazed by the conversation. His fork rattled against his fine china as he took another bite.

After a few more minutes of eating, the Sterns' butler entered the dining room with a slight bow. "Princess Roanna, your driver has brought a message from your train. Your presence has been requested."

Roanna feigned surprise. "Oh! Well, then, I suppose I should be on my way. My itinerary didn't include staying on for lunch, but I'm glad I stayed nonetheless." She stood, and the others at the table pushed to their feet the way they would do if she were royalty of their own country. "I hope we shall be in touch." She smiled.

Merry rushed to her side. "I will show you out, of course."

Roanna bid the rest of the table good-bye. Then Merry walked her to the door.

"I apologize for embarrassing you," Roanna said. "But I felt an urgency to put the issue in the open. It appears my instincts were correct."

Merry smiled. "I understand. Our cause could use the clout of the Chester's Wake royal family." She paused then bit her lip and looked down.

"What is it, Merry?" Roanna pressed. Whatever was going on in Merry's head was obviously causing embarrassment.

"Would you tell Gregory I said hello?"

Roanna's eyebrows stretched upward. "Gregory? Of course. I would be happy to."

Relief filled Merry's eyes. "Thank you. I would really appreciate it."

Roanna smiled and promised she would be in touch. At last, she left Merry behind as the white auto rushed her toward the train station.

70

Ben paced the train platform as Roanna approached. Was he upset with her for taking so long? When she drew closer, he stopped pacing and crossed his arms.

"I'm sorry." She hurried forward. She continued before he could interrupt her. "The Maynes were coming for lunch along with Dr. Presnell. I couldn't refuse the chance to meet him."

Ben's tight expression changed to surprise. "Did you learn anything?"

"About the Sterns' and Maynes' involvement? Yes." She paused, struggling for peace about her past. "About Dr. Presnell, no. He acted as if he had no idea who I was. In fact, he seemed to have little care about any conversation that went on. But I learned so much more about the rebel cause, and what they hope to accomplish." She didn't add that it scared her. That if they strove to stomp out anomalies, she might not be safe anywhere at all.

Ben took one of her hands and squeezed gently, but he quickly released her. "The queen hasn't awoken yet, but she will any minute. You need to hurry."

Roanna frowned. "What do we do now? They are guilty, but it's my word against theirs. How does this help us?" As soon as she finished speaking, an idea came to her. "I have to tell Katherine."

"What?" Ben shook his head. "That would be foolish. We even drugged her so she wouldn't know about the meeting. It will be better to give me the information, and let us continue to work on it."

But Roanna was resolute. Katherine was content with contributing little to the running of the country. However, desperate times called for desperate measures. The time had come for Katherine to awake from her slumber.

"I can handle Katherine. She will help me. I know."

Ben's frown changed from disagreement to confusion. "Why would she help you?"

Roanna's throat swelled with her answer, but she couldn't push the words forward. Ben might be disgusted if he knew the queen was her long-lost mother. "She will. You have to trust me. We need to go now."

He shook his head. "I'm not coming to Santa Rio. My absence is too suspicious. I have to get back to the palace."

He was right, but she wished he wasn't. She nodded. "I'll see you soon then."

He stepped away as Roanna climbed into the train car. The train blew a stream of steam into the air as she took her seat. Ben lifted a single hand in farewell, and Roanna placed her hand on the glass.

Ben's gaze seemed sad. Resigned.

The train moved away from the station.

Ben strode to the auto and hopped inside, and she watched him until he drove out of sight. She wasn't a fool—she had thought a hundred times about the marriage contract between Dawson's Edge and Lox—but things were different now. The Loxians had perfected the Termination technology to detect the anomalies. They wouldn't want an abnormal queen on their throne. Ben wouldn't want a woman with an anomaly ruling at his side.

Once the kingdoms knew she was Dawsonian, they would know she was wholly abnormal.

Katherine groaned as the train chugged away, and Roanna pushed her feelings to the side. She changed seats so she was sitting directly beside the queen. Someone had removed their tea and brought in fresh snacks.

Katherine's eyes fluttered open, and she gazed up at Roanna. "Did I sleep long? I don't even remember dozing."

Roanna considered her answer. She could lie and tell Katherine she'd only slept for a few minutes which would explain why they were still quite a distance from Santa Rio.

But if she wanted Katherine's help, she had to use the truth. Katherine would help her—she had to. She would understand the threat to her family if the rebels were successful in implanting Termination within the country.

Roanna swallowed her fears. "You slept for a time, yes."

Katherine sat up straight, stretching her back. "Then we're almost there, I suppose."

Roanna shook her head. "We made an extra stop, actually."

"Oh?" Katherine took a cookie from the tray and bit into it. "Why?"

"We stopped at the Sterns' estate so I could try tricking them into giving us information on the attacks."

Katherine's hand paused midway to her mouth, cookie dangling. "We what?"

Roanna's heart sped up. "It worked, Katherine. They admitted they were behind the attack at the Loxian border as well as the attack at the palace here in Dawson's Edge. They told me these things because I pretended to be working with my father. I said Chester's Wake wanted to form an alliance with them, to defeat Dawson's Edge."

Katherine's eyes had gone wide. She sat in stunned silence for a moment. Slowly, she returned her cookie to the tray. "Did you drug me?"

"No. Someone must have for you to sleep so long, but I wasn't aware that was going to happen, and I don't know who did it." The words were true, technically.

Katherine frowned, her brows lowered and her eyes sad—or maybe confused. "The king will be very angry," she said.

Roanna gulped. She had known this, but hoped Katherine would help him see the necessity. "But the mission isn't finished yet," Roanna pled. "We know they are responsible, but at this point it is my word against theirs. I need your help to trap them in their own plot. You must help me. For the sake of this kingdom. The rebellion is gaining followers and…and they want to implement Termination. They mean to kill off any who are found to possess an anomaly."

She could see the fear and horror in Katherine's eyes at this announcement. Katherine sat silently for long minutes. Roanna squirmed in her seat.

"I don't like getting involved." Her words were soft, but her eyes were fierce. "But I will do this because you ask. What do you need from me?"

Roanna stared in surprise but quickly moved ahead with her plan. "We need to invite the Sterns and

Maynes to Santa Rio. They cannot know of your presence. I'll tell them I've spoken with Chester's Wake, and my parents are agreeable. You will listen in to confirm my story. You might even broadcast it to the king."

Katherine's gaze intensified. "I do not like the position you've put me in. I do not like being deceived and practically blackmailed into going along with you."

"I'm not blackmailing—"

"You are telling me I may lose my kingdom, my family, and my freedom if I don't help you. That is blackmail, whether you know it or not."

Discomfort swirled in Roanna's gut. Was she manipulating Katherine? Bending her to her will? "No I'm not. The rebels are doing this. I'm trying to stop it from happening." Why couldn't Katherine see that?

Maybe Roanna was the conduit of the truth, but it wasn't her, personally, forcing Katherine to act against her personal wishes and beliefs.

"I'm sorry," Roanna said. "But I saw a way to mend the problems afflicting our kingdoms. I knew Merry Stern would confide in me, and I was right. Will you help me or not?"

Katherine's gaze moved to the passing landscape outside the window. "Yes, but I do not like it."

Roanna's stomach somersaulted. Katherine's judgment was unfair, but she was probably tasting a little of the anger Roanna had been feeling for weeks. Being forced into action was never appealing.

They didn't speak again until they reached Santa Rio.

71

Katherine instructed Roanna to do whatever she could do to get the Maynes and Sterns to Santa Rio. Roanna was to call Katherine when she was needed.

Roanna sent word to Ben immediately via a servant. She wished she could send word to her family.

Roland's offices occupied the top floor of the estate. If she could find a key, she might be able to use his technologies to send a message. But how likely was Roland to leave a spare key lying around?

Figuring it was worth a try, she tromped up the three staircases leading to his office with the fantastic view of the ocean. The halls were abandoned, and the door was locked as she suspected.

She returned to the first floor, defeated. She would need to wait at least a day to contact the Sterns, or her story wouldn't seem believable. In the meantime, she would relax at the beach.

Colorful wildflowers tumbled over each other, cascading in glorious decoration. Roanna breathed deeply of the scent. At some point, Roland had implied flowers enhanced their powers. Was it true? It could be why she'd always been drawn to the gardens at home.

Roanna didn't care. She didn't want her anomaly. She didn't want to be different, yet she was different.

Merry said there were some in the royal family who could enter people's minds and bend them to their will. Roanna had read that in the history book.

Could she do it, too?

She focused on exercising her powers. She felt with her mind, stretching the limits of the aura around her. It felt elastic. Bouncy.

Stretching farther, she felt for the aura of the nearest servant. There, in the hallway leading to the kitchens.

A woman was sweeping, pressing the bristles toward the corners, but they wouldn't reach. Her aura was stretchier than others Roanna had felt—not that she had much experience. How easily could she push the woman? Make her sweep to the left instead of the right?

The desire was there, just to see. But it didn't feel right. Didn't feel honorable.

Roanna jerked away before she could do something foolish. Something wicked.

The sudden movement caused pain behind her eyes, and she pressed the heels of her hands to her eyes.

Why must this be happening to me?

The thought was filled with anguish, but a new idea occurred. She didn't have to use the powers, ever. She didn't have to test them. Practice them. Employ them.

Ever.

She would keep her mind closed, never use it to mind read or communicate with other Dawsons. As long as the royal family was successful at stopping the rebellion, no one ever had to know she had the anomaly. It wasn't as if the Dawsons' powers were well known outside of their own country.

But could she keep the extent of her powers from Ben?

Roanna stood and hurried inside, eager to put the

unpleasant thoughts behind her. She smiled at the servant who swept near the door. The girl returned the smile and curtsied.

Supper would be served soon, and then Roanna would go to bed. She would send word to Merry Stern first thing in the morning.

The evening passed uneventfully. Roanna ate alone then retired to bed. She slept lightly, every sound disturbing her.

The next morning, Roanna was awoken by a knock on her door. Katherine came in without waiting for an answer, and Roanna hurried out of bed. "What is it, Katherine? Has there been another attack?" She grabbed for her robe.

Katherine held up a hand to stop her. "No, nothing is wrong. I came to discuss this plan of yours."

Roanna fumbled with her robe, slipped her arms inside, and then perched on the end of the bed. "What about it?"

Katherine fidgeted, clearly uncomfortable with the whole thing. "Have you contacted the Sterns yet?"

"No, I plan to send word this morning. I hope they will come for supper tonight, or at the least tomorrow night."

Katherine nodded once, her look thoughtful. "I will wait to tell the king until after we are successful. He will be furious." She shot Roanna a warning look, letting her know how dangerous this mission was. King Dawson might punish her for disobeying. What might he do?

Roanna squirmed. "I know, but if we are successful, the kingdom will be saved. If we're not, then your family could be doomed."

Katherine sighed. "The kingdom could be saved

this time, you mean. There will come another time, and another. Man does not live peaceably for long."

"Shouldn't we, though?" Roanna asked. Lox seemed to be peaceful. Queen Frieda and King Neville had done a marvelous job of keeping the peace. Of course, they still killed all fetuses with anomalies. How peaceful was that?

Katherine smiled sadly. "You are young and hopeful, and that is good. But there will always be differences among us. That is what makes us war, yet makes us beautiful."

The statement was profound and simple all at the same time.

Katherine was right. Differences were good— differences all around.

"Well," Roanna finally said. "We shall bring peace for this time, then." She moved to the desk near the window. "I will send word to Merry immediately."

72

The Sterns came for supper that very night. Merry expressed impatience to begin their alliance, and she asked if Roanna's family would entertain the Stern family in Chester's Wake. The rebellion was anxious to get started, Merry said, but Roanna suspected she only wanted to see Gregory again.

The Maynes came along with the Sterns, and Santa Rio was filled with guests for supper. The dining room bustled with activity as Roanna greeted each person. They ate happily together, talking loudly and excitedly.

"I've never been to Santa Rio," Merry said. "It's beautiful here."

"That's what I thought when I first visited," Roanna admitted.

"Perhaps you will be gifted the estate when this is finished, Merry," Lady Mayne raised her eyebrows and leaned close.

Roanna frowned. The supposed war hadn't even started and already Lady Mayne was giving away properties? Did she have an entire royal line picked out, as well?

It was time to get down to business. "Let us speak of why we are really together, shall we?"

The conversation around the table died down, and everyone looked to her.

"Chester's Wake has agreed to fund the movement, but we will offer no soldiers in the fight.

Do you have the soldiers you need?"

Lord Mayne was the one to speak. "We have soldiers in the south, Princess. We also have the hope of soldiers across the ocean."

Across the ocean? Roanna could only hope that arrangement fell through. She kept her face neutral, but she hadn't anticipated that the rebellion went so deep.

"Excellent. We need to know those in Dawson's Edge whom we can trust, and we need a contract of sorts, assuring our assets." She and Katherine had spent hours arranging the plan.

Baron Stern frowned. "You would ask us to divulge our allies to you, when our relationship is only just beginning? And you want to put it all down on paper? This creates unnecessary evidence."

She cast him a disdainful look. "I am a princess of Chester's Wake, and my father is its king. We do not take lightly to funding wars, so yes, we need to know who our own allies will be, and we need assurances."

Baron Stern nodded. "Of course, Your Highness. It makes perfect sense. It's only, we need to know we can trust you first. If Chester's Wake is to fund the movement, let us have a deposit of good faith first. We can agree on a payment amount, method, and schedule first. The contract will be drawn up. Once our funding is secure, we will freely give you all that you ask."

Roanna pressed her lips together, thinking. They needed the names of those involved in the attacks. They needed the names of inventors, builders, funders, commanders. Something concrete they could take to King Dawson, to Queen Frieda, and her own father, the King of Chester's Wake.

In her distress, she let down her mental defenses.

The aura of those around the table hit her dead on, a dull ache throbbing behind her eyes. The more she practiced her powers the stronger they seemed to grow. Was this how it would be for the rest of her life?

Baron Sterns's aura was more malleable than she would have thought.

A wicked urge took hold of her. The urge to win—to bring peace. It would take precious little pushing to bend him to her wishes. Her eyes slid closed in a slow blink as she felt the edges of his mind. She could push him toward surrender. He wouldn't even know she'd done it. And it was for the greater good.

The blink ended, and she studied the faces of those around the table. All of these people were traitors. Traitors to their country and to the peace. All for what? They wanted the palace for themselves and their own beliefs? They hated the royal family?

Perhaps she was brought here for this moment. So that she could mold these rebels to her will and end the bloodshed they wanted to cause. She was one of the anomalies they hated, after all. She would be justified in her use of power.

She pushed slightly, willing his mind to change.

The action brought a wave of nausea, but not because of the strength of her power. For eighteen years, she'd had her decisions taken from her. Did she really want to be that kind of person?

This wasn't who she was. She would not be the monster they expected her to be, whether they disgusted her or not. Whether she had the power to force them or not.

With a determined snap of her mind, she withdrew from Baron Stern's aura and closed her mind once again. She shook her head. "Then we have no deal. Father's instructions were clear. There will be no contract—no money—without assurance of our allies."

Baron Sterns's nostrils flared. He set down his silver fork and leaned back in his chair. "How do we know we can trust you?"

Roanna raised her eyebrows. "Do you need funding or not?" She prayed they wouldn't see her bluff.

Baron Stern huffed. "Very well. You shall have your list before we leave this night."

Roanna offered a curt nod. "Excellent."

If they had figured their plan correctly then Katherine had heard the conversation at the table and would relay it to the king. Roanna's job was done. She relaxed slightly, eager to get on with the evening.

They finished their meal and Baron Stern and Lord Mayne consulted over the list they would provide Chester's Wake.

Merry and Roanna sat quietly, speaking.

"Have you always heard them speak of this movement?" Roanna asked. "Have they tried other plots that failed?" She thought of Dr. Presnell's assumed kidnapping at her birth.

Merry sighed and shrugged. "More than I can count. Some have landed them in dungeons and others in gold. So far, though, none have been successful in bringing King Bartholomew Dawson to his knees."

Clarity washed over Roanna then. She was a pawn to them, and she had been since birth. Maybe Dr. Presnell had taken her to bring the king and queen to their knees. Perhaps he thought she would be tested and terminated in Chester's Wake. She was nothing to any of them, nothing but a means to an end, even as an infant.

"Is something wrong, Princess?" Merry asked.

Roanna smoothed out her features and smiled. "Nothing at all."

"They thought they had finally found success when they managed to persuade the prince's foreign bride, Princess Isabella, to help the movement, but that has brought them little resources. Her country is much more interested in scientific advances than in overturning a small, foreign monarchy."

Roanna pasted on a smile and listened to Merry's talk, but more than anything she wanted this night to be over. Time to end this, to end their movement, and to go on with her life. She would no longer be anyone's pawn—not the rebellion's, not Roland's, and certainly not the king's.

Roanna was ready to work for peace. True peace, without Termination or manipulation. And it would start with telling Ben the truth.

73

Roanna trudged up the stairs toward her room after the Sterns and Maynes had left for the train station. In the wee hours of the morning, her head pounded in sync with her footsteps.

As she reached the top of the stairs, a servant moved toward her. "Your Highness, the queen would see you now."

So late? Roanna wanted to ask to wait for dawn's light, but she sighed instead. "Very well."

The servant led Roanna to the stairs. Roanna frowned. "We're going up?"

"Yes, Your Highness. Queen Katherine waits in Prince Roland's office."

Roanna frowned but didn't question the girl further. They made their way up to the third-floor offices where Katherine had managed to unlock the door and waited inside at the desk.

"Are they finally gone?" she asked.

"Just left."

"Good. Come sit by me." She patted the extra chair she'd pulled near her. When Roanna sat, Katherine gripped her hand and smiled. "I managed to record your entire conversation with the Sterns. I've sent the file to the king."

Roanna bit her lip. "How did he react?"

Katherine rolled her eyes, a grin on her face. "How do you think? But he's grateful, all the same. He has arranged for us to return to the palace tomorrow. I fear the Sterns and Maynes will not like the company that greets them on their return to the Stern estate. I can't believe the things I heard from them."

No joy filled Roanna at Katherine's words. The Maynes and Sterns were the masterminds, but other nobles hated the royal family as well. As Katherine had said, they might have peace for a time. But how long would it last?

"Now," Katherine said. She powered up the Messenger. "I have arranged for you to send a message to you parents."

Roanna's eyes stretched wide. "My parents in Chester's Wake?"

Sadness filled Katherine's gaze. "Yes, those parents." She clutched Roanna's hands. "I'm sorry about all of this, my darling. You are an adult, and so I've given you space. You love your family, but you are my child, too, and I am overjoyed to have you back. It is a messy business." She shook her head. "I don't know who or what allows such things to happen. I see you praying, and it does make me wonder if Someone listens." She shook her head. "I'm sorry all this has happened to you, but I cannot deny that I am so happy you are here. I hope you will forgive us for taking you back, and even come to love us in your own time."

Pain sliced through Roanna's heart. Love? Dared she ever love King and Queen Dawson? She had felt kinship with them from the moment she'd met them, yet they were taking her away from all she knew and loved.

Tears pricked her eyes. "Thank you, Katherine. Your relationship to me is special. I hope we will grow close, as well." Emotions swelled her throat. "And thank you for letting me contact my parents. I miss them very much."

Katherine smiled, tears brimming in her eyes.

Roanna spoke into the Messenger, her words appearing on the screen. Her parents would receive the message in the morning. At Katherine's urging she invited them to Dawson's Edge. She said they had much to discuss. She could only hope they would be understanding.

When they were finished, Roanna walked Katherine to her room. Then she returned to her own room and fell into a fitful sleep.

First thing the next morning, they boarded the train to return to the palace. Roanna's stomach twisted at the thought of confronting her parents...and Ben. He deserved to know the truth—the full extent of her abilities. She also hoped he would consider working to ban the Termination practices. He didn't agree with them fully, anyway; it hurt to think that she would have been Terminated if she'd been conceived in Chester's Wake.

The train reached the palace after two hours, and King Dawson met them on the platform with a stern frown. He chided Roanna for her careless actions, but then assured her the guilty parties had been apprehended and were in custody for questioning and trial. King Neville also sent his blessings.

"Has Ben gone home then?" Roanna asked.

"No, he waits stubbornly with Prince Gregory." The king's tone let her know what he thought of that.

They entered the palace and headed for the king's offices.

Gregory and Ben waited for them.

Gregory stood when she entered.

"I wondered if I'd ever see you again," he said.

"My own sister, a hero." He managed a small smile, but his eyes seemed sadder than they should.

Roanna stepped closer to hug him. "Gregory, Merry Stern asked me to tell you hello. Did you know her well?"

Gregory's jaw clenched. "It doesn't matter now, does it? She's a criminal."

Roanna frowned. "A criminal against Dawson's Edge, but not Chester's Wake. And she was only following her father." While she seemed to agree with her father—that those with anomalies should be Terminated—Roanna had seen evidence that Merry wasn't always firm in what she said she believed.

Gregory's jaw clenched again, and he stepped away to speak with the king.

Katherine excused herself to rest in her room, leaving Roanna standing awkwardly near Ben.

"It worked," he said.

She gave him a small smile. "I was nervous, but it worked. We did it."

They faced each other without speaking.

Ben shifted, his look uncertain.

Roanna's heart tightened. She had seldom seen him anything but sure of himself.

"Won't you tell me what's going on?" he pleaded.

Roanna looked to the king. He and Gregory were deep in conversation. Her heart fluttered, but it was time. "Will you walk with me to the garden?"

Relief filled his eyes, and he held out his arm.

74

The flowers in the royal garden bloomed larger and more gloriously than any of those she had ever seen. They filled Roanna with a heady power, enlightening her senses. Filling her with fear.

She held Ben's arm, his skin warm under his thin linen shirt. They walked quietly for a moment.

Then Ben stopped her. "Tell me?"

She swallowed her fear. "It is better if I show you."

He frowned.

She nodded toward a gardenia plant. "Pick that flower on the very top."

He pointed. "This one?"

She nodded, and he moved his hand toward it.

Roanna pushed out with her mind, feeling his aura. It was strong. Hard. She pushed hard, harder still, and Ben plucked the flower at the bottom of the bush.

He frowned. "I don't know why I did that."

"I do." She held out her hand and took the flower. "It is part of my powers."

Ben's frown stayed in place, but uncertainty had returned to his eyes. "I thought you could read minds."

"I can. But Roland explained I can do more." She waited silently, hoping to gauge his reaction.

A line appeared on his forehead as he frowned, but he said nothing more about her powers. "You aren't marrying Roland, you said."

"No, I'm not." She paused. Could she really reveal to him what she'd learned? "Roland is my uncle."

The silence stretched to eternity. "I'm afraid I don't understand." His gaze pleaded with her to explain. To speak plainly and set things straight.

"Dr. Presnell kidnapped me." The words were choked. Whispered. "At least, I think he did. I still haven't figured out how it happened. I do hope to speak with him at length eventually. Maybe King Dawson can bring him in for questioning." She took a shaky breath and started again. "Regardless, I am the daughter of King Bartholomew and Queen Katherine. Genetic testing has proven it. I don't know why or how Dr. Presnell did it—maybe he thought I would be killed, or maybe he wanted to destroy them."

Ben opened his mouth as if he would protest, but she shook her head.

"Trust me. I looked for every other explanation under the sun. None were found."

He backed away from her, shaking his head. "You cannot be a Dawsonian princess. Surely, you don't believe this."

"Ben, the test was firm. It's true. And even if we thought the results were compromised, well, there's the truth of my powers."

Ben frowned. "Are you saying the other Dawsons have these powers?"

Fear came over her. Ben wouldn't accept her. He saw her, and the Dawsons, as something different. Ugly. He already disliked them, and now he would group her with them.

Their relationship would be over, and it would have nothing to do with a marriage to Roland.

"Yes, they do have powers," she admitted.

Silence continued between them. Finally, she could take it no more. "I'm telling my parents as soon as they arrive. I don't know how they'll react."

Ben looked to her, his face skeptical. "Are you saying you're the Dawsonian princess? The one I've been betrothed to my entire life?"

Roanna froze. She'd thought about it a thousand times in the last few days, but she'd never let herself hope. Now she held her breath, waiting for either his joy or his ire.

"And you have powers beyond mind reading? You can bend people to your will?" His eyes were wide, his nostrils flared.

"But I would never use that power, Ben. I had the opportunity last night, and I refused to use it on the Sterns. I used my wit, and my prayers, instead. I won't manipulate others to get my way. We are in agreement on that moral." She spoke vehemently, passionately. He'd known her their entire lives. Surely, he knew her well enough to know it was true.

He rubbed the back of his neck. "I believe you, but this is all very hard to hear."

"Trust me. I know." The short distance between them felt like miles. She wished he would take her hand, promise they were still the best of friends.

"Your family doesn't know yet?"

"No, but they're coming. We will tell them then."

"What do the Dawsons intend to do with you?" He spoke as if she were a pawn, or as if the Dawsons viewed her that way.

Maybe she wasn't one to them, though. Katherine seemed to truly love her.

Roanna shook her head. "I don't think they plan to do anything with me. They are happy to know what happened to their daughter."

"And what of the real princess of Chester's Wake?"

The words stung. How she longed to be the real princess.

She gulped then choked out, "I suppose we shall have to find out what became of her."

Something shifted in his expression then. A softening. He closed the distance between them and, after a short pause, crushed her to him in a tight hug. "I've been so worried about you."

Tears burned her eyes and flowed down her cheeks before she could stop them. A sob broke out. "I thought you would hate me. Be disgusted by me."

"Shh," he said. He held her tighter. "I believe you. You are my best friend, and nothing could ever change that."

Relief washed over her. The urge to cry harder hit her, but she pushed it away. She pulled back from him so she could see his eyes. "Thank you."

A slow smile crept across his face. "You owe me no thanks. I love you, Roanna. And I have never been so thankful to be betrothed to the Princess of Dawson's Edge."

Roanna gasped. "Do you mean that?"

He laughed and pulled her tightly against him. "Do I mean it?" His gaze moved to her lips.

She could hardly breathe. Would he finally kiss her? She half-expected someone to walk around the corner and interrupt them.

But then he was kissing her, softly at first then more fiercely. She kissed him back. Euphoria washed over her.

After a moment, he pulled away and looked into

her eyes. "I get to marry the woman I love and keep the peace all at the same time. Yes. I mean it."

More tears filled her eyes, but she pulled away from him and wiped them with her sleeve. "My parents will be devastated."

Ben took her hand and squeezed softly. "Yes, but they will love you still. As do I. It will work out, and we will have peace."

Katherine's word about peace passed through Roanna's mind. Peace was fleeting when left up to man—there were too many differences. But for this day, for this generation, she would relish it.

She smiled and leaned toward Ben for one more kiss. "So you would still marry me, Your Highness? Even knowing the truth behind my heritage?"

"If you would have me, yes." He pulled away from her. "Or should I shower you with compliments first?"

She laughed and shook her head as they headed back to the palace. "No, that won't be necessary. Instead, promise to work with me. And always to love me. The coming months will not be easy. Especially as word spreads that I am a Dawson with powers. What will Loxians think?"

A determined glint filled his eyes. "We will help them to see. Together." He kissed her again, and Roanna thought she would surely melt at any moment.

When he finally released her, Roanna clasped his arm, and they reentered the palace. Peace and happiness filled her like never before, and while she knew the meeting with her parents would bring many tears and heartaches, hope was renewed. Hope that their kingdoms would, indeed, enjoy peace. Hope that she and Ben could work to end Termination. Hope that others would see the beauty in differences.

And hope that she and Ben would live happily ever after.

Thank you…

for purchasing this Watershed Books title. For other
inspirational stories, please visit our on-line bookstore
at www.pelicanbookgroup.com.

For questions or more information, contact us at
customer@pelicanbookgroup.com.

Watershed Books
Make a Splash!™
an imprint of Pelican Book Group
www.PelicanBookGroup.com

Connect with Us
www.facebook.com/Pelicanbookgroup
www.twitter.com/pelicanbookgrp

To receive news and specials, subscribe to our bulletin
http://pelink.us/bulletin

May God's glory shine through
this inspirational work of fiction.

AMDG

You Can Help!

At Pelican Book Group it is our mission to entertain readers with fiction that uplifts the Gospel. It is our privilege to spend time with you awhile as you read our stories.

We believe you can help us to bring Christ into the lives of people across the globe. And you don't have to open your wallet or even leave your house!

Here are 3 simple things you can do to help us bring illuminating fiction™ to people everywhere.

1) If you enjoyed this book, write a positive review. Post it at online retailers and websites where readers gather. And share your review with us at reviews@pelicanbookgroup.com (this does give us permission to reprint your review in whole or in part.)

2) If you enjoyed this book, recommend it to a friend in person, at a book club or on social media.

3) If you have suggestions on how we can improve or expand our selection, let us know. We value your opinion. Use the contact form on our web site or e-mail us at customer@pelicanbookgroup.com

God Can Help!

Are you in need? The Almighty can do great things for you. Holy is His Name! He has mercy in every generation. He can lift up the lowly and accomplish all things. Reach out today.

Do not fear: I am with you; do not be anxious: I am your God. I will strengthen you, I will help you, I will uphold you with my victorious right hand.

~Isaiah 41:10 (NAB)

We pray daily, and we especially pray for everyone connected to Pelican Book Group—that includes you! If you have a specific need, we welcome the opportunity to pray for you. Share your needs or praise reports at http://pelink.us/pray4us

Free Book Offer

We're looking for booklovers like you to partner with us! Join our team of influencers today and periodically receive free eBooks and exclusive offers.

For more information
Visit http://pelicanbookgroup.com/booklovers